For the Love of Dinosaurs

THE ROYALS OF ISOLA NOSTRUM

BOOK TWO

TOMI TABB

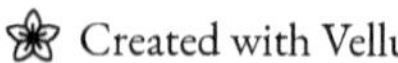 Created with Vellum

To my sister

Part One

CHAPTER 1

A Coffee Date in London

The doors of the red-and-blue Piccadilly Line train opened. A cool automated voice announced, "This is South Kensington. Change here for the District and Circle Lines. Alight here for the museums and Royal Albert Hall."

Passengers clamored to exit the train. Like a school of fish, a crowd of families, school groups, and tourists maneuvered their way through a series of stuffy, long, narrow tunnels. Standing on the right-hand side of an escalator, Nora Toscani reached into her pocket. The screen of her phone glowed.

Nine-thirty. Lucas said he'd be there close to opening. To him, on time was late. She should've tried to arrive by eight-thirty. She hated keeping people waiting. It was her own folly for forgetting how busy London was during the commute hour.

Near the surface, the temperature of the air changed from warm to bitterly cold. A light dusting of snow coated the street. She pulled the lapels of her plaid Burberry coat tighter to her body.

Mindful of her footing, Nora crossed the street and laid eyes on the terracotta-colored facade of the Natural History Museum. A marvel of Victorian architecture, its many windows, arches, and sweeping staircases reminded her of a cathedral.

She removed her gloves as she entered the building, and blew on her hands. The hall echoed with laughter and muffled voices. Teachers and school groups shuffled past. She squinted, scanning the entry hall for the chestnut-brown hair of her housemate from uni.

Should she send him a text message to let him know she'd arrived? Or would it be faster to search for him in the dinosaur gallery?

She glanced up at the skeleton of a giant blue whale suspended overhead. Her eyes traced over its elongated spine and powerful fins.

"Magnificent, isn't it? Her nickname is Hope. She's a blue whale, the largest mammal on Earth, and giant of the seas," a smooth bass voice said.

She spun and stared directly into the agate-blue eyes of Lucas Malcolm, the Earl of Merrick.

She grinned as widely as a Cheshire cat. "Lucas. It's so great to see you. How have you been?"

Rising onto the tip of her toes, the five-foot-two Nora wrapped her arms around her five-eleven friend. She breathed in the scent of cedar. The wool of his gray herringbone overcoat scratched against her cheeks.

"Nora. I've missed you too. I can't believe it's been an entire year." He hugged her back with equal enthusiasm. "It's good to be home."

"Y como va tu español? And how is your Spanish coming along?" she teased.

"Abismalmente. Abysmally." Twin patches of red

appeared on his cheeks. "I don't have the ear for languages like you." He rubbed the back of his neck. "You'd think after spending a year in remote Argentina, my language skills would've at least marginally improved, but they haven't."

She was sure he was being modest. He was able to answer her question. Growing up, it wasn't as if she had much of a choice. Mama and Papa insisted she learn Italian, English, French, and Spanish. "Give yourself more credit," she said.

Lucas squirmed in discomfort.

Nora changed the subject. "You know, I haven't been to the Natural History Museum or to London in ages. When do you suppose they switched out the monstrous dinosaur display?"

"The Diplodocus?" He slid his hands into his pockets. "It was retired from the Great Hall earlier this year. For the next year and a half, it's making a grand tour of the UK. Then, when it returns to the museum, it'll receive a new home in the dinosaur gallery."

"I'm happy to hear that. It was always a highlight for me."

Standing under Hope the whale, Lucas dove into a detailed explanation about the Diplodocus's history. Nora learned it wasn't actually an actual fossil, but rather a plaster casting.

"Finding an uncrushed Diplodocus skull is so rare. They were composed of a thin layer of bone and held mainly soft tissue. Fine sediments have been known to…"

Her eyes glossed over. She slid her hands into her own pockets as she tried to focus on what he was saying.

Lucas was so passionate and knowledgeable when he was in his element. Anyone watching him would be able to tell how much love he held for dinosaurs. It was a shame her brain shut off when he started launching into long-winded science-based explanations. Her brain wasn't wired for it. It was wired for music.

Lucas waved a hand in front of her face. "Sorry."

Nora blinked several times.

"Did I revert into professor mode?" He cocked his head sideways.

"Si." Nora nodded slowly. "You lost me when you started on about skulls."

The color of his eyes shifted to a murky gray color. "Your honesty is a breath of fresh air. That's more than some people have done with me lately." His brows knitted together.

She wondered what he meant by that. Was it something that happened in Argentina?

Her fingers were still numb from the cold. She opened and closed them several times, then rubbed her hands together.

Lucas nodded toward the café. "Would a hot chocolate with two extra pumps of chocolate help you regain some circulation?"

He remembered her favorite drink.

"Assolutamente," she replied in Italian. "My body isn't built for cold weather."

"It's been a shock to my system too. When I left Buenos Aires, it was a balmy twenty-nine degrees Celsius. Landing at Heathrow, it was eight degrees."

It was no wonder birds flew south for the winter.

They strolled to the east end of the entrance hall. Nora found a quiet, secluded table nestled against a wall in the dining area. Fairy lights were strung across the ceiling.

Holiday music played over a speaker, accompanied by the sounds of children laughing.

Lucas rejoined her carrying two steaming takeaway cups and an oversized chocolate chip cookie. He sat down and slipped his coat off to reveal a black cashmere jumper, which conformed to his broad chest and thick biceps.

Nora closed her eyes and inhaled the rich, creamy scent of chocolate, candy cane, and mint. Her eyelids fluttered, and she licked her lips. "Peppermint…" She moaned. "The way to my heart."

Lucas leaned his elbows on the table and chuckled. "I remembered from our time as housemates that you used to circle the date in your agenda to mark when the cafés would begin serving holiday-themed drinks."

She sipped the beverage and savored the rush of overly sweet chocolate. She hoped Lucas wouldn't mind that she'd be hyper from all of the sugar after this.

"Siobhan thought I was mad. A coffee purist through and through." She shook her head. "How are you two getting on? She and I are overdue for a chat."

He clenched his jaw and tightened his grip over the base of his cup. Bringing the lid to his lips, he took a long swig. "I haven't spoken to *her* in six months."

Nora grimaced. Had she just inserted her foot into her mouth? Now she was extra glad she didn't mention a wedding.

Unable to think of anything to say, she drank from her own beverage. Lucas's cup hit the table with a thud. She jumped and coughed on her drink.

His head turned in her direction. "I'm sorry." He offered her a napkin.

"It's fine," she croaked.

"My emotions are still all over the spectrum. I thought

I'd have better control over them by now. Siobhan and I are no longer together," he told her as he fussed with his hair.

Siobhan was the type of person who wouldn't let anything stand in her way when she had her mind fixed on a goal. She reminded Nora a lot of her brother Lorenzo's nasty new girlfriend. Lucas was more of a dreamer.

"While I was away, Siobhan was offered a job as the advertising director of European sales for a swanky Zürich-based luxury-watch company. I was thrilled to bits. It was a role that I knew she wanted. When we started talking about our future, somehow, we got into a nasty row about my wanting to go into academia." Lucas took a deep breath.

"She said I lacked ambition and that the job market was too full of uncertainty. She wanted me to quit my fieldwork and move to Zürich to be with her straightaway, but I refused. I wanted to finish out my research in Argentina and then for us to reevaluate where our relationship stood when I returned home."

Nora nodded emphatically. "That sounds reasonable. After all, what would happen if she hated her job? Relationships are a two-way street."

He hunched his shoulders. "Siobhan didn't see it that way. According to her, I lacked a commitment to us. We disconnected the call. About an hour later, she ended our relationship via text message."

Nora's mouth formed the shape of an O. "I don't understand how she could be so heartless and cruel."

"It's a mystery to me too." The muscles in his face tightened.

She could only imagine how devastating it would be to have to read a text that said it was over. Poor Lucas. He had such a big heart. Even with all her faults, he loved Siobhan so much. Nora would never be able to look at her the same again. She was done with her old housemate.

The muscles in her stomach tied themselves in knots. "Why didn't you reach out to me?"

"I didn't want to burden anyone. Admittedly, it was difficult to get through the first couple of weeks. But even now, I still see it as my problem to deal with," Lucas said, his eyes cast down as he drew circles on the top of his cup.

"That's such a typical male answer." She frowned. "You would never be a burden. Take it from a person who's been burned by past relationships not once, but twice—burying your emotions only makes it worse. It's not healthy to hold on to the anger, the resentment, the sorrow, or the pain."

It will only eat you alive, she thought.

He crossed his arms. "Have you been conspiring with Matthew?"

Lucas considered Matthew to be among his very best of friends. They had known one another since their boyhood days at Harrow.

"No." A look of confusion crossed her face. "Why?"

He stroked his jaw. "He gave me almost the exact same speech when I had lunch with him yesterday."

Nora never would have pegged Matthew, the king of parties, as a person to give out relationship advice. Maybe he had actually matured since uni.

"I promised Matthew that I'd arrange to speak to a professional about it."

Nora leaned forward in her seat. "And have you actually followed through and booked an appointment?"

"I have." He nodded. "He's been pestering me about it nonstop."

Brava.

Lucas offered her the monstrous cookie, as she

opened it, the plastic crinkling. Reading his body language, Nora steered the conversation off the topic of his now ex-girlfriend. "Is Matthew still living at his parents' flat?"

Lucas nodded. "Believe it or not, he's working as an estate agent in Gloucestershire. He's done well for himself."

Matthew had the right persona to build a strong rapport with people, but Nora wasn't so sure about the paperwork side of it all. He used to be horribly unorganized.

"There's hope for Matthew yet," she snickered.

Lucas smiled. "Tell me, what have you been up to while I was digging up old bones?"

Nora puffed her cheeks and blew out air. "I've spent the last few weeks attending auditions."

He raised an eyebrow. "How is it that an orchestra hasn't snapped up a talented violinist like you?"

"The field is oversaturated. If I played an instrument like an oboe or bassoon, I wouldn't be having so much trouble. Violinists are a dime a dozen."

Lucas leaned back in his seat. "What have your parents had to say about it?"

"Mama and Papa don't know," she said softly.

Nora relished the three years she had spent studying music at the University of Bristol. It had marked one of the first times in her life that she had been afforded the ability to live as an independent and "normal" person.

At Bristol, she wasn't Crown Princess Leonora Amelia Beatrice Toscani, the eldest child of King Lorenzo III and Queen Aurora from the European microstate of Isola Nostrum. Instead, she could enjoy the anonymity of being Nora Toscani, another international student. She had been given a taste of freedom, and she relished it.

Lucas scratched his head. "How have you been able to pop out to auditions?"

"I conspired with my cousin Giulia to hire me as a part-time front desk agent for her bed and breakfast." She chuckled.

"And how is that working out?"

"It's been the perfect cover. Giulia gets free labor, and I have an excuse to be out on the mainland. She's low-key and doesn't ask any questions when I ask if she minds that I disappear for a few hours. I think she thinks I have a boyfriend."

That wouldn't be happening anytime soon.

Lucas stroked his jaw. "Would your cousin consider hiring me?"

She arched her eyebrow. "How's your French and Italian?"

He sighed. "As superior as my Spanish—nonexistent."

"You *could* potentially slide by with only speaking English, but in hindsight, you'd have to relocate to Italy."

"It was worth considering." He leaned back in his chair and sighed again. "At this point, I'd be better off asking Matthew to train me up as an estate agent."

"Why all the questions? You've got your master's degree and you have a year of fieldwork under your belt. I bet you could apply to any museum or research facility involved in geology or paleontology, and they'd hire you straightaway."

He stared poignantly at his hands. "There's something I haven't told anyone about… it's the reason why I wanted to meet you here today. You always give such brilliant advice." Lucas swallowed hard. The Adam's apple in his throat bobbled up and down. "I thought it would be a long shot, but after Siobhan broke up with me, I decided to submit an application for a doctorate program. Three weeks ago, I had an interview. Then four days ago, I received a formal email welcoming me to the program with full funding."

The piece of cookie Nora held in her hands crumbled. "That's wonderful news."

"It's all well and good, but there's one complication." His facial expression remained grim, and he massaged his temples. "The program is in Australia."

"Ah." Finishing her hot chocolate, Nora patted her lips dry with the rough paper napkin and stood. "Let's take a walk. I need to think out loud and expend some of this sugar."

Plus, being among the dinosaur collection would help Lucas to relax a bit. This might even be his most favorite place in the world.

The dinosaur gallery was arguably the most popular area in the Natural History Museum. Bright interactive displays countered the dim purple- and green-hued lighting. Children nudged against one another, jockeying for the best position in front of a life-sized robotic Tyrannosaurus rex.

Its jaw opened and closed, displaying two rows of dangerously sharp teeth. Yellow eyes with narrow, thin black slits glared at the children. Its head turned with a roar, and the children screamed and jumped back in fright. Adults laughed in the background.

Nora gazed at her friend. The fine lines on the sides of his eyes were tight. His skin, like her own, was tanned from spending many hours outdoors in the sun. His hair had grown longer and was secured in an elastic hair tie. The scruffy, uneven beginnings of a beard covered his jaw.

Lucas and his father were going to have a row if he saw him like this. He was as conservative as they came.

"If I were a betting woman, I'd wager that your father

has hinted that he expects for you to start taking on more responsibilities on your family's estate."

"It may have come up as a topic of conversation once or twice." He clasped his hands behind his back. "Father, like Siobhan, has made it abundantly clear that he thinks all the work I've put in over the last two years is a colossal waste of time. Neither of them can understand why I'm drawn to spending weeks in the field sifting through rubble, wondering if I'm staring at a rock or a two-hundred-million-year-old fossil."

Nora shook her head. She was lucky her family encouraged her violin playing. It was her release from the world, and it had become such an important part of her life and her identity. Music was breathing for her soul.

"How did you convince your father to allow you to enroll in a master's course?" she asked.

"He was less than pleased, but eventually came around to the idea when I explained that I'd paid the full tuition from my inheritance, and it was nonrefundable." Lucas ran a hand through his hair. "I was supposed to spend the year doing the course, then when I came home, I was to start learning how to run the estate."

Something wasn't adding up for Nora.

"And the extra year in Argentina? When did that come into play?"

"Just before last Christmas." Lucas stared at the mechanical dinosaur. It turned its head and glared at the duo. "I received an email from the head of the geology department attached to the University of Buenos Aires. He was so taken with the article I published from my MA dissertation that he offered me a funded spot on his excavation team. They'd uncovered the remains of a gargantuan sauropod fossil from the late Cretaceous period near the province of—"

"Lucas," she interrupted. "Focus."

"Right." He rubbed the nape of his neck. "Um… I explained to Father how highly unusual it was for a non-doctoral student to be offered an opportunity like that. Our conversation turned heated, and we had a row about my 'lack of dedication to my birthright,' as he said. Our relationship has remained strained."

They started moving to the next display. "That's one conversation I know all too well. Mama and Papa have been disappointed with my own lack of enthusiasm toward my duties."

He raised an eyebrow. "Really?"

"Si. It goes back to our earlier conversation. I'm not ready to give up my life as Nora Toscani and become a full-time working royal. I want to know that I can make my own way in the world. I want the freedom every young adult craves—to live in my own flat, pay my own bills, cook my own meals, et cetera, et cetera. I just can't think of any way to make it happen."

Nora folded her hands in front of her body. "There are times where I've given some serious consideration to stepping aside and allowing my brother or sister to become the heir apparent. I'd be free to do as I please without any strings attached. But I always stop short of making any drastic decisions. There is this switch that flips in my brain that yells at me to do my duty."

They walked in silence for several moments.

Lucas shoved his hands into his pockets. "Duty is a part of our DNA."

"Si. Despite what I may want, in my heart, I can't bring myself to let my family and the people of Isola Nostrum down." She lowered her voice. "I'll be the first queen in over two hundred years. There are so many little girls who tell me I inspire them."

"There is so much pressure riding on your shoulders."

Turning the corner, they encountered a brachiosaurus. Its telltale long neck and tail extended floor to ceiling. Nora's gaze traveled upward. She could picture the dinosaur munching on leaves from the branches of a tall tree, not unlike a giraffe. They paused in front of it.

Nora turned and leaned her back against the protective railing. "Why do you want a doctorate degree?"

Lucas took a moment to consider her question, then replied, "Some children dream about becoming doctors. Others might long to become policemen or firefighters. For me, all I have ever wanted was to become a paleontologist. Every class I've taken in school, all the hours I've spent studying, were so I could make my dreams of working with dinosaurs a reality."

He blew out air. "With my father being who he is . . . I never thought I'd actually get this far. But now that I have my MA and have had a chance to work in the field, I have a thirst I can't quench. A PhD is required to be hired anywhere worthwhile. I've never wanted anything so badly."

She could see the burning flames of desire in his eyes. "How long would your next program be?"

"Three to four years if I enroll on a full-time basis, and up to six years part-time."

Every time he spoke about these creatures, Lucas glowed and radiated an energy that made Nora excited, and she wasn't even a dinosaur person. It physically pained her that all his hard work could be for naught. That a dream so close to being realized could be crushed if he wasn't able to go to Australia. He had to be able to follow his heart. She couldn't even imagine him doing anything else with his life and being happy.

"Thinking out loud… let's pretend I was a secret agent writing up a dossier on your father."

Lucas frowned. "Nora, be serious."

"Humor me. I promise there is a method to my madness," she said gently. She walked over to him and placed her hand under his chin, lifting his head. "I need you to think long and hard. What is the one goal your father wants to see you accomplish more than anything else in the world?"

Lucas scratched his head. Nora could picture the cogs of a well-oiled machine turning inside his mind.

"He wants me to marry and start a family. He wants the dukedom to stay within the Malcolm line and pass from him to me, and eventually, to a future grandson."

The English peerage system was so different than the peerage system on Isola Nostrum. Her life would be so different if she weren't in line to inherit the crown.

She clapped her hands together. "There's your answer."

"Getting married?" Lucas shook his head. "Impossible."

"It sounded better in my mind." She pursed her lips. "I admit, it sounds crazy, but it isn't impossible."

"It is for me." He crossed his arms. "Siobhan put me off the notion of ever dating again. I don't see myself caring if I never marry. All that matters is moving step by step from point A to point B."

The wounds were still too raw. He needed time to heal and to learn that the hurt wouldn't be there forever. But in the short-term, he was wrong. This was the best answer to bribing his papa into letting him move to Australia to chase his dream.

Nora stood still as Lucas sunk onto a bench and held his head in his hands. "Look, even if I found a willing accomplice and we tied the knot, none of it would matter. Father is like a scent hound. He can smell a fib a mile away and would see right through the charade. It's hopeless."

Nothing was hopeless. Nora believed the right woman was out there who would appreciate Lucas's sense of humor and encyclopedia-like brain. With the largeness of his eyes and puffy lips, Lucas reminded her of a lost puppy who was eagerly sitting by the door, awaiting the return of its beloved master.

She couldn't handle seeing him so depressed. He was a shadow of the happy-go-lucky man he once was. She had to do something. Maybe she'd have better luck finding an orchestral job in Australia than in Italy. She couldn't believe she was even about to suggest this.

Her pulse began to race. Her breath hitched. "I'm willing to marry you if it means you'll be happy."

CHAPTER 2

The Idea

Lucas's head snapped up. "No. I can't do that to you."

"The only person who decides what I do is me." Nora stuck her hands on her hips. "I'm willing to go all in. I'm a dreamer and I can't stand to see you so miserable. This is your out."

"I won't be responsible for ruining your future," he said.

Her future was not as free as his. Nora frowned. "When I was sick with a high fever our second year at uni, you ran to the corner store—through the snow, mind you—and bought me hot soup, crackers, and meds. When Fred decided that I was too high-maintenance a woman to be around, you popped out to buy me ice cream and rent a DVD of *Emma*. You've always been a loyal friend who has stuck by my side through the ups and downs, highs and lows. You're one of my closest friends. Let me return the favor to you.

"If you want to be real about the future, remember, *I* am a crown princess. I can't go on dates without the guy being vetted by the palace. I've never been able to have a long-term serious boyfriend because of all the baggage that comes with me being me. Did you know that when I ever decide to marry, my husband has to be approved by Parliament? The monarchy is still deeply entwined in the day-to-day running of Isola Nostrum."

Lucas swallowed hard. "That's a lot to take into consideration."

It felt as if an iron weight were pressed upon her own shoulders. For the first time, she'd realized exactly what the implications of getting married entailed. Her future was all too real. Ironically, Lucas was exactly the type of man Parliament would want her to marry. For the country to have as her consort.

Was this how her favorite leading Austen gentlemen like Mr. Darcy or Mr. Knightley might have felt during the Regency period? Having to pick a wife who they knew would be able to handle the weight of the responsibility of their positions and the duties that running a grand estate entailed?

Silence passed between them as they were each lost to their own thoughts. The T. rex roared. Lights flickered, and the imposing silhouette of a Triceratops appeared on the wall. Glancing upward, Nora took notice of an enormous skull suspended overhead.

"Triceratops dinosaurs had a generally gentle disposition, with strong protective instincts. They were herbivores and lived in herds. They remind me a lot of deer."

Lucas reverted to reciting random facts when he was nervous. How could a creature that large remind him of a deer? She would've thought they might be more like elephants due to their sheer size.

She glanced back at the skull, trying hard to picture how the millennia-old reptile as a deer.

Nope. I can't see it. I'll have to take his word for it. In fact, trust was going to be what this sham marriage was built upon. No. Not sham. It was more of a modern-day marriage of convenience. It sounded as if she were writing her own Jane-Austenesque novel.

Lucas took a deep breath. As if reading her mind, he said, "We both know getting married in a month isn't feasible. It would raise red flags to both your parents and mine. But what if we considered this from another angle?"

She'd do it for him. He was a person who went above and beyond for others. The Charlotte Lucas to an Elizabeth Bennet. No. The Knightley to an Emma would serve as a better comparison.

Nora tilted her head to the side. "What did you have in mind?"

"What if we were to become engaged? With any luck it *might*—and the keyword is *might*—be enough to convince my father I'm thinking about the future. It would only be until I graduate. Then we could call the entire thing off."

She was locking herself into a three-to-five-year commitment. She knew she wouldn't be able to date anyone or be in a relationship for the duration of the engagement.

I can handle that. It's not like my love life exists to begin with. It's a complicated mess. I can use the time to really build up my career. Actually, being an engaged woman would give me some extra freedom. Mama and Papa are much more likely to agree to let me live on my own if I make the case that this might be the only chance I'll ever have to do so.

Nora's thoughts turned to her own family. She was also going to have to live an enormous lie for the next few years. She gulped. She was close with her papa. Did she have the inner strength to look him straight in the eye and blatantly lie to his face? Her stomach muscles clenched as she looked back at Lucas. Her heart was being torn in two different directions. What should she do?

Nora and her parents had first met Lucas when they had been on an official state visit to the UK. What was it? Ten years ago? Nora had been enamored with his dimples and the awkward choices he selected for their conversation. He was the only person who could ever make sediment deposits sound so interesting.

Mama and Papa met the Duke and Duchess of Trent a second time when she, Lucas, and Siobhan became house-mates. They got on well. Nora felt horrid at the time that she and Lucas kept Siobhan in the dark about their "secret" lives. In hindsight, she was glad she never told Siobhan she was a princess, although Siobhan had later learned Lucas was in line to become a future duke.

I lived a lie with Siobhan during uni. If I've done it once I can do it again. I have to remember we're talking about the man's livelihood and his chance at getting a happily-ever-after ending. After the crap Siobhan put him through, he more than deserves a fresh start. Papa will understand in the end that it was all for a good cause. Jane Austen would yell at me to not even question the matter and just to get on with it.

"I think it could work. But our engagement *has* to be believable. We can't leave anything to chance," Nora said.

If Lorenzo were to accidentally spill the beans to Mama that she and Lucas had been dating under the radar, a seed would be planted in her mind. It wouldn't take long for it to take root and grow. Mama would be planning their wedding before the engagement was ever official.

"From here on out, we're going to have to spend as much time together as possible," she said. "We need to get to know one another more intimately than we do now. When would your semester start?"

He muttered in a tone so low that she couldn't hear him.

"What did you say?"

The tips of his ears turned red. "In February."

"That quickly? When would you have to notify them of your decision?"

"Before the end of the year," Lucas replied.

Nora rubbed her temples, the dull throb of a migraine beginning to take hold. "By my count, that means we would have about two and a half weeks to become engaged and convince your father we are the real deal. With any luck, you would have all of January to establish yourself in Australia before the term commences."

Lucas stood slowly. He picked up Nora's hand. "I want to reiterate that this is only until I graduate." His intense blue eyes bore into her. They'd turned from fire to ice. An element that could take on many forms and constantly differ in appearance depending on how it was viewed in the light. "I'm just putting this out there, but if any time you want out, say the word and it's over." He snapped his fingers together. "Just like that."

"Understood."

He hugged her tightly. Unlike earlier, it felt more intimate. Through the fabric of his jacket, she could feel the rise and fall of his chest and hear the steady beat of his heart. In his arms, she felt warm and comfortable, like a ship being guided into a harbor by the flash of a lighthouse beacon.

"Thank you, Nora," Lucas whispered in her ear. "You are the most amazing person there is."

She wondered what it would be like if he kissed her.

Would his lips be soft and tender? Would he dip her romantically?

That can't happen. We're only friends.

He released her, and they stepped back from one another. He turned his head, but not before Nora could see him wipe a stray tear from the corner of his eye. Her cheeks warmed.

She cleared her throat. In an even, dry tone, she challenged him. "I just hope you'll continue to retain that mindset when you learn about my quirks."

"What quirks?" He chuckled. "I lived with you for two years. I doubt there's much left about you that might surprise me."

She crossed her arms, and a lock of hair fell in front of her face. "I bet there is."

"I know you cannot resist the urge to set foot into a used bookshop and walk out with your arms laden with books, even if you already own a copy of what you've purchased." Lucas gently reached for the lock of hair and placed it behind her ear. "I know that every Sunday, you would visit the antique market to search for any items shaped like a cat."

Fair enough. Nora never had enough space on her IKEA bookcases for her massive book collection. But how did he know about her guilty pleasure of shopping at the market? She had always made an effort to sneak out before he and Siobhan were awake. They were never home when she returned to their flat with her treasures.

"You left out my Jane Austen obsession."

"Jane Austen." Lucas arched an eyebrow. "Score one for Nora. What's this about the author?"

"You'll have to spend more time with me if you want to find out."

Around them, the skeletons grew smaller in scale. Overhead speakers played haunting music and a series of high-pitched clicks and squeaks, similar to the sounds made by whales. A re-creation of a Stegosaurus nest revealed fossilized eggs as large as dinner plates.

Lucas gestured for them to continue through to the dinosaur hall. "If I'm to put together a secret-agent dossier on you, I'll need every moment you can spare. How long do you think you can stay in London?"

"Three days?" Butterflies fluttered in her stomach. Her throat grew dry. "I counted on spending the rest of today with you. Tomorrow, I had hoped to do some holiday shopping and catch a show in the West End. My air ticket is open-ended. So long as I'm back on Isola Nostrum on Sunday for a charity concert I'm playing, I doubt my parents would notice I'm MIA."

"Three days should be enough time to scratch the surface. If you're up for it, I'd like to take you out on a series of proper dates." Lucas rubbed his hands together. "I'll book myself into the Saint George Hotel. There isn't any sense in driving back and forth between here and Lincolnshire. You know I dislike driving. It's more trouble than it's worth."

Wait a moment. Lucas loved going out on long drives to remote places. It was one of his favorite ways to unwind. Why did he suddenly say he didn't care for it?

Reading between the lines, she narrowed her eyes. "You haven't told your parents you're back from Argentina, have you?"

He hunched his shoulders. "Mother and Father are on holiday in Jersey. It didn't seem right to spoil their fun until I'd had a chance to speak to you and Matthew and figure out what to do."

She understood. Once the words were spoken, they couldn't be taken back. It was like opening Pandora's box. The level of trust he had in her was almost frightening. The stakes were so high. Lucas was a private man. She was one of the two people he chose to speak to about his situation. Her body warmed at the thought.

If they were to maximize their time together, they had better crack on with it. She had a lot more to learn about him. What made his heart sing besides dinosaurs? *What secrets are you hiding Lucas?*

She cleared her throat. "Okay, Lord Malcolm. Starting now, we're on the first official date of our fake relationship. Let it be known that I fully expect you to make a grand gesture to me when you propose."

"I already have a few ideas on that front." Lucas offered his arm to her. "And if we're being technical, my courtesy title is Lord Merrick. Malcolm is my surname. Shouldn't you know that from reading Jane Austen stories?"

"Oh, I'm aware." She felt her cheeks burning. "If you must know… your nickname in my head has always been Lord Malcolm. I refuse to change it now."

"Very well. For you, I shall be Lord Malcolm. But only you."

Nora's heart fluttered.

CHAPTER 3

Winter Wonderland

Nora's head shot up like a cannon as they arrived at their destination. Green and white neon lights illuminated the entrance to the Magical Ice Kingdom area of Hyde Park's annual Winter Wonderland carnival. A series of tall Douglas fir trees surrounded them as if they'd left the festival behind and were entering a dense forest.

As they walked through the tent's entryway, the temperature dropped to a frigid level. She rubbed her hands over her forearms. Yet her discomfort was forgotten the moment she laid eyes on the first ice sculpture.

"Oh wow, look at these!" Nora gasped, rushing up to a white picket fence protecting the icy likeness of a squirrel perched upon a log. "Everything looks so lifelike."

Lucas chuckled. "The sign here says there are over five hundred individual ice carvings to see."

Nora shook her head in disbelief. Her eyes roamed over a pack of wolves and settled on a Victorian house constructed from hardened snow. "How long do you reckon it took to build or create all of these?"

"Weeks and weeks."

Pausing in front of a cluster of dancing polar bears and curious foxes, Nora held out her phone. "Let's take another selfie. We already have a couple of decent shots from the museum."

They might have to wait a moment for a break in the human traffic, though. She'd always heard the Winter Wonderland carnival was popular, but she never knew the extent of it. Next time, she'd come during the day, when most people were at work and there weren't as many families with large buggies. She hated the feeling of having to shuffle when they walked because of the crowds.

Nora passed Lucas her phone. They poked their heads together, and his scruffy facial hair scratched the soft skin on her chin. The flash clicked off, temporarily blinding them.

"How'd I do, Lady Nora?"

She reviewed the selfies, then handed him the device. "See for yourself. Not bad. Only two people in the background. Although, the lighting washed us out a little bit. Maybe I can add a fancy filter to the photo."

Lucas pointed to the screen. "I like the falling snowflakes. Brilliant."

She saved the changes and pocketed her phone. "I was thinking that we could spend tomorrow morning on an impromptu photo shoot. If we find some indoor locations like the greenhouses at Kew Gardens, we could get away with pretending the pictures were taken in spring or summer. But that means you're going to have to shave and get a haircut if we want to pretend that we're stepping back in time."

"No problem." Lucas stroked his beard. "I was going to

have to do so before facing my father anyway. He might refuse me entry into the house if I came like this."

They entered the next room and spotted a larger-than-life snow maiden clenching the reins of a horse. It was illuminated in peony-pink and raspberry-red lights.

"This one reminds me of you. With her cape and her angelic expression, she could be one of your Jane Austen heroines." Lucas stopped next to Nora, his body providing a comforting warmth.

"Almost." She tilted her head to the side. "The only problem is that she's riding astride in the saddle. A Regency gentlewoman would ride a horse sidesaddle. Unless she was being scandalous."

Lucas arched an eyebrow. "Details. Details."

Nora smirked. "Historical accuracy is what makes or breaks a Regency story, my dear Lord Malcolm. You may not pay attention to the nitty-gritty details, but us readers do."

Especially when it came to fabricating a mental image of a gentleman's tailored attire. Lucas had the perfect physique for a tailcoat, waistcoat, and breeches.

"Explain to me, Lady Nora… exactly how deep does your interest in Austen run?"

What was that American saying? Go big or go home? *If Lucas wants to know about the real me, he's about to get more than he may have bargained for.*

Nora brushed her fingers along the rough, curved top of the fence protecting the ice sculptures. "The works of Jane Austen and books set in the Regency era have been one of the most influential factors in shaping the person you see before you today."

She stared at the ice sculpture of a mythological satyr holding a panpipe to its mouth behind the snow maiden.

"She's the primary reason I devoted myself to studying English. The driving force behind my decision to attend uni in the UK."

"I still don't understand. That doesn't seem out of the ordinary. Authors have always inspired their readers. Look at J.K. Rowling and the Harry Potter series. When I was in sixth form, we had an influx of international students applying to Harrow simply because they wanted the British boarding school experience."

"It goes beyond having a normal fascination. It's more of an obsession." Nora dropped her hands by her sides. "What would you say if I told you that I owned two trunks packed full of Regency clothing costumes? Or that I spend most of my free time researching and writing fictional stories about the main characters from *Pride and Prejudice,* Elizabeth Bennet and Mr. Darcy?"

Go ahead. Say what you will about it. I have an Austen addiction.

His hand took hold of hers and guided her to a secluded corner in front of a centaur poised to shoot a bow and arrow in their direction.

"Nora. I understand *exactly* how you feel. It isn't anything to be ashamed about. Look…" He retrieved his mobile phone from his pocket and unlocked the screen. Opening the photo album, he rotated the device so it faced her. "This morning, I dropped about a thousand quid on a rare, limited-edition *Jurassic Park* Tyrannosaurus rex figurine set and a hand-painted 3-D printed model kit of a Stegosaurus."

Above his scarf, Lucas's neck and ears flushed deep red. "Everyone has different interests that bring them joy. Look at your brother and his love of all things *Pokémon*. You and I just happen to be the type of people who choose to express our enthusiasm at a different level than the rest of society."

When he framed it in that light, they almost sounded sane. Here he was again, trying to lift her mood.

"Where do you store all of your toys and collectible items?" she asked quizzically.

"In the basement flat of a brilliant property Matthew found on the outskirts of Cheltenham in Gloucestershire."

"And how many rooms do they occupy?"

"One? Possibly two rooms?" He rubbed the back of his neck. "The last time I was there, the boxes of things I'd ordered were stacking up. I haven't exactly had time to stop by and open them all or unpack my flat, mind you."

She blanched. "Wouldn't it have been easier to rent a barn or a warehouse if your plan was to use the flat solely for storage?"

"In hindsight, that would've been the smart move to make, but Matthew sold me on the notion of purchasing the property as an investment. The remainder of the dwelling is rented out. It brings in a tidy income."

Nora wrinkled her nose. Did he own a house or a flat? Never mind. It was better if she didn't know. She hoped that he'd consider cleaning the flat, or at least sorting out whatever mess was there before he left for Brisbane.

They stood in silence for several moments. The lighting of the room shifted between hues of purple, blue, and green, and the track of music repeated itself. Nora watched a thin layer of frost form intricate patterns each time she exhaled.

"Tell me more about your stories. Have you ever published them?" Lucas asked in a hushed undertone.

"They're just some rubbish I scribble down for my own enjoyment. Nobody would want to read them. The type of people who write Regency stories have the ability to suspend reality and ensnare the five senses. I don't have that gift."

"I beg to differ. How do you know they are rubbish? I wouldn't mind reading them. Remember, my father is keen on studying the Napoleonic Wars. Over the years, some of his knowledge has rubbed off on me."

Nora chewed on her lip. "I'll consider your proposition, Lord Malcolm." She wondered if he actually wished to read her stories, or if he was just humoring her.

Lucas flashed her a rakish smile. "That's all I ask."

"On the count of three… two…one!" Lucas roared.

Nora couldn't believe she'd let him talk her into this. *Lord Malcolm, in the future, I shall have to be extra wary of your way with words. I don't do ostentatious things like this.*

She screamed as she gripped the squishy handles of the rubber inner tube as tightly as she could. All her muscles clenched. Cold air numbed her face. The world rushed by as she slid down the forty-five-meter ice slide. She squeezed her eyes shut until she felt the inner tube gently come to a stop on top of a rubber mat.

"What a rush!" Lucas said. She opened her eyes to see him springing up from the end of the slide. "Shall we have another go?" His gloved hand assisted her to her feet.

Her pulse pounded against her ribs, and she shook her head. "You go. Once was more than enough for me. I'm not really a thrill-seeking person."

"Are you sure?"

"Positive. I'll meet you at the exit when you're done."

Without another word, she watched Lucas take up his

inner tube and jog to the end of the queue ten people deep. Her boots crunched over the thin layer of powdered snow as she went to stand beside a set of parents waving to their children at the top of the slide as they took their turns.

Was that how fast she traveled? It seemed as if she were going over one hundred kilometers an hour. From down here, everyone looked more like they were only going ten.

A few minutes later, Lucas claimed the center lane. To Nora's amusement, he angled himself backward, gave her a big thumbs-up, and took his second run down the ice slide. She could hear his deep laugh.

She had never seen Lucas so relaxed. Since they'd been at the carnival, he'd been so carefree and had shown such a zest for life. When he smiled, it was a million-watt smile—the type that could easily provide enough energy to power all the fairy lights of the carnival. He'd transformed into a child again.

Lucas joined Nora after returning the inner tube. "Shall we grab a bite to eat?" He sniffed the air. "I can smell the cinnamon churros and waffles from here."

Nora's stomach growled on demand. Her cheeks warmed. "I wouldn't say no to a snack and something warm to drink."

"More peppermint hot chocolate? Or can I tempt you to venture beyond your comfort zone?"

"I'd be keen to try the carnival's mulled wine or hot cider."

Lucas snapped his fingers. "One of each coming up."

She blanched. "I can't drink both!"

"Whichever one you don't finish or enjoy, I'll drink up." He winked.

Like a real couple, she thought. Her nose wrinkled.

Lucas stopped walking. He scratched his head, and lines

of worry crossed his face. "I shouldn't have assumed. I mean, if you don't care to share like Siobhan… She never would be one to…"

He was in such a wonderful mood, and she had spoiled it.

She placed a gloved hand on his. "I'm more than happy to share. My brother and sister and I do it all the time."

Lucas let out a sigh of relief, and his facial features relaxed. "Excellent."

A cold breeze tickled her face as she looked around. The sky was an inky black covered by wispy patches of fog. Strings of popcorn lights flickered atop the game booths. Opposite the street-food village, a small gathering of families and couples snacked on pretzels as they watched a three-person band singing a cover of ABBA's "Dancing Queen" on the main performance stage.

"If the queue is long, you know the food is delicious," Lucas said as they approached a booth.

After picking up a mulled wine, a piping-hot apple cider, chicken sausages, and two churros, they seated themselves across from one another in the center of a long picnic table.

Lucas removed his gloves. "It's your turn to pick our next adventure."

Nora blew on the mulled wine. The pine-and-citrus scent of the spices tickled her nose. "How do you feel about ice skating? I haven't been in ages and the rink we passed earlier is decorated so beautifully."

She bit into the crunchy churro and let the sweet cinnamon melt on her tongue.

He grinned. "So long as there is a barrier wall for me to cling on to, I'm game."

Nora snorted. "Stop exaggerating. I bet you're a natural on the ice."

"While I appreciate your vote of confidence, this is going to be my first time." He shrugged.

Her eyes widened. She placed the churro on her plate. "You've *never* been ice skating?"

"No," he confirmed, swirling the hot cider around in his cup before taking a drink.

"I don't believe it. Every person should experience it at least once."

"It wasn't by choice." He drummed his fingers on the table. "Growing up, my father always said outdoor winter activities like ice skating and building a snowman were unbecoming of a future duke. That was the end of the discussion. There was no room for negotiation or a counterargument."

What else had he been deprived of? What kind of childhood had Lucas had?

Nora, Lorenzo, and Lucia were encouraged by Mama and Papa to explore and try anything that interested them. She couldn't imagine how crushing it would've been on their spirits to be told they couldn't do something for the sake of appearances.

"Try the cider before I finish it all. It's delicious." Lucas slid the cup toward her, and she offered him the mulled wine.

Nora took a drink and smacked her lips together. "It's good. A little stronger than I'd expected."

They exchanged drinks once more. The wine brought back a memory of her chasing her brother while running wildly through the rows of endless grapevines in the Toscani family vineyard. Her father yelling at them to mind the plants. She pictured a young Lucas stoically watching the chaos unfold from behind a window, wishing he could partake in the fun.

This will not do.

"Before we leave Hyde Park, tonight is the night you're going to build that snowman, ice skate, and even learn how to carve ice." Nora hesitated. "Is there anything else you always wanted to do as a child?"

Lucas's eyes darted back and forth, glancing over the parents sitting with their children. "Will you promise not to laugh?"

Did he think she was asking him because she saw this as a game?

"You can trust me. Whatever you say to me will stay between the two of us." She zipped her lips closed and threw away an invisible key.

He stared at the rim of his cup. "I'd like to write a letter to Father Christmas."

Nora's heart dropped. She swallowed hard. It was even worse than she'd imagined. Reaching for her handbag, she unzipped the top and stuck her hands inside it. She felt around the interior for her pen and the spiky coil of her notebook. Wordlessly, she placed them on the table, passing the items to Lucas.

"We'll have to find an envelope before we drop it in the post box."

He rested a warm hand atop hers. Its weight was comforting. His eyes shimmered like liquid aquamarine gems. He didn't need to speak for Nora to understand how grateful he was to her.

CHAPTER 4

Shopping at Harrods

Two days later, a doorman in a hunter-green cap and jacket opened the door to London's world-famous Harrods department store for Lucas and Nora.

"Thank you," she called out over the sea of shoppers swarming into the store like a school of fish.

"I didn't think it would be so busy right at opening." Lucas took hold of her hand. They walked single file past the beauty and perfume concessions straight through to the black-and-white-checked floors of the food halls.

Standing pressed against the wall, she saw glass cases elegantly displaying everything from cheeses and charcuterie to Middle Eastern, Asian, Indian, Italian, French, and British sides and entrees. Nora's eyes, however, bore into the dessert cases of fruit tarts, airy cakes decorated with powdered sugar and raspberries, and rounded rainbow macarons.

"There isn't much time left before Christmas. The rush is on to purchase last-minute gifts," she said, inhaling the savory scent of fresh bread, coffee, and chocolate.

As if to prove her point, they observed a man with a strained expression video chatting with an exasperated blonde woman. "I told you three weeks ago to order the Victorian dollhouse for Emma," she said. "If Harrods has sold through their stock, *you* can be the one to explain to our daughter why Father Christmas didn't bring the *only* item she's asked for."

"I told you I was sorry. Emma is six. She'll understand she can't always have what she wants."

"That's what *you* think. You're not the one who is home with her most of the day."

The man apologized again. His power walk became a steady jog as he disappeared up an escalator.

Lucas stepped away from the wall. Nora grabbed his sleeve. "I wanted to order a hamper and pick up a few tins of chocolate. Would you rather I order it now or before we leave?"

He glanced at the large face of his silver Cartier tank watch. "Before we leave. It'll be less to carry. In the meantime, we have an appointment to keep."

As they turned down the corridor to the right, the throngs of shoppers thinned. Rubies, peridots, diamonds, emeralds, sapphires, and pearls shimmered under the soft overhead lighting of a crystal chandelier.

"Are we shopping for your mother? What style of jewelry does she prefer? An everyday item like a necklace or bracelet? Does she tend to favor something that makes a statement, or is she a person who wears daintier pieces?"

"So many questions." Lucas rubbed the back of his neck.

"Finding the right piece of jewelry can be tricky and time-consuming. When I'm shopping for jewelry, I want the person who's receiving it to know how much thought and care I put into selecting a piece when they open the box."

His lips twitched. "Then it's a good thing you're here to pick out your engagement ring."

Nora dropped his hand and took two steps backward. "Lucas. No." Her pulse began to race.

"If you're going to go through this farce with me, I want you to have a piece of jewelry that speaks to you. I'm rubbish at understanding what the difference is between all the cuts, the settings, and whatever else there is to choose from."

"This is too much. We don't have to be so traditional. I'd be happy with a candy ring or something durable, like a silicone ring," she sputtered. "At Giulia's B and B, you'd be surprised by how many couples have lost their engagement and wedding rings swimming in the Mediterranean."

Lucas crossed his arms. "An expensive designer engagement ring is one of the few things that's non-negotiable. The first question my mother is going to ask when we meet my parents is to see the rock on your ring finger." He frowned. "Both your parents and mine will expect to see a piece of jewelry fit to our stations in life. There is no way around it."

As much as she hated to admit it, he was right. Mama and Papa might be modern royals, but in anything related to marriage, they were going to take a traditional stance. They'd want a lavish church ceremony, Nora wearing a frilly dress, a carriage, the whole works. The opposite of everything she wanted.

"If you can handle wearing a priceless, multimillion-euro heirloom tiara, you can handle a ring." Lucas cupped her cheeks. "Our engagement and all that it entails is going to be a long-term commitment. It could be three, four, maybe even five years before we break it off. Consider this to be a thank-you present from me for all the mess you're getting involved with."

Her cheeks warmed. She breathed deeply and splayed a hand on her chest. "Let's get this over with."

"That's the spirit." Lucas slid his hand down her arm and squeezed it. "Our first appointment is at Picasa's, but if you don't find a ring there, the Harrods' personal concierge assured me that we could have standby appointments at any of the other luxury jewelry concessions they have here. Take your pick—Cartier, Van Cleef and Arpels, Harry Winston, Tiffany and Co.—the world is your oyster."

In the rear of the jewelry area were the high-end designer stalls selling items that required an extra set of security guards. As they walked through the glass doors of the Picasa concession, a woman in a crisp white shirt, black blazer, and pencil skirt stood and greeted them. Her hair was slicked back into a severe updo. "Welcome to Picasa and Co. How may I assist you two this morning?"

Nora saw royal-blue boxes held up by the company's famed lion, topped with gold-red bows. In the center of the small room stood a tall tree trimmed with red, blue, green, and gold baubles.

Lucas held up Nora's hand and kissed it. "We're here to shop for our engagement ring."

"I see." The woman walked out from behind the desk. Nora felt as if she were entering an X-ray machine as she appraised them. She glanced down at the couple through her nose and asked in a condescending tone, "Do you have an appointment?"

Nora hated it when a salesperson gauged how someone was dressed to decide if they were worth their time. It shouldn't matter if she wore an expensive Balmain blazer or a black rubbish-bin bag.

"We do, but I don't know if you have what we're looking for. I'm a woman who admires simplicity," she answered.

The saleswoman blinked twice. "You must have an appointment with one of our sales associates who sells our reasonably priced *stock* pieces of jewelry. This area is only for our VIP clients, sweetie."

Nora internally winced. She abhorred that name. She plastered a disappointed expression on her face. "Oh, what a shame," she said with a false note of regret, then turned to Lucas. "It looks like there isn't anything for us here. Come on, *darling*... let's try Cartier."

With a straight face, Lucas agreed. "If you wouldn't mind canceling the consultation for Lord Merrick and Her Serene Highness Princess Leonora, we'd appreciate it." He waved at the stunned saleswoman. "Cheers." They walked out the doors as quickly as they'd entered.

"Her attitude just rubbed me the wrong way the moment we walked in." Nora shivered.

Lucas rubbed her shoulder. "I couldn't agree with you more. We'll take our business to a place that knows how to provide *all* of its customers with decent service."

Two and a half hours later, Nora and Lucas were browsing through the selection of Van Cleef and Arpels jewelry when she spotted a yellow-gold ring with a striped brown, black, and reddish-orange gemstone shaped in the form of a clover-flower. In its center was a dainty diamond.

Their gazes met. Lucas's lips curved up in approval.

"That's the one," Nora confirmed.

The patient sales associate slipped on a single white glove, opened the case, and removed the ring from the display. "Ah, an excellent choice," he said. "This is one of our tiger's eye pieces. It's a gemstone that represents bravery, strength, and courage. No two stones are cut the same way."

Nora held out her hand and tried the ring on. *Most people may go for large diamonds, but this little baby has an understated style, flair, and uniqueness to it,* she thought. This ring was her as a piece of jewelry.

"What do you think?" She modeled it for Lucas.

"It's perfect." He took hold of her hand and studied the ring up close. "I like the striped bits. Its color reminds me of the shade of the wood that your violin is made from."

"Funny. I was thinking that it resembles amber. It's a nod to your love of fossils."

The sales assistant chuckled. "I can see you two are on similar wavelengths. Once I log in to the computer, I can advise you on how long it'll take for your order to arrive to the store."

"Would it be possible for us to walk out of the store with this ring?" Lucas stroked his chin. "I can pay any price."

The sales assistant hesitated. "Unfortunately, we generally aren't able to sell our display pieces. If you place the order today, we must wait until your item arrives from our artisan workshop in Paris. Then we will ring you to come in for a fitting. Last time I checked, for rings, the turnaround time is roughly four to six weeks."

They didn't have the luxury of waiting that long.

Nora removed the ring and gently laid it on the tray, feeling slightly disappointed. "Do you have *any* rings in stock? We're working with a short time frame."

"We have a few necklaces and earrings in stock, but hardly any rings. Compared to a full-service boutique, our stock is limited. Your best bet would be to visit the flagship VCA shop in Paris if you need it straightaway."

"Would it be possible for me to have a private chat with your store manager?" Lucas asked. He reached for his wallet and discreetly slipped the man a card Nora couldn't see. "This is my business card."

The sales associate read it. His eyes widened. "Excuse me for just a moment. I'll see what I can do." He stepped away from the counter.

"You have a business card? Fancy," Nora said in a hushed tone.

"It has my courtesy title and our family crest printed on it."

It was like a Regency calling card.

"I try not to pull it out often, but I have to admit, it comes in handy in certain situations every now and again."

If that didn't do it, Nora had her passport. Having an official government document that identified her as a princess might help fan the flames of the proverbial fire they were igniting.

The sales associate returned with a curvy woman wearing a black-and-white silk scarf and a pair of scarlet-red cat-eye glasses. "This is our manager, Kelly Simms. If you'll follow her, she'll be happy to assist you two in any way she can."

She guided them into a private room with gold walls and soft LED lighting. Placed in the center of the room was a white chaise lounge, a glass table with a tea service, and a black desk. The door clicked shut behind them.

"Lord Merrick, it's a pleasure to see you here today. Your mother is a frequent patron of ours. I'm thrilled that you've chosen to visit us."

"Thank you for seeing us on such short notice. This is

Crown Princess Leonora Toscani of Isola Nostrum, my fiancée."

"Your Highness." She flashed the pair a bright smile. "Congratulations."

Handshakes exchanged, Lucas and Nora sat on the chaise sofa and Kelly behind the black sales desk.

"Thank you," Lucas said. "I'll cut right to the chase. My lovely princess has settled on your tiger's eye ring for our engagement set, but your sales associate told us we would have to place an order and wait for it to arrive. Unfortunately, we must have our ring today. Is there anything you can do to help us out?"

"We're expecting word to leak out about our engagement at any time. With that in mind, it's likely to incite a maelstrom of unwanted attention." Nora placed her hand on his knee. "It's only by happenstance that we've been able to shop and enjoy London incognito as long as we have. Neither one of us is going to be able to make a return trip to Harrods anytime soon."

"I understand, and again, we're honored you've selected a piece from VCA to represent the love you share with one another," the store manager said. "Owing to your high profiles, I'm more than happy to accommodate you."

"That's the best news we've had today." Quickly, Lucas added, "May I inquire about adding a pair of earrings, a bracelet, and a necklace to our purchase? My princess requires a full set." He smirked at Nora's discomfort.

"Of course. Let me pop out into the showroom to pick up a few pieces. Our corporate office would be thrilled to see our jewelry in your official photos. Please help yourself to some tea in the meantime. I can also have some sparkling wine and chocolate-covered strawberries sent up."

"Thank you, we'd both appreciate it," Lucas replied.

Once they were alone, Nora clapped the palm of her hand against her forehead.

So much for keeping it simple. At this rate, Lucas would be on track to spend well over one hundred thousand pounds. Luxury jewelry was categorized as luxury for a reason.

~

Later that afternoon, Nora and Lucas sat in the tea salon of a boutique hotel in South Kensington, a stone's throw away from the Museum of Natural History.

"I think we've made decent progress over the last few days. We have a stockpile of cutesy photos of us as a couple, we've covered our interests and quirky habits, and now, I have a ring." Nora scrolled through the notepad app on her phone. "Is there anything we're missing?"

"I think you've covered the majority of it. The next big hurdle is our families." Lucas tapped his fingers on the table. "When my father returns from holiday, I'll schedule a meeting with him and tell him point-blank that when you and I were reunited at Heathrow, I decided I couldn't wait a moment longer to propose to you."

Nora glanced up from her mobile's screen. "You have to schedule a meeting with your father?"

"Generally." Lucas shrugged. "Leave him and my mum to me. How should we handle your parents?"

"If you want to stay in my papa's good graces, he'll expect you to ask for his permission to propose to me." Nora clicked the screen of her phone off and placed the device facedown on the table.

He winced.

"Papa isn't scary." Nora rolled her eyes.

"I beg to differ. He's the king and a head of state," Lucas muttered, scratching his head. "Would it be best if I booked an airline ticket to Isola Nostrum for an in-person chat? Or do you think a phone call from me might be an option?"

"Knowing Papa, he'd make do with a video conference."

She picked up her phone once more, then the mobile in Lucas's jacket pocket chimed. His eyes traveled to the pocket.

"I sent you Papa's private mobile number. Ring him after tea. Pretend that you thought I'd given you his private secretary's mobile number. It'll soften him up, then you can swoop in for the attack."

"Right."

They decided it would be most effective if Lucas would emphasize that he didn't want to begin the next major chapter of his life without ensuring that Nora knew exactly where their relationship stood. He would tell her father that an engagement between the two of them would signify that she was an important priority in his life.

"We should also arrange for our parents to meet at least once before I leave. Maybe a lunch in a neutral location like Paris?" Lucas suggested.

Nora shook her head. "My parents will insist on hosting your parents as our guests for a long weekend."

"That should work." Lucas rested his head on his hand. "There are so many minute details that are going into this. Imagine if we had an actual wedding to plan."

It was only going to get tougher. Mama would hire a wedding planner not even a day after she heard the news from them.

"There is another matter to settle." Nora cleared her

throat. "What's your workload going to be like with your move to Brisbane? Will you be up for a video chat, say, once a month? Even if we are in a long-distance relationship, we'll have to make a show of spending time together. I'd like to establish good habits right from the start."

"Once a month sounds brilliant." He rubbed his eyes. "On day one, I'll be jumping straight into my research on sauropods that lived approximately ninety to ninety-five million years ago. Sauropods were herbivorous dinosaurs that constitute the largest fossils to have yet been discovered in Australia. There is a theory that—"

"Lucas," Nora warned gently. "Focus."

His eyebrows knit together. "Where was I again?"

"Discussing your availability for monthly video chats."

"Right." Lucas snapped his fingers together. "Um… there shouldn't be any classes for me to take. More than likely, my advisor is going to have me spend most of my time the first six months reading and building up my litera-ture review."

Nora scrunched her nose. "Which is what? It sounds as if it's a summary of sorts."

"That's exactly what it is. The literature review is a compilation of what other researchers have done in paleon-tology in the past. It's intended to help a student identify a gap in the research where their own project fits in. A PhD project is, after all, supposed to be an original contribution to the field."

Nora's brain ached thinking about reading so many books. "It's not my cup of tea, but it makes sense."

A waiter rolled a trolley with squeaky wheels into the room. Lucas perked up and watched with rapt attention as a three-tiered dessert stand, teapot, and two cups were placed on the table.

On the lower tier, steam from dry ice swirled around a selection of round scones. The top tiers contained macarons with dinosaur footprints and chocolate desserts shaped in the form of a volcano, rocks, and dinosaurs.

"What is this?" he asked with wide eyes, carefully picking up a tiny green chocolate stegosaurus.

"This is the Ampersand Hotel's Jurassic Afternoon tea service. I knew as soon as I saw the pictures on their website that we had to come here. The scones are supposed to be dinosaur eggs, and the top layers are a Jurassic mountain and volcanic eruption. I hope it tastes as amazing as it looks."

Lucas placed the dinosaur on his plate and poured himself a cup of tea. "The last few days with you have been some of the best of my life. You're one of the best friends a man could ask for."

Nora's throat constricted. "A girl could cry."

Lucas placed his hand upon hers. "I mean it."

"I know you do." She picked up her teacup. "Remember this when you're ready to make that grand gesture." She winked.

He pulled at the collar of his shirt and quickly drank from his own cup.

He was nervous again. *What do you have planned for me, Lord Malcolm?*

CHAPTER 5

A Room Full of Treasures

"Can I remove the blindfold now?" Nora's hand traveled up to the silky soft yet slippery fabric covering her eyes. Putting one foot in front of the other, she trusted Lucas to guide her to wherever their intended destination might be. Since they'd entered the mystery building, the sounds around them had grown steadily quieter. She could hear people speaking in whispers.

"Give it two more minutes. We're entering a lift." As Lucas spoke, she heard the ding of a bell and an automatic voice warning them that the doors were about to close.

With a jolt, the lift moved. A minute later, the doors opened. Lucas interlaced his hand with hers. She could feel calluses on the tips of his long fingers.

"Is this the lucky lady?" an alto female voice asked.

"It is."

Nora held her hand up to wave.

I hope I'm facing the right direction.

The woman chuckled. "I left two pairs of gloves on the table for you. Please put them on before handling the artifacts. You'll have fifteen minutes to do what you need to do. I'll be just outside the room. Let me know if you're finished early."

Nora's curiosity grew. Where were they? She sniffed the air, but all she could make out was the scent of fresh paper.

A door clicked closed.

"*Now* you can remove it."

Nora reached up and slid the blindfold off. She and Lucas were in a room devoid of furniture except for a single white table. On top of the table were the two pairs of gloves and a curious-looking wooden box containing a frayed, yellowing packet of papers. The walls of the room were adorned with framed posters of the covers of Britain's most famous novels.

A Midsummer Night's Dream. Alice in Wonderland. Jane Eyre. The Lion the Witch and the Wardrobe. Oliver Twist. Pride and Prejudice. All iconic works of British literature.

Lucas cleared his throat. Nora turned. Lowering himself down onto one knee, he held out the light-green Van Cleef and Arpels ring box. She inhaled sharply.

"Princess Leonora Amelia Beatrice. You are one of the most kindhearted, generous, and considerate people of my acquaintance and a person who I'm so proud to call one of my very best friends. You have done so much for me in the short span of the last few days, and now, I'm here to ask you, are you still willing to be my fake fiancée?"

Nora smiled. "Si, Lord Malcolm. I am."

He stood, and with unsteady hands, slid the engagement ring onto her left ring finger. She smelled the light scent of his sandalwood cologne as he wrapped his arms around her.

"Thank you. You've made me one of the happiest men alive."

The door creaked open. Nora heard a woman sigh in contentment. "Young love," she muttered. The door clicked closed.

Lucas pinched the bridge of his nose. "I hope she wasn't privy to the part about my being your fake fiancé."

Her body shook with silent laughter. "I think we're safe."

Lucas pointed to the white gloves. "Put these on, and then we can have a look at the desk and manuscript."

Nora tilted her head to the side. "To whom do they belong?"

He smirked. "My dear Lady Nora. I thought you of all people would recognize the swirly handwriting."

She punched him lightly in the shoulder and picked up a pair of gloves. "If you must know, I have a difficult time deciphering English words written in cursive."

His eyes widened. "You speak English so effortlessly; sometimes I forget Italian is your first language."

"Attending international schools in Italy, Switzerland, and the UK will have that effect on a girl."

She found that the gloves were heavier than she expected as she pulled the rough, thick cotton fabric over her fingers. She moved closer to the table. The so-called desk looked more like a box.

Behind her, in a quiet tone, Lucas said, "We're inside one of the off-exhibit research rooms at the British Library. We had to wait until the treasures room was closed to the public to see this baby in person."

Nora's pulse began to race. The treasures room had so many amazing treats inside of it, including…

She gasped. "Is this the Jane Austen writing desk?"

"Ding. Ding. Ding. Ten points to Lady Nora."

Instinctually, as if it were made from glass, she gently ran her fingers over the fine wood and brass hinges of the desk. The top sloped up, giving its owner the perfect angle to write.

I'm dumb, she thought. This would have been a small, portable writing desk. Jane might have sat under a tree writing about Marianne and Elinor or Lizzy and Jane with this little artifact on her lap.

The desk's interior was lined with a thick navy fabric. Storage compartment slots at the top held a pair of thin wire spectacles, an empty inkwell, and a penknife.

Jane's eyeglasses. She was never formally portrayed with them on. They were so dainty. Did she only use them for reading? For everyday activities? If her sister Cassandra had not burned all the correspondence between them, there might have been an answer.

"I can't believe I'm actually touching this," Nora breathed.

"Don't forget about those." Lucas gestured to the packet of papers. "Fifteen minutes was the longest span of time I could arrange with curators to see these. I think the woman I spoke to over the phone said they were from a set of writings called *A History of England* and *First Impressions*? I've never heard of either one of those."

Nora grew light-headed. "*A History of England* was a private satirical story written by Jane and her sister in their youth. It's better known as *Juvenilia*. *First Impressions* was the original title of *Pride and Prejudice*."

"Ah. That makes sense," he mused.

With hands quivering like a leaf, she picked up the papers and scanned over the text. Although her brain couldn't process the words, what intrigued her was a small colored portrait of a woman at the top. The writing was dense and crammed onto the page, leaving no room for margins.

"Would you like me to read one of the pages aloud to you?" Lucas asked.

Her tongue was glued to the roof of her mouth. Still in shock over what she held in her hands, all she could manage was a weak bob of her head.

Lucas started to read in his professor voice. "The History of England from the reign of Henry the Fourth to the death of Charles the First. By a partial, prejudiced, and ignorant historian. Henry the Fourth ascended the throne much to his own satisfaction in the year thirteen ninety-nine…"

Nora giggled. Hearing Lucas read the text aloud, she could picture a young, witty teenage Jane, quill in hand, penning whatever popped into her mind's eye.

She was so talented with words. She rarely made any mistakes in her manuscripts. Jane knew exactly what she wanted her characters to say and how the scenes should unfold. The world was so lucky these papers survived. They gave so much insight into Jane and her personality. In this day and age, most documents were electronic. The people of the future wouldn't be afforded the same window into the past that a handwritten note or document might provide.

A knock sounded on the door. A woman with shoulder-length auburn locks and rounded glasses entered the room. "How are you two getting on? Are you enjoying the Austen writing box?"

"I'm living every Janeite's dream," Nora gushed.

The woman gestured to the box. "It's really a stunning piece. It's hard to fathom that Miss Austen penned the first drafts of *Pride and Prejudice, Sense and Sensibility,* and *Northanger Abbey* on this very surface between seventeen ninety-five and seventeen ninety-nine."

Nora agreed. "And the manuscripts. What a treat!"

"That was all Lord Merrick. He personally requested that you be able to see one of the manuscripts in our holdings. We have several, but these two are my personal favorite. They paint a rather intimate portrait of a young Miss Austen and the writer she would later become."

Nora blinked twice. Lucas looked away from her. *Lucas went to all this trouble for me? He truly is among the best of men.*

The woman sighed. "I came into the room to advise you that we are closing. Unfortunately, these precious objects must be returned to their cases."

They thanked her and left via the same route they had entered.

Nora shook her head. "That was much more than a grand gesture—it was a mammoth gesture."

Hands in his pockets, Lucas studied the tile patterns on the ground leading from the entry hallway to the exit. "I'm fortunate that I have connections to mates in high places. There are Harrovians scattered throughout London."

Nora furrowed her brow.

"The name of former pupils of Harrow School."

"Of course," she said.

"It was easy to pick up the phone and call in a favor or two."

They walked in silence, Nora's mind still whirling over Lucas's ability to continually surprise her.

The next evening, home again on Isola Nostrum, Nora sat in front of her bathroom mirror and tapped the excess powder off her makeup brush. Musical notes and phrases flashed through her mind as she mentally prepared to play Tchaikovsky's *Violin Concerto Opus 35*.

A knock sounded at her door. Without glancing away from her reflection, she called out, "Come in."

The door creaked open. Stiletto heels clicked against the tiled floor of Nora's bathroom. "Leonora! I heard from the servants that you'd arrived home," her mother said.

"Ciao, Mama." She set the brush down and pivoted her body to face her mother. They kissed one another on the cheeks. "I'm sorry I didn't come down and see you. I was running short on time to dress for tonight's concert. First, my flight was delayed. Then, Lorenzo was late to pick me up." She shook her head in disbelief. "We only docked at the harbor a half hour ago."

Her mother shot her a look of sympathy. "Is there anything I can do to help you?"

Nora lined her lips with a matte blush-pink lipstick and smacked them together. "No. All that's left for me to do before I head down to the conservatory is to warm up with Roberto, tonight's pianist."

Her mother checked the time on her watch. "You have about twenty minutes. It's a full house tonight. The president of the Ananostrum Royal Hospital believes we've raised over fifty thousand euros for the new children's ward."

Nora grinned. "Eccellente."

"The crown will match the proceeds, of course." Mama leaned against the door frame.

Nora picked up her hairbrush and quickly secured her

hair into a low, slick chignon. "Is there anything else, Mama?"

"Can't a mother just wish to spend a few minutes of time with her eldest daughter?"

She resisted the urge to roll her eyes. "Mama. What is it that you've been wanting to ask me? Can it wait until later?"

Her mother's eyebrow twitched. "Your sister showed me the most peculiar photo of you and your friend from university… what was his name again? Alfred? Michael?"

Mama was brilliant at remembering faces, but names, not so much.

"Lucas," she automatically corrected, reaching for some bobby pins.

"Si, Lucas." Mama snapped her fingers together. "Lucia said the photo was taken this past week. You have to admit, it is *quite* a coincidence that the two of you were able to meet one another in London after two years. I wasn't aware you were still in contact with him."

"Lucas and I never lost touch. He's always been a very special person to me."

"Is that so?" Like a sponge, her mother absorbed the information.

"Lucas just returned to the UK, and I thought that since I had a few free days in my schedule, it would be fun to spend some time with him." She shook a can of hair spray.

"Uh-huh. And did anything else happen in London?" Her mother took a step closer to her. "Your father received a curious phone call from a UK number. I know it didn't come from Buckingham Palace…"

"Mama, I know this might come as a shock to you"— Nora checked her appearance once more and stood to face her mother—"but Lucas and I have been seeing one another in a committed long-distance relationship for more than a year. The call Papa received was from him. He wanted Papa's blessing before he proposed to me."

She internally cringed at the lie, but knowing why she was doing it helped lessen some of her guilt. It wasn't only for Lucas. It was also for herself. She could almost picture herself living in the flat away from Isola Nostrum. A place where she could be free from the burdens of being the crown princess for a little bit longer. A place she could feel as close to normal as possible.

"Pardon me?" her mother sputtered.

A digital alarm beeped on Nora's phone. She tapped the screen and silenced it.

I couldn't have timed it any better. Go me.

"That was the ten-minute warning." Nora gently guided her mother out of the bathroom and into her sitting room. From her writing desk, she picked up a folder of sheet music, and the handle of the case for her precious three-hundred-year-old Guarneri violin. "We can chat more about it after the reception."

Her mother managed a dumbfounded nod. "Yes. After the reception."

Together they walked out of Nora's rooms to the lift, her mother mumbling under her breath in Italian about when she might be able to invite Lucas to visit.

Nora had never seen Mama so stunned, but by the time she played the last note of the concerto, her mother would have her wits about her. She hoped Lucas was not going to have too much trouble with his parents.

CHAPTER 6

Stick to the Plan

Close to midnight, Nora unlocked her tablet as she lay on her stomach atop her bed. Lucas's face appeared on her screen. His eyes were puffy, his jaw lined with scruff.

"Hello, stranger," she said.

"Hello yourself." Sitting in a wingback chair, he balanced his own tablet on his lap while scratching the head of his family's black-and-white border collie. Rex's head rested on Lucas's knee and his tail wagged slowly from side to side. A log burning in a fireplace crackled. "How did your concert go this evening? Sublimely?"

"It wasn't anything to write home about." She shrugged. "Not my best performance, but certainly not my worst. The most important bit is that we raised enough money to fund the expansion of the children's wing of the Ananostrum Royal Hospital."

"Brilliant." Lucas gave her a thumbs-up. "Now that you're finally able to have some downtime; I bet you are just as physically and mentally exhausted as I am."

"Assolutamente. From the moment I stepped off the plane, I had to run with all cylinders firing to get from point A to point B." She propped her head up, resting it on her elbows. "I'd hoped to avoid Mama and Papa until after the concert, but Mama cornered me when I was getting ready."

"I'm not surprised. She's like my father. She has a sixth sense." Lucas snickered.

"Si. Mama had it all planned. She asked question after question about you, London, and about your phone call to Papa. She instinctively knew something was up, but she wasn't exactly sure what it was."

Nora moved a lock of hair behind her shoulder. "Since you spoke to Papa, I didn't see any need to prolong the news, so I told her you had proposed to me. She went into shock, but it didn't last long."

At least Mama's shock wasn't as bad as Papa's. When Lucas rang him after tea, he dropped his phone into the pool. I'm just glad he made it clear that he would support whatever decision we make.

Lucas raised an eyebrow.

"By the time the concert and reception were finished, Mama was already in full-on wedding-planning mode. I'd expect an invitation for you and your family to visit Isola Nostrum within the week." Nora shifted her position and sat crossed-legged on the bed. "Have you had a chance to make an appointment to lower the boom on your parents as of yet?"

Lucas's fist clenched. "No appointment was needed."

She repositioned the tablet closer to her face. Reading his body language, she said, "It went that poorly?"

"I arrived home about an hour before my parents

returned from their holiday. They were in a jolly good mood. We spent the afternoon catching up with one another. Everything was going well until dinner." He breathed out sharply. "That's when Father started in about my future. He said now that I am home, I can finally put all the paleontology nonsense behind me. He planned to arrange for me to start shadowing the estate manager as early as tomorrow."

Nora's stomach dropped. The Duke of Trent certainly didn't waste any time.

"Father caught me off guard. I was both hurt and angry that he considered all the hard work I'd put in to be nonsense. In the heat of the moment, I threw out that he shouldn't bother making plans for me because I'm moving to Australia to pursue my PhD." Lucas's chin lowered. "We exchanged harsh words, and he stormed out of the room, leaving my mum and me alone. I haven't seen him since."

Poor Lucas. Nora wished she could reach through the screen and give him a hug or rub his shoulders in a show of solidarity. Rex licked his hand.

"Was your mum on your side?"

"I would like to think that she is." Lucas shrugged. "She hates being caught in the middle whenever Father and I have a row. She's taken to walking on eggshells around the two of us and refrains from mentioning her direct opinion about anything these days. After Father left the room, Mum gave me a hug, said welcome home, and left for the quiet sanctuary of her study."

So he hadn't mentioned their engagement to his father.

Nora's jaw clenched. "You definitely sound as if you are going to need reinforcements when you confront your father again. Uno momento." She padded over to her desk and retrieved her mobile phone. Unlocking the screen, she opened her calendar app and reviewed her planned engagements for the week.

Giulia needed her tomorrow and Tuesday, and she had auditions set for Wednesday and Thursday. She'd told Papa she'd be shadowing him on Friday and was supposed to attend the last Parliamentary session of the year. She couldn't bail on Giulia or Papa, but if she canceled her auditions, that would give her two potential days to jaunt over to the UK. This was just bad timing. The end of the year was busier than any other time.

Glancing up from her mobile, Nora placed it down on the bed and picked up the tablet. "Do you know if your father is free on Wednesday or Thursday?"

"Father's diary varies week to week, but Thursdays are generally open. Why?"

Nora bit her lip.

"You aren't planning to come to Rosewood Hall in person, are you?" Lucas abruptly stopped scratching the dog's head and leaned his face toward the camera. "You just obliged me by rearranging your entire weekend to spend time with me in London. I can't ask you to drop everything and fly back here a second time."

"If you think my presence will make a stronger statement to your father, it'll be worth the trip." Nora crossed her arms. "I can be *very* convincing and argumentative when I set my mind to something."

"It's the week before Christmas." Lucas massaged his temples. "I'll only agree to you coming out here if you promise I'm not taking you away from anything pressing, like an audition."

You're not making this any easier, Lucas.

He furrowed his brow at Nora's hesitation.

"They haven't been on the books too long."

"No."

"Lucas," Nora pleaded.

"N-O. No." He rubbed his hands through his hair. The static electricity caused its ends to stand up wildly. "I need to grow a backbone and stop being such a coward when it comes to dealing with my father. If he chooses to completely cut me off financially, so be it."

Nora watched a string of conflicting emotions play across Lucas's face. She'd known that he'd always been afraid of the man. His father pushed him hard. The duke was a man who lived more in the past than the present. Appearances were everything to him.

"How much of your trust fund and your inheritance do you have remaining?" Nora asked softly. "Is it enough to see you through your studies? Why did you spend so much money on the jewelry?"

"Because you deserve it. It's my small way of paying you back for what you're doing. Don't even think of saying we can sell it or return it. It's my gift to you." Lucas's shoulders hunched. "To answer your other questions, I spent the majority of what was remaining in my account when I bought the property in Cheltenham. If I rein in my spending and stick to a budget, I'll have just enough money in the bank remaining to put down a deposit on a flat in Australia."

"Are you going to receive a stipend from the university? I remember you saying that your place in the program was fully funded."

"Graduate students are only paid a small pittance. If I've reviewed the figures correctly, my stipend will cover the cost of rent on a flat and groceries. My bills and other living expenses I'm hoping will come out of the rent I'm receiving from my property investment."

"Would you accept a loan from me?"

Lucas's jaw clenched. "No."

Nora exhaled deeply. "Forget I asked."

He pinched the bridge of his nose. "Money will be tight, but manageable. There are ways to supplement my income. Teaching, for example… I can always pick up some tutoring hours."

They'd already had this conversation about how busy he was going to be. Like it or not, Lucas was going to have to remain in the good graces of his father. Or accept a loan from her. As much as he might wish it, he couldn't afford to become financially independent with the path he'd chosen to walk. At least for the time being.

The fire crackled. In the background, Nora could hear the faint sound of holiday carols playing from a wireless speaker somewhere in the room.

"As well and good as your intentions are, Lucas, one of the reasons I agreed to this entire charade was to soften your father to your cause. Have some faith and stick to the original plan. As crazy as it is that we're 'engaged'"—Nora used her fingers to make a pair of air quotes—"you weren't wrong when you said it was the one thing your father wanted for you."

She took a breath. "Give you and your father both time to cool your tempers overnight. In the morning, let him know that you have some other news to share with him. I'll book myself a flight to the UK when we get off the phone. What's the closest airport to you? Bristol?"

"Yes. That would be the closest major airport."

"What about regional airports?" She thought there was

a low-cost carrier or two that operated flights between Rome and places like Nottingham.

"Uh … I think it'll be the East Midlands Airport."

"Got it." Nora nodded and made a mental note to learn more about Lincolnshire and the area where Rosewood Hall was located. With the passion Lucas's father held for the family estate, a little knowledge might go far in helping gain some extra brownie points with the duke.

"Nora. You are a gem. If we were truly engaged, I'd give you the fiancée of the year award."

"The day will come when I need a favor from you." She waved him off with her hand. "Besides, you spent a hefty amount on jewelry for me."

"I'll speak to Father in the morning." His cheeks flushed cherry red. "Did you have a chance to check your email before our chat, by any chance?"

"No, I haven't, but I will when we're done."

"If you have any questions, let me know," Lucas said cryptically.

They spoke to one another for a few more moments before ending the call. Backing out of the video chat app, Nora tapped the envelope icon and noted she had a message from Lucas.

To: bennetgal06@email.com
From:theroarsomemalcolm@email.com

Nora laughed upon remembering his email handle. *Roarsome. If there were ever a word to describe Lucas to a T, this is it.*

Dear Nora,

Thank you for entrusting me with a copy of the latest *Pride and Prejudice* variation story you have written. Although it has been many years since I've read through Ms. Jane Austen's novels, it was easy for

me to become immersed within the reimagined world of the Bennets, Darcys, and Bingleys that you've seen fit to create. I am incredibly impressed with your writing style and ability.

Her body warmed. She'd never let anyone read her writing before. Her stories and her writing had always been a fun hobby solely for her own personal pleasure. Was it good enough to share with other Jane Austen fans?

In fact, I don't remember either Mr. Darcy or Colonel Fitzwilliam having such developed personalities. You truly turned these two-dimensional literary characters into men I could imagine myself conversing with and spending time with.

Nora laughed.

If she were to sketch Lord Malcolm's character á la Lizzy Bennet, the result would be a man who was a living, breathing hybrid of Colonel Fitzwilliam and Mr. Darcy. Colonel Fitzwilliam was often overlooked. He might have been written to be a minor character, but she had always firmly believed his being named a co-guardian of Georgiana Darcy spoke dividends about the type of man he might be. He was a man who had seen and experienced war, and yet he was still able to be witty, well-mannered, and full of heart.

I hope you don't mind, but since I needed a distraction tonight, I've made a few corrections to your grammar and spelling. The content of the story remains largely untouched. I hope you might consider sharing your writing with others. If you have any questions, please let me know.

Yours,
Lord Malcolm

Nora clicked on the attachment to the email. As it loaded, her eyes widened.

When did Lucas have the time to go through and proofread my manuscript? She scrolled through the document quickly. *He's left corrections and notes for me in the margins on all three hundred pages?*

She returned to the email and read it over a second time. Her gaze stopped on the phrase "earlier this evening." Had Lucas done all this for her within a few hours? She looked at the time stamp on each edit.

Talk about impressive. It took her just over three months to write this. Lucas had not only read the entire document within the span of a week, but all these notes were from today. This must be one of his magical graduate-student skills. Did he ever sleep?

She sighed. If Lucas was going to fight one of his internal demons and stand up to his father, perhaps she should consider taking a lead out of his book.

With a rush of adrenaline, Nora logged on to the Jane-Austen-themed message board Never Far From Netherfield. Holding her breath, she hit "compose" and began to type a message.

BennetGal06: Hello, everyone. For the last two years, I've been a frequent visitor to the stories sub-forum, but this is my first time posting. I have a P & P variation story I've written that explores what might have happened if Mr. Collins was the negligent master of Netherfield and sought to rent the estate out to Mr. Bingley to inject some much-needed capital into his coffers. The Bennets are tenants of Netherfield, and Mr. Bennet its steward. Would any of you be interested in reading this story? Please share your thoughts.

After proofing her message for errors, Nora clicked "Post."

Within ten seconds, she already had a reply.

AustenAddict: Yes! Yes! Yes!

A ghost of a smile crossed her lips, then she turned her tablet off.

Let's put your suggestion to the test, Lord Malcolm.

CHAPTER 7

Rosewood Hall

Nora glanced out the airplane window as a combination of rain and half-formed snowflakes fell upon the wings of the midsized eighty-seat regional jet. Outside, a worker wearing a bright yellow vest and holding two orange batons safely guided the airplane into position as it taxied into the gate. As it was one of the busiest travel weeks of the year, every seat was filled. Christmas was just four days away.

Following the antlike line of passengers to the arrivals area of the East Midlands Airport, she held her hand to her forehead before spotting Lucas engrossed in work on his black laptop computer. His hands flew furiously across the keys as if he were playing a piano.

An announcement over the speaker said, "Now arriving from Rome, flight number two-seven-six-three. Please expect your checked baggage to arrive on carousel six."

Glancing up in surprise, Lucas removed a pair of rounded black glasses, rubbed his eyes, and took a deep breath.

Nora's body shook with laughter. He was adorable

when he was working. She hadn't seen him wear glasses too often. They added to his attractiveness.

"Malcolm," she called out.

Lucas looked over at her. She waved.

"You forgot the 'Lord' bit," he said cheekily as he closed the computer and tucked it into a black traveling case. "You made good time, all things considered."

"Apologies, *Lord* Malcolm." Nora curtsied and flared out the sides of her trench coat.

They shared a laugh.

"I was fortunate to get put on the earlier flight. It helps to travel solo sometimes. My originally booked flight was going to be delayed four hours because of all the heavy snow." She rubbed her hands over her forearms. "The cold weather is a nasty shock every time I set foot in the UK."

"So long as you don't mind dog hair, I have a blanket in the car you can make use of while I drive us to Rosewood."

They exited the terminal and headed toward the car park. Tiny snowflakes landed on her nose and eyelashes.

"And how is Rex, my favorite border collie? This will be the first time I've actually met him in the flesh."

Lucas pulled the key fob out of his pocket with a click, and the doors unlocked and lights flashed. "He's excited to meet you. I've been working on sorting all his veterinary paperwork out while waiting for you. He'll be coming to Queensland with me. We've been separated for too long, and I can't bear to leave him again. He's turning ten this year."

"I'm looking forward to seeing that impish grin and giving him belly rub after belly rub." She opened the door and spied the red-and-black tartan blanket sitting on the passenger seat. As she picked it up, she felt the coarse fabric under her fingers. "I miss having a dog around the house.

Mama and Papa never had the heart to let Lorenzo, Lucia, or I get another dog after our last set of greyhounds."

"It's a tough commitment to have a senior dog, but they just stare at you with those sad eyes and it is all over." Lucas slid into the driver's seat. "Rex hasn't let me out of his sight since I've been home."

Nora sighed. She swore dogs could understand humans better than other humans could.

Lucas started the engine, checked the mirrors, and slowly backed up the SUV.

She cleared her throat. "I've been doing some reading up on Rosewood Hall this week, and before we meet your father, I thought I might have you correct and fill in any gaps in my knowledge."

The turn indicator clicked as Lucas changed lanes and entered the motorway. "You are always so prepared."

She grinned. "It's in my DNA. A princess always has a few basic facts prepared for any situation she is about to enter. Papa claims it's one of the reasons why Isola Nostrum has been so successful when it comes to diplomacy."

He raised an eyebrow. "Doesn't Isola Nostrum always try to present itself as a neutral country?"

"Precisely."

He chuckled. "Okay, Lady Nora. What questions do you have for me?"

Nora closed her eyes and recited from memory. "The original Rosewood Hall dates from the sixteenth century. But unfortunately, in the seventeenth century, it suffered from a horrid fire. The current structure was rebuilt in the eighteenth century and has a Georgian facade." She opened her eyes and glanced at Lucas for confirmation.

"So far, you are spot on."

"Additionally, Rosewood Hall has always been the seat

of the Duke of Trent, and Hollyrose House the seat of the Earl of Merrick. Yet during World War I, due to a lack of funds, Hollyrose House was sold to the National Trust. It's now a private school."

"Spot on." Lucas nodded and added, "Queen Elizabeth I granted the dukedom to the Malcolm family in fifteen seventy. While it may not be a royal dukedom, the title has been passed down from father to son in an unbroken chain. It's a fact my father is exceptionally proud of."

"The Toscani family only predates yours by fifty years," Nora mused. "We became the ruling house of Isola Nostrum in fifteen twenty."

The car slowed as the snow began to come down harder.

"What was the reason for Queen Elizabeth awarding your family a dukedom?" Nora asked.

Lucas flicked the wipers on and glanced at her. "The Malcolms were renowned dog breeders. According to family lore, we were one of the first families to bring border collies down to England from Scotland."

Nora let out a long whistle. "Wow. That's impressive."

"Our kennels are one of the most profitable enterprises of the estate. There is a long list of individuals waiting to adopt a border collie puppy." He drummed his fingers against the steering wheel.

Nora read it as a sign of his irritation. "What do you find frustrating about it?"

He frowned. "Having a purebred puppy is all well and good, but there are also so many dogs waiting in shelters to find their forever homes. I wish Father would consider taking in some rescue dogs and helping them find families." He huffed. "A lot of people pass through the estate. If they could see and interact with the rescue dogs, it could make a world of difference."

"I'd be happy to bring that up with you father if you'd like," Nora suggested.

She pictured Lucas dressed in a khaki-colored ensemble, leading two lines of dogs to a dig site. When he blew a whistle, the dogs would go to work sniffing out and digging up fossils. She wondered if the dogs, however, would bring the bones to Lucas, or if they might ignore him and start chewing on them.

It sounded like a wonderful project they could start on Isola Nostrum. Lucia would be the perfect person to spearhead the endeavor. She'd always been passionate about animals. As for Rosewood Hall, if Lucas didn't want to speak to his father, they could casually hint to his kennel manager about the idea.

She stopped herself short. Her cheeks warmed. She'd almost forgotten that they weren't a real couple.

"Maybe. If the notion were to come from you, he might be more receptive to it. It would depend on his mood."

The snow began to come down harder against the windshield. Lucas slowed the car.

Nora adjusted the blanket over her legs. She changed the subject. "Do you think I've studied enough in order to make an impression on your father?"

"I'd say so."

She chewed on her lip. "Is there anything else I should know or be aware of when it comes to your father or the estate?"

"No. Just be the charming Lady Nora that I've grown to love."

The way he called her Lady Nora sent a tingle of delight through her spine.

~

As the car turned off the motorway, they entered a long gravel drive. Trees on either side were decorated in twinkling gold fairy lights. It gave off the effect of them driving through a shimmering tunnel. Emerging from the tunnel, Nora stared in awe at the sand-colored limestone facade of Rosewood Hall. It was much grander than she'd imagined.

"This is a larger building than the palace at Isola Nostrum. It could double as a stand-in for the grand estate of Chatsworth." She squinted. "I can't tell with all the snow covering the ground, but is that a frozen lake or a fountain?"

"At one point in Rosewood's history, the water feature was a pond. My three-times great—grandfather had it transformed into a proper fountain. It's one of the characteristics I love best about the estate. In summer, it's brilliant when the fountains are running."

Lucas positioned the car into one of the covered porticos to the side of the manor home's entrance and turned off the car's engine. An assortment of Christmas trees of varying heights, dressed in multicolored lights and colorful round ornaments, created a festive ambiance.

Nora opened the car door and stepped out. "I didn't expect to see so many decorations."

He shrugged. "It's primarily for show. Every holiday season, Rosewood hosts a milelong holiday trail of extravagant light displays, food offerings, and entertainment for visitors to the estate to enjoy."

"And I'm only hearing about this now?"

"It's something I've grown up with and am immune to. I was never allowed to attend or partake in it." He slid out of the car, closing the driver's side door. "Father is only keen on it because of how lucrative the financial returns are. We have more visitors to the estate during the holiday season than any other time of the year."

Nora bit her tongue to keep from lashing out against Lucas's parents. It just seemed wrong to her that the Duke of Trent would go through the trouble of hosting such a lavish holiday affair at Rosewood Hall, and at the same time, would actively seek to keep his only child from experiencing the joys it might bring him.

She rubbed her hands together.

"Would you care for something warm to drink before I take you up to greet my parents?" Lucas asked as they ascended the steps together to the side entry door connected to the kitchens. Nora could smell mulled wine wafting through the air.

"No. I'd rather face them now." She removed her scarf and her gloves. "But if we have some time afterward, I'd like to sneak a peek at the holiday trail with you over a glass of mulled wine."

"It's a deal. We'll both need the respite after what's to come." Lucas removed his gray overcoat.

As he guided them through a maze of corridors, they passed a tour group and pressed their bodies up against the wall to let them by.

A guide in a navy-blue pinstriped suit walked backward as he said, "This hallway will lead us up to the portrait gallery, where you will find a magnificent portrait of the first Duke of Trent commissioned by Queen Elizabeth I herself. It was painted in the—"

To Nora's amusement, she overheard a woman near the back of the line declare to her companion, "I read online that the current duke's son is unmarried. Wonder if there's any chance of either of us catching a glimpse of him. Who knows, with any luck, maybe he'll take one look at me, and we'll fall madly in love with one another."

"As if there's any chance of that." The other tourist snorted. "The duke's son probably isn't even home."

Nora watched two patches of red appear on Lucas's cheeks. Her body shook with silent laughter.

"Not a word from you," he murmured.

"Spoilsport."

Lucas rapped his knuckles on a dark cherry door and paused, fingering the zipper of his knit jumper.

"Enter," a baritone voice called out.

Nora wiped her hands against the fabric of her tweed skirt. Plastering a pleasant expression onto her face, she nodded to Lucas. "Andiamo. Let's go."

Lucas turned the knob, and the door creaked open. Together, they entered the room. His Grace, William Malcom, the eleventh Duke of Trent, rose from his seat behind an elongated wooden desk. Standing about five foot ten, Lucas's father had salt-and-pepper hair, a neat beard, and was impeccably dressed in a white-and-blue window-pane-striped suit.

"Ah, Lucas, have you finally come to your senses? I knew it was only a matter of time before you'd come seek me out to have a man-to-man chat—"

"Father," he interjected, "I brought a visitor to say hello. You remember Nora, from my uni days."

Standing beside him, she could feel the tension Lucas held in his body. A flicker of surprise flashed behind the duke's eyes.

"Your Grace." She inclined her head. "It's wonderful to see you again."

The duke cleared his throat and walked out from around his desk. "Princess Leonora. Welcome to Rosewood." He shook hands with her. "Lucas failed to mention you'd be gracing us with your presence today."

Nora smiled. "Forgive me, Your Grace. Lucas wasn't aware I'd be coming to visit until early this morning. I wanted to be here in person when he was ready to share our exciting news with you."

She nodded encouragingly to Lucas and intertwined her hand with his. His face was pale.

"Father, after our, er… discussion two nights ago, I never had the opportunity to share with you that I had one other bit of important news."

The duke's eyebrow rose. He crossed his arms against his chest. "Oh? And what is this news?" His gaze traveled to their hands.

Nora could sense Lucas's courage was fleeing. With as much warmth as she could muster, she said, "Your Grace… I am thrilled to be able to tell you that Lucas has made me the happiest woman alive." She paused for dramatic effect. "He's asked me to marry him, and I've said yes."

The lie is almost easier to accept and slip into the more times it comes out.

Lucas placed a gentle kiss on Nora's cheek. His lips were warm and his chin was scratchy. She could smell the slightly fruity and earthy scent of his cologne. It all felt so natural and made her body tingle.

The duke leaned against the edge of his desk. With a clang, a frame toppled over. "Lucas… my son… has asked *you* to *marry* him?"

She nodded patiently. "Yes, sir. My parents were just as

surprised as you are." She and Lucas exchanged knowing glances. "We've always been good friends, and after being in a long-distance relationship with one another for over a year, we both can say in no uncertain terms that we want a future together."

The duke was still processing the information. Nora lifted her chin. Her eyes locked on to his icy-blue orbs. "Your Grace, it's important for me to let you know that this isn't a decision that either of us has made lightly. I take my duties as the crown princess of Isola Nostrum seriously. Lucas is one of the few men who will understand the weight of the responsibility that comes with having a title."

Nora's words caused the Duke of Trent to perk up. She squeezed Lucas's hand and attempted to send him a mental message. *Come on, Lord Malcolm, I've set the table for you. This is where you plead your case.*

Lucas blinked twice and returned the gesture. Rubbing her thumb over his wrist, Nora could feel the rapid beat of his pulse.

"Leonora is one of those women whom a bloke might meet once in a lifetime," he said softly, angling his head in her direction. "From the moment I first laid eyes upon her, I knew she was special. Nora is the only woman I could ever picture having in my life. I love her so much."

Her body grew warm. He almost sounded so genuine. For a few moments, she found herself believing the words coming out of Lucas's mouth. He was a far better actor than she'd given him credit for.

Lucas brushed a stray lock of hair behind her ear intimately. His attention turned to the duke. "Father, I proposed to Nora because I didn't want to take the risk of losing her to another man. Regardless of what you say, I am leaving for Brisbane to enroll in the paleontology doctorate program at the University of Queensland on the fifteenth of January. Brisbane will be my home for the next three to four years whilst I complete my studies. We've both agreed that right after I officially graduate, we'll marry."

The duke's brows creased. His face grew a deep shade of red.

Oh, too much at once. It's not going well. We're losing him. What else can I say?

"Your Grace, I hope you can find it in your heart to forgive me." Nora let go of Lucas's hand and placed her hand upon the duke's arm. "I'm the one to blame for encouraging your son to rush off to Australia."

Think about Lizzy and Mr. Darcy never being able to be together. Think about the courage you would need if you were Georgiana Darcy and had to tell your older brother that you'd eloped with Wickham.

The corners of her eyes grew moist. Her lips quivered. "Sir, I'm not sure if you're aware, but this is your son's dream. He's worked harder than any person I've ever met to achieve it. Lucas has already had an article published in one of the top journals in his field *and* he's been notified that he has earned one of two fully-funded places for his doctorate. Both of those accomplishments speak volumes about him."

She sniffled. "The paleontology department at UQ is world-class. The department sees so much potential in him and in his work. They could have selected any other number of applicants but didn't. They chose him. You may not see eye to eye with your son, but he doesn't deserve to be mocked. In fact, you should be proud. He's going to be one of the leading experts in the paleontology world."

The waterworks turned on. She started to cry. She couldn't stand to see Lucas belittled and just take it. She'd known he'd been treated this way his entire life, but hearing about it and seeing it in action were two separate things. It hurt her.

Lucas took her into his arms and hugged her. "Thank you," he whispered into her ear.

The duke sighed. Wordlessly, he reached into his pocket and offered her a tissue. "My dear, no tears."

Nora and Lucas broke apart. She accepted the tissue from the duke and patted the corners of her eyes. From under her eyelashes, she observed Lucas had turned his body. He stared into the crackling fireplace with his hands placed behind his back. She could hear a dog scratching at the door and high-pitched whimpering.

The duke cleared his throat. In a sharp tone, he said, "Lucas, let me be clear. When you leave for Australia, you are on your own. I refuse to offer you any sort of financial support. I am extremely vexed. I thought I had raised you better, to be a leader and to know your place as a future duke. You can't even stand up to me and make your case."

Poor Lucas. His father sounded so cold and distant. Nora's eyes widened. She inhaled sharply and backed away.

The duke's face softened. "Princess, I mean no disrespect toward you." He swallowed hard. "Your engagement to my son is the only thing he's done right these days. I hope he doesn't do anything to muck it up. You may call me Bill."

Her eyes fluttered. "Please, sir, I prefer Leonora or Nora."

"Very well." He nodded. "Leonora it shall be." The duke walked back around his desk.

Nora made her way back to Lucas. He wrapped one arm around her shoulder. His hands trembled. "Father, Nora and I are going to head up to speak with Mother. Is there anything else you need from either of us before we leave?"

"No." The duke's jaw clenched.

Lucas grit his teeth. He and Nora moved to leave the room.

Just before reaching the door, Nora stopped. She gestured for Lucas to wait a moment. "Thank you for meeting with us, Bill. It was a pleasure. I hope we can count on taking tea with you before I leave today."

"Of course, Leonora. I'd like nothing better."

She nodded, and Lucas opened the door. Rex barked and padded over to him. "Hi, boy." Closing the door, he knelt down to scratch his loyal friend. Rex licked his face.

Rex instinctively knew Lucas needed him right now. He'd known Lucas longer than Nora had.

Her own pulse was still beating at a rapid pace. "Your father is an intense man."

For all the courage she'd been able to muster, she'd fought hard to hide the fact that the man frightened her too.

"For him, that went about as well as I could've hoped for. There was no yelling or destroying of objects… just another dressing down." His throat constricted. "Thank you for standing up for me, Nora. I appreciate it in more ways than you'll ever know." Lucas was still focused on Rex. "I can never find my voice with him."

"It was painful for me to watch. You don't deserve to be treated so abysmally." Nora knelt down next to Rex and let him sniff her hand. He licked it. "Are you doing all right?"

"I'll be fine." He stroked the dog.

But he wasn't fine. He was angry and hurt. It was all over his body language. She was slowly beginning to understand why her friend had always been so private and closed off. For so much of his life, he must have been alone. The dinosaurs, she surmised, had been his coping mechanism. They'd brought him comfort and were his distraction from the world.

"Lucas?"

"Give me time. Being here always drains me both emotionally and physically. I'll recover. I always do." His eyes locked on to hers. They were large and sparkled with longing, as if the sun were shining through the Hope Diamond. Her stomach fluttered. There was something different behind them. A deep emotion she couldn't put into words.

Moving his body close to hers, he whispered, "I just… I just… " Her eyes closed. Her lips parted. She felt the tender brush of his lips against her cheek. "I'm so grateful you're here. I would've been lost without you. You've been my rock over the last week."

"You deserve to be happy." Her eyes opened. All hopes of receiving a kiss from Lucas faded. It was all a charade. She had to remind herself that everything Lucas had told his father about them was a part of the act. Their relationship was supposed to remain platonic.

Rex barked as they stood. "If I were to translate dog speak into English, I think Rex would say forget everything your father said. What matters is you are going to Australia."

He smiled weakly and rubbed the back of his neck. "Shall we go up and see my mum?"

"Lead the way," Nora said.

CHAPTER 8

Musings in Milan

Two weeks later, Nora stood on an empty stage in a dim and eerily silent theatre. Her pulse was racing wildly in her chest, and her throat was parched. Her eyes traveled to the rows of empty maroon velvet seats. A black screen hid her from the view of the three-person selection committee occupying the center front row.

Suddenly, a male voice announced, "Candidate number seven-four-two, we'd like you to play excerpt numbers six, ten, and eleven."

She opened her mouth to reply but stopped herself just in time. Speaking aloud would immediately disqualify her from the audition process. Her thoughts turned to Lucas.

What would he make of seeing how an orchestral audition unfolded? Would he laugh that she removed her shoes so the panel wouldn't hear the click of her high heels and realize she was a woman?

To ensure that both male and female musicians were afforded equal treatment, the only sound the members of the audition panel were supposed to hear was the playing of her violin.

Nora took a deep breath. Her hands shook as she selected and arranged the three pages of music on the silver music stand.

They wanted to hear selections of concertos by Tchaikovsky, Sibelius, and Brahms. Her eyes skimmed over the pieces and she bit her lip.

Of all the rotten luck. She'd spent hundreds of hours practicing, and one of the three was a piece she never thought in a million years that she'd have to play—Brahms's Violin Concerto in D Minor. What was the tempo? The style? The speed?

In her heart, she knew no matter what she did, she wouldn't be offered a spot with the prestigious La Scala Opera Symphony. It would go to a person who was much more experienced and less nervous. She stared at the door, wondering if she ought to leave the room before she had even played a single note.

She didn't want to sully any future audition opportunities that might arise. The music world was so small. This was where having a royal title worked to her disadvantage.

She weighed the pros and cons.

She supposed today's audition was technically anonymous. If she was only seen as candidate number seven-four-two, then she wouldn't technically build a reputation around herself as being a violinist who came unprepared. Plus, she had traveled all the way up to Milan.

"Candidate seven-four-two, whenever you are ready," the male voice said.

Placing her violin under her chin, she took a deep breath and began to play the opening set of notes of an excerpt from Tchaikovsky's Violin Concerto in D Major.

Orchestral audition panels always looked for a musician to have good rhythm, technique, and intonation when they played. Nora never worried about her fingerings or her bowing when she was hidden from view. At the end of the day, the audition panel cared only about a person's ability to create a beautiful sound. If she was successful, she would be a part of an orchestra. One violin among many.

Within the span of three minutes, Nora found she'd finished the first and second excerpts. Coming to the third piece, her brain moved at warp speed. When was the last time she'd heard Brahms's concerto?

Every key had a different meaning in classical music. A C major was tied to purity, D major to victory, and an E minor to grief and mourning. The great composers all used these to signify great phenomena. But what was D minor? Happy? Sad? Indifferent? She was drawing a blank.

Taking a complete shot in the dark, Nora made an educated guess and approached the D minor with a jovial air. Her fingers moved up and down the neck of the violin. She opted to add a little extra oomph to her vibrato as she played the last chord.

I hope this is passable.

When she finished, she tucked her violin under her arm, and exhaled sharply.

She heard whispering on the other side of the screen and the scribbling of pens against paper. "Thank you, candidate seven-four-two. You should expect to hear the results of your audition within the next two weeks."

Fleeing to the backstage rehearsal room, Nora quickly packed her violin away, slipped her shoes on, and bid the next candidate good luck. Outside in the freezing-cold fresh air, Nora finally felt as if she could relax for the first time all day. There wasn't any more she could do in Milan.

As she walked along one of the roads that formed the Piazza della Scala, the imposing white-and-gold facade of the Teatro alla Scala grew smaller. Tourists crowded the square, purchasing hot mulled wine and sweet panettone and pandoro cakes. Decorative Christmas trees lit in bright golden lights flickered despite being covered in a dusting of snow. She heard the cooing of pigeons meandering near the covered statue dedicated to Leonardo da Vinci.

Nora reached into her pocket for her mobile and unlocked the home screen. She found the contact she wanted and pressed the green button. The phone rang for a few moments before Lucas's face appeared on the video screen.

"Bon-journee, Nora." Rex barked in the background. "Shh… quiet boy. How was my pronunciation? Did I say it right? I'm rubbish at trying to roll my Rs."

"Ciao, Lucas." Nora giggled. He wanted so hard to be able to speak a few words of Italian. It endeared him to her. "That is a very nice touch. It is pronounced buongiorno, but it doesn't matter. Among family and friends, you would say ciao."

"Ciao, I can manage." Lucas laughed. "Where are you today?" He squinted at the screen. "I'm surprised there are still so many Christmas decorations up. Father had the staff remove all of our decor the first Monday of the new year."

"I'm in Milan. Wait a moment." Nora tapped the camera and slowly panned her phone around the piazza. "The decorations will be up for one or two more days, until La Befana. In English, that would be Three Kings Day or Epiphany."

Lucas frowned. "Wait a moment. Can you pan the camera back to that last stall? It looked like it was selling something like a hag or a witch doll, but that can't be right."

Nora's body shook with laughter. She moved closer to

the stall selling puppets of an old peasant woman clutching a broom in one hand and a basket laden with gifts in the other. "This is not a witch. It is the Befana. She is very much like your Father Christmas."

His eyes sparkled with mirth. "I've never heard of her. This is fascinating."

"Every year on the night of the fifth of January, the old maid known as la Befana enters a home through the chimney, bearing gifts for good children or a lump of coal for those who have been naughty."

They talked for several minutes about the differences and similarities of various holiday traditions in the UK versus Italy and Isola Nostrum. Lucas learned that many families often left wine and small morsels of food for the Befana instead of sherry and mince pies.

"In America, they leave cookies and milk out overnight for Father Christmas." Lucas wrinkled his nose. "I could never understand why. The milk is so cold. Why would Father Christmas choose to drink a cold beverage? And there are the health risks to consider with milk being left out at a temperature of…"

Nora let Lucas rattle off a few scientific facts as she entered the Galleria Vittorio Emanuele, a walkway connecting the Teatro alla Scala to the Duomo Cathedral, two of Milan's greatest landmarks. Overhead, glass-vaulted and cast-iron roof arcades adorned in thousands of blue Swarovski crystal lights gave off the effect that she had entered an ice palace. High-end designer shops lined the walkways.

"… and that's my opinion on the matter," Lucas finished.

Nora changed the subject. "How has your packing been going? Are you all set for the big move next week?"

"More or less. My life is packed into one large suitcase and Rex is crate trained."

"Only one suitcase?" Nora chuckled.

"All I need are my electronics and a few pieces of basic clothing. It's summer in the Southern Hemisphere right now. I'll be living in shorts and T-shirts. Anything else I require, like furniture, I'll purchase once I'm settled and have a flat."

She conjured an image of Lucas in a form-fitting white T-shirt, the thin fabric clinging to his chest, revealing long, lanky muscles built up from long hours of digging and lifting heavy rocks.

"Smart thinking." Her cheeks warmed. "Um… how is your search for a flat coming along?"

"I have a few promising leads. Out of pure happenstance, Matthew has a mate based in the Saint Lucia area, where the university is." Lucas adjusted the glasses that had slipped down his nose. "Enough about me and the move. I should've thought to ask you earlier. Why are you in Milan today?"

Nora switched the camera view back to her face. She glanced wearily to her left and made her way to a café. A hot beverage sounded like the perfect way to warm up. "I just completed an audition with La Scala."

"Crackers. I've heard of La Scala. It's one of the most celebrated opera houses in Milan, is it not?" He clapped his hands together. "Well done you!"

Nora sat down, setting her mobile device on the table and the violin case on the empty seat beside her. "Si. It is, but nothing will come of it."

He furrowed his brow. "What makes you think that? You are highly talented. You graduated with a first-class degree from a top-rated university music program."

"I messed up." Nora explained to Lucas that out of fifteen possible compositions, the audition committee selected three at random for each candidate to play. "One of the excerpt pieces should have been played solemnly, but instead I played it with a gleeful tone. From the perspective of the committee, making a mistake like that paints me as a musician who showed up to the audition unprepared."

A waiter approached. She ordered a latte and a slice of fresh pandoro. Lucas used the interruption to let the excited Rex out of his room. Nora heard a door open and close.

When he sat back down, he said, "Maybe you playing the composition differently is *exactly* what the committee needed. If I were hearing the same music compositions played over and over again, I'd certainly appreciate a musician who put an original stamp on it."

She loved how optimistic the man was. It warmed her to hear him trying hard not to crush her hopes, but she knew the painful reality of the situation—there wasn't room for originality at La Scala. The entire purpose of the audition was to prove she could fit in, not stand out.

"Perhaps." She rubbed the nape of her neck. Her entire body felt stiff, her limbs heavy. "At this point, I'm beginning to question if I should even spend the time auditioning. Maybe fate is trying to send me a subtle message that being a concert violinist is not in the cards for me."

"Nora. This isn't you." Lucas leaned in closer to the camera. "You have wanted to play professionally since uni. You can't give up now."

"I'm so tired of it all." She slowly closed her eyes. "The sneaking out, the rejection. It stresses me to the limit every time. I'm constantly having my hopes rise, only to be turned down. The worst bit of it is that I never know why I'm no longer in consideration."

She opened her eyes. Lucas's agate-blue orbs bore into her body as if he were X-raying her. "You've told me that your parents have always supported your music."

"Mama and Papa *do* support me, but in a different way than I want. They see me as a part-time musician performing to raise money for various charitable groups on Isola Nostrum. Like your father, my papa expects me to expend all my energy as a working royal. It makes me feel like I'm trapped."

The waiter brought her order to her. She thanked him and placed her hands around the hot ceramic cup, staring at the likeness of a Christmas tree in the foam.

"I thought, against all odds, that if I could earn my way into an orchestra, then maybe I could play full-time and layer in a few royal responsibilities here and there. My nonno only stepped down from being king five years ago because of his health. When Papa was my age, he was spending all his time clubbing with friends on the mainland."

Lucas drummed his fingers on the arm of his chair. "Nora, you sound utterly exhausted. You're running yourself ragged. When was the last time you've taken a real vacation?"

She stayed silent. She *was* both mentally and physically drained. She never felt as if she could take any proper time away. She had too many commitments to see through.

"My own selfishness and your visiting Rosewood has set you back at least two weeks. I remember you having to rearrange your schedule for me." He ran a hand through his hair. "You've been there for me every step of the way."

"Lucas, you mean well, but I'll be fine. You're right. I'm just tired. I'll nap on the train ride to the Cinque Terre."

"Nora, it isn't healthy. You're acting like… me."

A ghost of a smile crept onto her lips.

"If I could take away some of your worries…" He stroked his jaw. "There has to be a connection I have that can at the very least get you another audition."

She didn't want any handouts. She wanted to do this on her own.

Nora took a sip of her coffee. The espresso gave her a much-needed jolt of energy. "How about this? I have one more audition booked next week. If I go through with it and still find myself unemployed, I'll let you scroll through the list of contacts in your mobile to see if anyone knows about an audition outside Italy."

She'd wanted to stay within a half-day train ride of Isola Nostrum. But if she wanted a chance to be a professional violinist, perhaps it was time to cast a wider net. After all, life never moved in a straight line. It was always full of twists, turns, and unforeseen surprises.

This time last month, she was replying to a text message from Lucas, saying she would be more than happy to meet him in London. Look at them now, in a fake relationship.

"You have a deal."

Lucas and Nora chatted for a little longer before he let her go. As she sat in the café, she surveyed the towering Gothic Duomo cathedral and its pointed-arch windows, statues, little pinnacles, and reliefs. The sky was just beginning to darken. She watched pedestrians stroll past her, walking at all speeds. She wondered where they were going. Who were they meeting? Were they just as lost as she?

Lucas knew exactly what he wanted and the type of future he wished to have for himself.

Where did she see herself? In a large city like Milan? On a small island like Isola Nostrum? If she was being realistic, if she did find herself playing in an orchestra, how long could she sustain it?

She had no trouble speaking her mind in front of Lucas's parents, yet she couldn't do the same with her own family. Mama and Papa wanted the best for her and her siblings. But she couldn't tell how they would react to her dreams.

She had always been held to a different standard than Lorenzo and Lucia. Was that how it always was with the eldest child? Did Mr. Darcy feel as if he had the weight of the world on his shoulders when he inherited Pemberley estate and the guardianship of a younger sister?

She made a mental note that she wanted to explore a young Mr. Darcy learning to navigate his many responsibilities in a future story.

She knew she was going to have to have a discussion with Mama and Papa. She was making herself sick with the extra stress of being afraid to talk to them. She was an adult, and she did have a say in the life she was going to lead. She was a future leader. She could do this.

With a goal firmly fixed in her mind's eye, Nora pulled out her phone and sent a text message to her parents asking for a meeting after dinner that evening.

Part Two

CHAPTER 9

A Visit Down Under

SIX MONTHS LATER

Nora rubbed her hands over her arms. She'd never expected it to be so chilly in Sydney. Then again, she'd forgotten that the seasons were the reverse of what she was used to in Europe.

"Nora, over here." She turned her head and spotted Lucas waving his hands wildly in the passenger meetup area.

A smile crept onto her face. She hadn't seen her fake fiancé in person for several months. He made his way through the crowd and wrapped his firm arms around her. His chest expanded and contracted. She smelled a clean, woody scent. "Welcome to the land Down Under. Did you have a good flight?"

"Lord Malcolm, it's so good to see you."

He released her. She blinked several times as she got her first up-close examination of Lucas. He was very much the same man she was used to seeing through the video chats, and yet physically, she could tell he'd changed. His skin was much more tan. His body, while it had always been fit, was leaner. Yet the most recognizable change was his posture and the shimmering in his blue orbs. Lucas was happy. Truly and utterly happy.

"I did have a good flight, but ask me again in a few hours. I'm sure I'll be hit with some jet lag. I'm excited to see what you have lined up for me. This is my first trip to Australia."

Lucas reached over and took her rolling suitcase. They walked out of the arrival terminal to the car park. "I have a confession to make. This is my first time in Sydney. Everything we see and do will be my first time too."

Nora chuckled. "How has your first semester been?"

"So far, it's been heavy on the reading. But that should change in a few weeks when we drive out to a few of the excavation sites and start on with our fieldwork." Lucas stopped in front of a blue sedan. "This is us." He clicked a button on the key fob. The boot of the car opened, and he placed her rolling bag inside. "Anything else?"

Nora shook her head, starting for the front seat.

"Other side, Nora. Unless you wish to drive."

Her cheeks colored. "Non grazie. No thank you."

He chuckled and started the engine. Carefully checking the mirrors, he backed the car out of its parking spot. "If you're up for it, I thought we could spend the day with a cycling tour of the city. It's received some rave reviews online."

She appreciated how Lucas always went outside of his way to try and find unique tour offerings.

"I'm up for it, but disclaimer alert . . . I haven't ridden a bicycle in years. Do you know if they happen to offer any bikes that come with training wheels?"

He laughed. "Once you hop onto the bike, you'll be

just fine. Muscle memory is more powerful than people give it credit for. But if it might make you feel more confident, we can check into the tour early and you can practice cycling."

"Yes, please." She glanced out the window. They'd hopped onto the motorway. "What about you? When was the last time you cycled?"

"This morning."

"Oh? New hobby?"

Lucas glanced to his left through his mirrored sunglasses and changed lanes. "Two of the other grad students in my department participate in triathlons. It sounded interesting, so they invited me to one of their training sessions to see what it was all about. I really enjoyed connecting with new people and the physical and mental challenges the training presents. So I joined the UQ triathlete club. In about ten weeks, I'll be swimming, biking, and running my way through my first triathlon."

That explained the change in his body's physique. She wondered what lay hidden underneath his jumper and jeans. She pinched her forearm. She shouldn't be harboring thoughts like that about him.

"Um . . .what does Rex make of all this? Is he jealous you aren't taking him out on the runs with you?" Nora knew Lucas's beloved border collie was getting on in years and had developed some arthritis in his paws.

Lucas snorted. "Rex may not be able to run with me, but he joins me on the cycling rides. I bought him a little buggie that attaches to my bike."

Nora tried to picture Lucas cycling intensely through a park with Rex sticking his head out from a little wagon attached to the back of it. In her mind, the canine would be wearing a matching pair of dog-sized sunnies similar to what Lucas owned.

She cocked her head to the side. "Does he stay still in it? Or do you have to have the buggie covered?"

"I have a cover so Rex doesn't jump out, but if we're going for a leisurely ride, I remove it. Rexie loves to nap while I do all the work."

Just like a little child.

~

Over the course of three days, they saw the Opera House, climbed to the top of the Sydney Harbour Bridge, and even sampled Vegemite. Much to Lucas's amusement, Nora enjoyed the Aussie spread. She'd heard that most foreigners couldn't stomach the salty-meaty flavoring, but to her, it tasted a lot like an unsweetened version of Nutella.

On her fourth day Down Under, Lucas and Nora were in the state of Queensland, with plans to spend the next two days exploring the sites around Moreton Bay, a picturesque stretch of coastline just outside Brisbane.

They walked past a stretch of cafés and small family-owned souvenir shops in Woorim on Bribie Island.

"Hold on. How is it that a woman who has grown up on an island has never been surfing?" Lucas stared in disbelief, his hands on his hips.

"I don't know," she sputtered. "I just haven't." Her face seared with heat. Why wouldn't he just let the subject drop?

"Change of plans." Lucas pivoted and jogged up the steps of the surf rental shop they'd just passed. Pausing on the top step, he said, "That is, if it's all right with you." He scratched his stubble-coated jaw and looked to Nora for permission. "I'm not used to having another person around to make decisions with."

"Understandable." Nora blinked lazily. "Si. If you're willing to teach me, I will give it a go. Being here is all about trying new experiences."

Lucas flipped his sunglasses up. "I love that about you. You're one of the most easy-going people I've ever been around. I'll be right back."

Butterflies fluttered in her stomach. Lucas's words were starting to have an effect on her. She cared about his opinion more than she should. In Sydney, he'd been so patient as she struggled through relearning how to cycle. He jogged alongside the bike, making certain she'd found her balance and didn't fall over. Then, at the end of the day, when her leg muscles had turned to jelly, Lucas had booked her in for a massage.

She fell asleep in the spa and never questioned how she ended up getting from there to the hotel room. He must have carried her and put her to sleep before sneaking into his own hotel room.

Lucas returned carrying two wet suits. "I guessed on the size. If it doesn't fit, the bloke inside said to just let him know. I went for the short-sleeved option since the water should be pretty warm."

Nora took the wet suit from his hands and held it up against her body. Her hands brushed over the rubbery fabric. It ended just shy of her ankles on her petite frame. "This should be fine."

He nodded. "The surfboards we can pick up around back. The four-hour rental was the best deal."

After finding a spot on the beach to stow their belongings, they slipped the wet suits over their swimsuits. She'd opted for a cute red-and-white-striped bikini with straps that crisscrossed in the back. She was amused to see Lucas discreetly watching her as she shimmied into the tight-fitting garment.

Is it wrong that I am enjoying the little extra attention he's giving me? It's only fair I return the favor.

The ever-practical Lucas had opted for a pair of multipurpose swim, run, and bike shorts. As he removed his shirt, Nora caught a glimpse of a body packed full of elongated, toned muscles. She licked her lips. She never expected to see such defined arms and chiseled abs—the result of triathlon training.

"Do you like what you see?" he joked.

She nodded, quickly glancing away. The memory would linger in her mind for weeks to come.

"Good to know."

Nora touched her hands to her still-flushed face. "Can you demonstrate what I'm supposed to do when we're out there?"

Lucas zipped up his wet suit and set one of the surfboards down flat. "Once we're out past the breakers, all you have to do is lie on your stomach, and from the push-up position, jump to your feet and stand. Give it a go."

Nora felt foolish as she pretended to swim, then popped to her feet. "Like this?"

"Exactly like that, but you need to distribute your weight more evenly. The stance is one foot in front of the other, with your body slightly angled."

She glanced down. "Which foot goes in front?"

Lucas walked behind her and gently pushed her back. She stepped forward with her right foot. "You're what they call a goofy foot. For you, you'll place your right foot forward, left foot back."

She raised an eyebrow. "A goofy foot? Huh. That's a curious name."

He shrugged. "You ready to crack on with it?"

"I guess. Just don't laugh when you find out I'm the world's worst surfer."

"You'll be brilliant. Trust me. My gut instinct is never wrong." Picking up the other surfboard, he tucked it under his arm. "Let's go." He charged toward the water.

"Lord Malcolm. . . that's cheating. I've got much shorter legs than you." She chased after him, her feet sinking into the soft white sand. His laughter only grew louder.

Wading into the water, Nora observed Lucas and the handful of other surfers and tried to emulate their movements.

She caught up to Lucas, who sat atop his board. "What's that face for?" he asked. She stuck her tongue out. "I'm sorry if I offended you. I can't help being competitive. I thought that since you have siblings, you wouldn't make much of my egging you on."

"Not you. It's the salt. Pleh." She shuddered. "I grew up swimming in the sea, but I'll never grow used to having that bitter taste in my mouth. Or to it getting in my eyes. It stings."

Lucas laughed.

They floated along in the water lazily, the gentle swell of the waves rising and falling. It was a slightly overcast day, with a hint of sun beating down upon the turquoise water.

"Do you want me to go in first, or would you like to do the honors? I default to you, Lady Nora."

She splayed a hand on her chest. "Why, Lord Malcolm, a brave and noble gentleman *always* goes first. I'll be right behind you."

Lucas bowed awkwardly and flopped onto his stomach, moving his board perpendicular to the incoming set of waves. Nora watched carefully, noting when he turned and let the wave carry the board toward the shore. Lucas stroked, jumped to his feet, and was knocked aside spectacularly not a moment later.

Nora held her breath as the white water washed over the board at the same time his head emerged. He picked up the board and walked into the shallow water, waiting for Nora to take her turn. She exhaled.

I can do that. I think.

Gauging that the next set was coming in her direction, Nora positioned her body onto the board and paddled fast.

It didn't feel that different from kayaking with Lorenzo. With kayaking, you let the waves do the work and used your paddle as a rudder to steer. If she applied the same rule of thumb, theoretically, all she had to do was get into a balanced position and gently lean one way or another to steer the board.

Gripping the side of the board, Nora found her footing and planted her right foot in front. She made it to her feet, enjoyed three seconds of perfect Zen, and subsequently found herself tumbling back into the water. She'd tipped her body too far on the back of the board.

Nora met Lucas on the shore. His arms were crossed. "Lady Nora. . . am I mistaken? That was your *first* time surfing? Ever?"

"Yes."

"You were exceptional just now. Watching you from the beach, it looked as if you were a seasoned pro." He ran a hand over his jaw. "I should be taking lessons from you."

"Maybe I'm not the world's worst surfer after all." She grinned. "Can we do it again?"

"Lead the way, Lady Nora."

With her board in hand, she sprinted to the water. "Catch me if you can."

Nora carried her sandals in one hand and held a soft-serve raspberry ice cream in the other. It wasn't a gelato, but after surfing all afternoon, it was the perfect refreshment. "How's your death-by-chocolate soft serve?"

"Chocolatey?" He held the cone to her. "Would you care to try some?"

She shook her head. "No. Chocolate doesn't mix with fruit flavors."

He shrugged. "Your loss."

She bit back a giggle at seeing a small chocolate mustache coat his upper lip. The day had been full of fun and adventure. For all his bragging, she'd bested Lucas's surfing skills by a long shot.

"What are you thinking?" he asked.

"That when I'm with you, I'm the best version of myself."

Lucas slowed his pace. "Funny. I was just thinking the same thing earlier. When I'm with you, I can be Lord Malcolm."

She gently elbowed him. "Cheeky, aren't we?"

"Call it cheeky if you will. But this is me. The real me." They stopped and watched as the first set of the sun's rays began to slowly slip behind the horizon. He breathed deeply, and his playful tone turned thoughtful. "Aside from Matthew, you're the only person I can joke with. The only person I am relaxed and at ease with. You've become one of my best mates. I'll never be able to repay you for everything that you've done."

She licked her lips, savoring the sweet berry taste of the dessert. "You can repay me by earning that PhD."

"Nora. That's not what I meant."

"I know." She placed a hand on top of his. As her fingers brushed over his, she felt an excited energy grip hold of her body, propelling her to him.

Suddenly, movement caught her eye on one of the sandy dunes close to the water. "Is that . . ."

Lucas squinted. "It looks like two roos and a wallaby?"

They stood still for a moment and watched as the creatures with powerful legs, pointed ears, and long tails dug into the sand, foraging for plants to eat. The smallest of the three animals, the wallaby, placed its arms on the ground and used its tail as an extra leg. Waves crashed against the beach. The sky was now a brilliant shade of purplish orange.

"They move slower than I would've thought."

"Only when they're grazing. They can move bloody fast when they need to escape." Lucas shook his head. "I haven't seen any roos on the island the handful of times I've been here. I wonder if they crossed over from the mainland during low tide. I'll have to ask one of the blokes on the triathlete team."

The sun was now nearly out of sight, replaced by a shimmering field of stars. As she stood with her hand still laced through Lucas's, Nora knew without any shadow of a doubt that her feelings for him had begun to change. She'd started to fall for him.

CHAPTER 10

An Afternoon With Lorenzo

ONE YEAR LATER

Nora walked out through the bifold doors leading to the rooftop terrace of her family's home. She would never grow tired of seeing the endless turquoise expanse of the sparkling Mediterranean Sea. A lazy spring breeze brought the scent of salt and seaweed.

Off to the right-hand side, she spied her two siblings. Lorenzo sat on the ledge of the infinity pool with his legs pulled into his body. He rested his forehead on his knees, and his wavy caramel locks hid his eyes. His neck was sunburned and red. His clothing was a mess of wrinkles.

How long had he been sitting there feeling depressed and sorry for himself? Everyone had been walking on eggshells around him since the breakup with Noemi. He needed to be treated like an adult, not a child.

Nora placed her hands on her hips. "Lorenzo, you have been moping around the palace for three months. You are driving me mad."

From a beach chair under the shade of a giant red-and-white umbrella, Lucia lowered her magazine. "It's a lost cause, Nor. Nothing you say will penetrate that thick skull of his."

"Not helping, Lu."

Lorenzo hadn't moved a muscle. The old Lorenzo would be firing back a witty insult, not frozen in place.

"Where's my wet suit? Let's go out on your kayak," Nora said with a grimace.

Slowly, like a meerkat ascending from an underground tunnel to check for any signs of danger, he raised his head. His eyes were wide. "Kayak?"

Lucia sat taller in her beach chair and lifted her sunglasses.

Nora's eyes darted between them. She tapped her foot. "Si. This is the one and only time I am willing to voluntarily go out with you on the water." She bent over and attempted to pull her brother by the arm to a standing position. "Now get moving. You're too heavy for me to lift." She shook her arms. This was their workout for the day.

Lorenzo grunted and struggled to his feet. At his full height, he stood six feet tall, dwarfing Nora's five-foot-two frame.

"You're in charge of prepping the two-seater. I'll oversee the packing of some snacks for the excursion," she said.

All Lorenzo could do was nod. He stumbled through the bifold doors in a daze. When he had disappeared from sight, Nora wafted the air with her hands. "When was the last time he showered and shaved? He looks like a caveman."

"That's why I'm sitting way over here." Lucia snorted. "At least he'll have to take a sea bath to get the kayak out into the surf."

Nora crossed her arms. "I'm counting on it."

"You must really love our brother to be going out on the water with him. No one in the family likes to accompany him anymore with the punishing pace Lorenzo sets with his paddle. He's like a human speedboat."

"Hopefully I won't have to do any paddling. That's why I asked him to set up the two-seater." Nora winced remembering how sore her body had been for days afterward the last time she'd been out in a kayak.

"Not likely." Lucia rolled her eyes. "As soon as Lorenzo gets going, he's going to need to expend all this angry energy that's been building over the last few weeks. I wish you all the luck, sister." She resumed reading her magazine.

Nora remained rooted in her spot. Now to deal with her other sibling.

The pages of Lucia's magazine rustled. She glanced at Nora over the top of it. "Was there something else you wanted to ask me?"

How could she put this delicately to Lu?

"I thought you had your end-of-term exams to sit next week? You're an adult, and how you spend your free time is entirely up to you, but as your loving, caring older sister, I just want you to get the best possible marks you can achieve."

Lucia took the hint and sheepishly closed her magazine. Sighing, she silently stood and disappeared into the palace, heading up to her rooms to study.

Satisfied, Nora turned and set out for the kitchens.

My job here is done.

As Lucia had predicted, turned loose on the water, Lorenzo paddled the kayak as if he were a shooting star traveling two thousand miles per hour. Nora gripped the sides of the boat tightly, frightened that with his aggressive strokes, Lorenzo might flip the kayak over. She stayed silent as they circled the island twice, then cut through the water toward some of the smaller uninhabited islands.

Finally, after a marathon of three hours, the watercraft started to slow. Releasing her death grip, she felt a sensation of pins and needles in her hands. She opened and closed the appendages several times, in hopes of regaining some blood circulation.

Behind her, Lorenzo rested his paddle on his lap and panted. Reaching into an insulated nylon tote bag, she offered her brother a water bottle. "Drink slowly. We can't have you making yourself ill. Who knows how far we are from home, and we both know that if I had to steer this boat, we'd be lucky if I could get it pointed in the right direction."

Lorenzo half laughed and half coughed. She had his full attention. Now, she had to maintain it, and hope that he would continue to engage her in conversation.

Nora prattled on. "I will deny this story if you ever repeat it, but when I went to visit Lucas in Brisbane last fall, we decided to spend the weekend driving up the Sunshine Coast toward Great Sandy National Park. Lucas had heard rave reviews about the scenery. I was supposed to navigate—"

"Lucas trusted you to navigate?" Lorenzo's voice came out hoarse.

"My sense of direction isn't *that* bad."

He glared. "Where did you actually end up?"

Her face burned hot. "In a charming city called Coffs Harbour, about a half day's drive in the opposite direction of Great Sandy National Park. We were nearly halfway to Sydney."

Lorenzo cackled with laughter. "And neither one of you thought to use a mobile phone to check your progress?"

"His phone was dead, and my mobile couldn't lock on to a signal." Nora rubbed her temples. "In spite of my humiliation and driving three hundred and fifty kilometers in the wrong direction, Lucas took it all in stride."

She would never live it down, but Lucas was always a gentleman. Even when he was angry, he stayed deadly calm and never raised his voice.

"Your secret is safe with me." Lorenzo wiped a tear from his eye. His gaze traveled to the spot near Nora's feet. "Did you happen to bring any snacks?" He rubbed his stomach. "I'm a little hungry."

Nora's eyes lit up. "Si. You've been going nonstop all morning. I had the cook pack some of your favorites—there are a few protein bars, a takeaway container of lasagna from Giulia, a chicken-and-avocado panini—"

"You brought enough food with you to feed a small army. I'll have the lasagna, per favore."

"Do you wish to eat here, or picnic on one of the outlying beaches?"

Lorenzo took hold of his paddle. "Fair point. Let's eat over there near Parvus Nostrum." He pointed to a white sandy beach about a quarter mile long. Nora recognized the second-largest island in the Isola Nostrum chain by its single white Greek marble temple column, standing tall amid the toppled remains of the other columns.

She hadn't realized they were out this far. To think, in ancient times, mariners used to row between Parvus Nostrum and Isola Nostrum daily. It was sad to think that a once-bustling island was now uninhabited.

Nora's eyes glanced at her paddle. "Do you want some help?"

"No. You'll just slow me down," Lorenzo said in a cheeky tone.

This was the facet of his personality she'd been sorely missing. She secretly enjoyed their banter. Nora had always been closer to Lorenzo than Lucia.

With ten confident strokes, he had them in the shallow water. He hopped out of the kayak, walking it onto the shore.

Nora moved to follow his lead. As she jumped into the water, she yelped. "Too cold." She scrambled up from the water to the beach.

Lorenzo burst out laughing. "You have a wet suit on. How can you be cold?" He removed the kayak from the water and placed it out of the reach of the surf.

"My wet suit is cut with short sleeves and short legs. You, my *dear* brother, are fully covered."

"I should've worn my short-sleeved suit like you. I'm too hot."

"I'm only wearing this one because I couldn't find my other," Nora muttered, rolling her eyes.

Shrugging, he pulled the zipper and peeled off the sleeves of his wet suit, exposing his skin to the cool air. "Much better." Lorenzo's head and neck were cherry red, kissed by the sun. The rest of his body, however, was pale white.

He had gotten too thin. He was usually much more built. Now, he looked like Lucas.

Nora's mind turned to the memory of the afternoon she'd spent surfing with Lucas. It seemed like a dream. Seeing him on video chat was not the same as being able to see him in person. She couldn't fully appreciate his dimples when he smiled. Or the ringing sound he made when he laughed. She missed the tenderness with which he stroked her hand. All of those small mannerisms melted her insides.

She sighed. Each time they spoke, it became increasingly more difficult for her to downplay the stirring sensations she felt for him. She saw him as much more than a friend. But she knew those feelings weren't something she could put a name to or ever act on. They could never be more than just friends. Their arrangement was only a business transaction until he graduated. Nothing more. Nothing less.

Nora shook off all thoughts about Lucas and busied herself with preparing the cutlery and meal for Lorenzo. Just as one of the men in her life was en route to finding happiness, another was tormented by bitterness and dark clouds.

As she turned, she saw her brother sitting on the rim of the kayak. "You're thinking about him, aren't you?"

His statement caught her off guard. Nora handed him a plastic container, knife, and fork. "I don't know who you mean."

"Leonora… really? You're going to play this game?" Lorenzo took a large bite of the lasagna. "Anyone can see by reading that glassy-eyed expression on your face that you miss Lucas. You're engaged to the man, and you have only seen him in person once in nearly two years. I get it."

"Fine. I am thinking about him." She kept her head lowered, taking a keen interest in the insulated bag. "But I'm also thinking about you. I'll be the first person to tell you point blank that you have had everyone concerned by your depressed behavior of late."

Noemi, her brother's second-ever serious girlfriend, had been caught maxing out his credit cards on extravagant designer clothing and accessories in excess of two million euros. When confronted, she confessed she'd never loved Lorenzo and had pursued a relationship with him for access to his wealth and his royal title.

"I'm not ready to have a conversation with you about Noemi." He clenched his jaw and chewed slowly. "You wouldn't understand. You haven't had your heart ripped to shreds and your trust betrayed like I have."

She could sense a sudden shift in her brother's mood. She wasn't about to let him withdraw into himself again.

He sounded as broken as Lucas did the day they met at the Museum of Natural History in London. Siobhan destroyed Lucas's confidence the same way Noemi did her brother's.

She stood up, holding a half-wrapped panini for herself. With a slight hesitation, she said to Lorenzo, "Let's say that I *did* know a person who had once been in a relationship that ended in a similar manner as you and Noemi." He winced upon hearing her name. "Would you consent to speaking with them?"

"That depends on who it is." His brow furrowed.

"Lucas?" she offered.

Lorenzo nodded subtly and continued to eat his meal. Nora calculated the time difference. The last time she checked her phone, it had been close to ten in the morning. In Brisbane, it would be around seven in the evening.

That couldn't have been more than an hour ago. Lucas should still be awake if she rang him now. He usually spent his Saturday nights watching television or playing *Final Fantasy* on his PlayStation.

Decision made, Nora walked to the back of the kayak and opened the storage compartment. She located her phone inside the front pocket of her backpack.

"I never thought I'd have a signal out this far," she mused aloud.

"We aren't that removed from civilization," Lorenzo said sarcastically. "Only a few miles."

Nora ignored him.

Unlocking the screen, she took a chance and clicked on Lucas's name. She trusted and valued her fake fiancé enough to know that whatever he said to Lorenzo would help set him on the path to healing.

"Here. I'll be taking a long walk over there by the temple ruins. Come find me when you're done." She tried to hand the phone to her brother.

"Hello? Nora?" a familiar voice asked quizzically.

Lorenzo stared at the phone.

"Hello?" Lucas's voice repeated.

She shoved the device into her brother's hands and nodded to him.

Lorenzo switched to English. "Ciao, Lucas. This is Leonora's brother, Lorenzo."

Lucas sucked in air sharply. "Is everything all right with Nora? Has something happened?"

"No. My sister is fine. She rang so I could speak to you…"

"Of course, anything for Nora. What's on your mind, Lorenzo?"

Walking in the surf, she moved across the beach away from the two men she loved the most. Having a rare moment of time to herself, Nora welcomed the quiet. She could hear the sound of waves crashing against the beach and numerous species of seabirds calling out to their mates and newborn chicks.

Ascending a set of worn steps, she stared out at the ruins of the Greek temple to Neptune, the god of the sea.

Pieces of broken marble and golden coins were scattered throughout the remains of the treasury and high altar.

If Papa ever opened Isola Nostrum to archaeologists, they would have an absolute field day combing through the ruins. There were hundreds, maybe even thousands, of artifacts buried here that had been left to be reclaimed by the Earth.

Papa was so afraid that any excavations might destroy the ruins, but what good were they just wasting away? The artifacts could tell them so much about the ancient history of Isola Nostrum, a thousand years before the Toscanis ever arrived.

Nora walked the perimeter.

There was much she and Papa couldn't ever seem to see eye-to-eye on. He was a progressive royal, but there were some areas where he was also out of touch with reality. The monarchy was his life, but it wouldn't be able to survive as an institution unless he learned to accept that the crown would have to make concessions and modernize with the times.

Perching herself atop the steps looking out at the sea, Nora bit into her sandwich, wondering if her father would ever come to see that she did care about the crown, just in a different way from him. She wanted to be more than just a crown princess. A year after Lucas was finding his stride, Nora felt as if she was still flailing.

Falling

Lorenzo found Nora watching the birds settle on the beach between wave sets, hunting for crabs, shrimp, and other small sea creatures to eat.

"Leonora, I've been calling your name for the last few minutes. Didn't you hear me?"

Nora stood, brushed the sand off her legs, and faced her brother. "Sorry, I was lost in my thoughts."

"Clearly." He appraised her.

She rubbed her hands over the goosebumps on her arms. "Did you have a meaningful chat with Lord Mal—with Lucas?"

Nora hoped Lorenzo wouldn't notice the slip of her tongue.

"Si. He gave me some thoughtful advice." He handed her mobile phone to her.

"Grazie." She clicked the button on the side, and the time glowed. "It's three in the afternoon? I hadn't realized we've been here so long."

"That's my fault." Two round patches of bubblegum pink appeared on his cheeks. "Lucas and I got off track. We have quite a few interests in common. We started discussing the news that Nintendo is going to end production on the DS gaming system next year. We're both worried about what it means for the *Pokémon* games. He's just as keen on playing them as me. Although, he is a purist and doesn't care much for the Pokémon beyond the Kanto region. His favorite character, Professor Bill…"

Nora's brain clicked off. Lorenzo had lost her.

She didn't know Lucas liked those little monsters. He continued to surprise her at every turn. She hoped he was prepared for her brother to latch on to him. Finding another like-minded male for him to bond with was rare. Like Lucas, Lorenzo didn't have the easiest time growing up. Children could be so vicious and cruel to one another.

Heading back toward the kayak, Nora indulged her brother as he recounted his conversation with Lucas about the merits of dinosaur fossils serving as a source of inspiration for the creation of the so-called "ancient Pokémon."

As they settled themselves into the kayak, Lorenzo said, "He's a good man. From the way Lucas spoke about you, it's clear how much he adores you. I'm thrilled to bits that he's going to officially become a part of the family, and I'll finally have the brother I've always wanted."

Nora's heart fluttered. It warmed her to hear him refer to Lucas as his brother. "Lucas spoke about me? What did he say?"

"All bad things."

"Lorenzo," Nora whined.

He chuckled. "I promised Lucas that what we spoke about would stay between us. He swore me to secrecy, and I respect that."

She crossed her arms and huffed. How did Lucas see her? What did he say to give Lorenzo the impression that he clearly liked her? Had he started to see her as more than a friend too? Or experienced the same stirring sensations when they spoke for hours on end?

Lorenzo steered the kayak past the waves and toward the calmer water, staying quiet for several moments. Nora glanced behind her.

Her brother's forehead was wrinkled with deep lines. "Seeing the deep bond you share with Lucas has caused me to reevaluate and question everything I thought I knew about love. I was so blind that I couldn't see it was all one-sided. I never want to feel so vulnerable ever again."

She placed a hand on his forearm. "Give yourself time to grow and heal. The pain won't always be so sharp." She sighed. "I have no doubt that the right woman is out there waiting for you to find her. When the time is right, fate will bring you two together."

"Not likely," her brother mumbled.

Her chest grew uncomfortably tight. She couldn't help but feel pangs of the guilt and anxiety she'd been working to overcome. It had become so easy to live the giant lie that she and Lucas had cultivated. But Nora was aware that as more time passed, her resolve was beginning to weaken. She *wanted* their relationship to move into the stage beyond friendship.

The irony of their entire fake romance was that she could speak with Lucas about everything except what her feelings were for him. She couldn't tell him that he was constantly on her mind. That she had started conjuring fantasies about the adventures they'd have as a couple when they were together. That she dreamt about seeing him running shirtless on the beach, his taut muscles glistening in a thin sheen of perspiration.

No. Lucas was just about at the point where he was

finishing his research and was about to direct all his energy into writing up his findings. He had told her this was going to be the most stressful part of his entire program. She couldn't be a distraction to him. He might even grow to resent her for it. Romance was the absolute last thing he'd ever think about or have time for.

~

Later that evening, after dinner, Nora knocked on the door to her father's study and was invited inside. Her papa reclined in a plush black office chair, legs crossed on the desktop, perusing a file. Across his desk were three red boxes containing confidential parliamentary papers.

"Leonora. Right on time." Locking eyes with her, he removed his reading glasses from his face and feet from the desktop. "I noticed a stark change in Lorenzo's demeanor over dinner this evening. Whatever you did, well done, my little principessa."

Nora's cheeks warmed. "I'm not a little principessa anymore, Papa."

"You will *always* be my little principessa, regardless of what you might say."

She walked around his desk and kissed him on the cheek. Then she settled herself in the worn maroon velvet chair across from him.

"What will we be working on tonight?"

"I thought I'd have you start by reviewing the list of candidates recommended by Parliament for the Order of the Golden Lark, and the proposed list of topics that Isola Nostrum will be discussing with the president of Spain during his state visit next week."

"Of course." Nora nodded. "He'll be here for three days?"

"Si," her father confirmed, rubbing his eyes. "It's been a while since we've played host to any visiting dignitaries, and I always seem to forget just how much preparation is required, even for such a short visit."

"We have highly trained and capable staff. They'll work their magic as they always do to make the Spanish president's stay with us seamless." Nora folded her hands and settled them on her lap. "If you'd like, I can take charge of drafting the welcome speech."

"That would be helpful. You have a natural way with words." Papa smiled at her warmly.

The time I spend writing Austen fan fiction seems to be paying off.

"Will you be delivering it in English or in Italian?"

"Actually, I won't be delivering it at all. I'd like you to do the honors."

Nora's pulse began to pick up. "Me?" She blinked twice.

"Si. It will mark your first official duty as the Principessa dei Fiori. Your mama and I have been discussing it for some time. We feel that you are overdue to receive the title that is traditionally bestowed upon the female heir apparent."

Her throat grew dry. "I don't know what to say, Papa. Grazie. I didn't expect to receive any titles of my own until —" Nora stopped herself short of saying until she was married. "For several years yet."

Her father stood and stared out the window, hands clasped behind his back. "It is my hope that as the Principessa dei Fiori, I can count upon you to begin taking on some of the higher-level engagements on the calendar on behalf of the crown. We've had a request from the ambassadors to France and Switzerland for—"

The muscles in her stomach clenched. Nora scooted to the edge of her seat. "Papa," she interrupted, "have you timed this rather sudden decision of styling me as the Principessa dei Fiori to delay my move to Florence? I would hate to think of you breaking your promise to me."

She had an arrangement with her father. When Lucas finished graduate school, and before they called off the fake wedding, she'd become a full-time working royal. Until said time, she was supposed to be free to live and work as Nora Toscani. The public engagements she attended were her decision. Not Papa's. Not the palace's team of public relations officers. Hers.

Papa turned to face her. His jaw was rigid. "Leonora, I've tried my best to honor our agreement, but please understand that I am fielding all kinds of questions from Parliament, from the public, and even other family members about why the crown princess of Isola Nostrum is barely present. They see more of Lorenzo and Lucia than they do you."

"Papa…"

"Do you realize that the most conservative members of the government have begun using your nonattendance at events to illustrate that you are not invested in the future of Isola Nostrum? They've always sought to amend the line of succession to exclude a female heir, but this is the first time that members of the public have actively voiced some support for it."

"But that's not true. I do care. Deeply," she sputtered.

"You know that, and I know that, but others don't. As I was so eloquently reminded of by our PR team yesterday, your absence has been viewed outside the palace as a sign that I lack the confidence in you to succeed me."

Papa rubbed his temples. "As much as I loathe the media, it cannot be ignored. The media is too powerful a tool when it comes to swaying people's thoughts and actions. We are no longer in a situation where I can sit by the wayside. I must intervene."

Nora's own head began to ache. Was that truly how the outside world had come to view her? Her own people? What about all of the hard work she had been putting in behind the scenes?

She had always liked to keep her appearances and charity events under the radar. She didn't need the recognition or the acknowledgment to know that it was a job well done. But in doing so, she'd been hurting her public persona. *Now, I'm in this precarious situation where I'm darned if I do and darned if I don't.*

"This is a lot for me to process," she said.

Papa was the king, but when he was crowned as the sovereign, he pledged to do whatever was in the best interest of the people. The king had always attempted to follow the directives of Parliament. As the heir to the throne, she had to learn that what she wanted, she couldn't always have. She had to be willing to make some concessions and compromises.

"You are stuck performing a delicate dance of diplomacy," Nora whispered.

"Unfortunately." Her father sat back down in his seat and looked attentively at her. "If our roles were reversed and you were in my position, what would you have me do?"

What would she do? Her first inclination was to issue a vehemently worded statement and declare to the world that her personal life was off-limits. But she'd be lying to herself if she truly thought that to be the case. The price she paid for being a royal was that she didn't get to have a private personal life. Everything she did would always be examined under the microscope.

"I suppose the first thing I would do is take control of the situation by acknowledging my absence. Knowing that I'd have to appeal to those who feel entitled to an explanation for why I haven't been in the public sphere"—she rubbed the back of her neck—"I'd pen a statement that highlights the fact that I've always firmly believed that the monarchy must continue to evolve with the times if it wishes to be able to best serve the people and country of Isola Nostrum."

She took a deep breath. "I'd make the case that as the future queen, I firmly believe it is essential that I come to the throne with some real-world experience. The Toscani family may be financially well off, but that's not the case for many of the people on Isola Nostrum. I want to understand what it's like to work for an honest wage and see how that income gets chipped away into bills, groceries, petrol, insurance, et cetera, et cetera. The best leaders are those who can rely on their own life experiences. I aspire to be the best queen I can be."

Papa arched an eyebrow. "So in other words… you wish to claim that the monarchy is an archaic, money-sucking institution."

Their family's private wealth came from the wine they produced. Mama and Papa gave more than half of what the vineyard earned to charity. They didn't live that extravagantly compared to other royal families.

She winced. "Not archaic, per se…"

Papa chuckled. "That's how the conservatives might see it."

"Si, but…"

"You are passionate when you speak." The corners of her father's mouth curled up. "We've had discussions in the past about your wish to live and work in Florence, but until now, you've never been able to fully articulate why you wanted to do so."

She stared quizzically at her father. "Were you testing me, Papa?"

The laugh lines around his eyes told her he was. "I'm sorry, Leonora. But Mama and I needed you to be able to prove to us why you wanted to move out on your own. It's been difficult for us to be stern with you because we want you to be happy. No matter what, in the end, we would've supported and respected your decision to live on your own."

Mama and Papa had been just as bad as her and Lucas. She couldn't believe they'd been pretending to be cross with her for months. She should be angry. But she wasn't.

"I have a confession to make, Papa." Nora shifted uncomfortably in her seat. "Until now, I've only thought about me. I wanted to prove to myself that I could make it as a violinist and as a normal person, so to speak. It's only your putting me on the spot that has forced me to voice how and why my time in Florence could also be advantageous to my future."

"The mind is a curious thing. It works in mysterious ways. The reasoning has always been within your exceptional brain." Papa's blue eyes danced with mirth. "When I was your age, I wasn't nearly as intelligent or as grounded as you. I wanted to race cars professionally on the Formula One circuit and be anywhere other than Isola Nostrum. I wasn't prepared in any way, shape, or form to become king. Fast forward twenty years, and from time to time, I still harbor lingering doubts over my fitness to serve as a head of state. It has taken me decades to get to the place where you are now."

Papa stroked his chin. "I love you, Lorenzo, and Lucia equally to the ends of the Earth and back. But neither Lorenzo nor Lucia is cut from the same cloth as you, Leonora." Her father walked around his desk, standing across from her. He picked up her hands and squeezed them as his eyes bore into hers. "You were born to be queen. You have an inner strength and compassion that shines through whenever you enter a room. You command the attention and respect of those around you."

From his pocket, Papa removed a small golden signet ring engraved with three intertwined roses—the symbol of the Principessa dei Fiori. He pressed it into her hands and puffed out his chest, beaming with pride. "You, Principessa Leonora Amelia Beatrice Toscani, the Principessa dei Fiori, already speak as a leader. I couldn't be any prouder of you. It's evident to me that you are ready to formally receive the responsibilities that come with being heir to the throne."

Nora's fingers closed around the ring. It was still warm. A few tears flowed down her cheeks, and her throat felt raw. Her father's words surrounded her like a warm, protective cocoon. "Papa." She buried her face into his fleece jacket, soaking in the scents of grapes and fresh lavender.

His arms wrapped around her body, holding her tight as he kissed the top of her head. "There will be times when I may not always agree with your thoughts and opinions, but you are the future of this country. After your mama, you, my eldest child, are my closest advisor and confidant. The best decisions are formed out of arguments and debates. Together, it is how we'll propel Isola Nostrum forward and lead her in the direction it needs to go."

"That sounds bellissimo, Papa."

Near midnight, as she lay in bed, Nora reflected on how strangely the day had unfolded.

She never thought that Mama and Papa would be on the same page as her when it came to her moving to Florence and working at the Tuscan Museum of Music. To think that all along, they'd trusted her. And now, she was the Principessa dei Fiori. She was truly to be the next ruler of their country. She'd learn from her experiences working and living in Florence and use them to craft the best possible future for their people, for their country. She couldn't wait to share the news with Lucas.

Her eyes closed. Her breathing started to even out. As her body entered the first REM cycle, she dreamed of Lucas escorting her to a Regency assembly. She wore a lovely cherry-blossom-pink ball gown, and Lucas a hunter-green and silver ensemble. The orchestra began to play a lively reel. His gloved hand touched hers. Just as he'd led her out onto the dance floor, a swarm of a thousand angry wasps invaded the ballroom.

Guests were screaming, running chaotically in every which direction. Lucas gallantly jumped in front of her. Yet the wasps merely flew around him. Coming together in the shape of a giant hand, they surrounded her. Helplessly, she swallowed hard as the buzzing grew louder and darkness encroached. Her eyes opened. She jolted upright and gasped, taking several deep breaths. On her desk, her phone vibrated.

"It was all a horrible nightmare," she said to herself, her hand splayed on her chest. "I must have subconsciously heard my phone and mistaken it for the sound of a wasp swarm." She laughed nervously at the ridiculousness of the situation.

She lay back down, rolled onto her side, and nestled her head into the pillow. Her phone continued to vibrate. Annoyed, she threw back the covers, turned the bedside lamp on, and climbed out of bed to silence it.

Who was trying to reach her so late at night? It had better not be another telemarketer trying to tell her that the warranty on a car she didn't own was about to expire.

Tapping her home screen, Nora scrolled through the alerts to see five missed phone calls from Matthew and a string of text messages. Not bothering to read the messages, she angrily tapped his name. It rang twice before she heard his voice.

"Nora, I'm so sorry to call you so late. But I didn't know what else to do—"

"Matthew Wheeler, you had better have a brilliant excuse for waking me up at"—she glanced at the clock on her desk—"two in the night, or morning, whatever time of day it is."

"Have you read through any of the text messages that I've sent you?"

"No."

Matthew inhaled sharply. "I'm ringing you because about two hours ago, I received a call from the Queensland Fire and Emergency Services. Lucas is missing!"

CHAPTER 12

Missing

All the air fled Nora's body. Her muscles clenched. "Missing? What do you mean by missing? I don't understand. My brother just spoke to him this afternoon. He was fine less than twelve hours ago."

"I'm deeply sorry that I have to break this to you over the phone, but one of the fire service teams fighting the bushfire ravaging the outskirts of Carnarvon National Park discovered the charred remains of his Jeep on the side of a road."

"But the Jeep could belong to anyone." Her heart began to beat faster. She was now fully awake and on high alert. Placing Matthew on speaker, she pulled up a blank text message and started to type as fast as her fingers could move.

Nora: Lord Malcom, you are hereby ordered by the Lady Nora to please text or call me as soon as possible. Are you okay? I need to hear your voice and confirm you're in one piece.

"Nora…" Matthew said gently. "The Department of Emergency Services was able to run the license plate—the car was definitely registered to Lucas. Moreover, they found a semi-destroyed mobile phone not far from the car. Surprisingly, they managed to power it on, and were able to retrieve the contact information of the last person he spoke to. That was me."

She slowly sank onto the rim of her bed. Her hands shook, and she put her phone down. A dark sense of foreboding gripped hold of her.

This isn't happening right now. This can't be real. Lucas will text me back straightaway, and everything will be fine.

"I've been up the last three hours ringing my mates in Australia, calling in favors for any scrap of news. From what I've been able to piece together, Lucas had planned to drive out west to a fossil excavation site near the town of Winton, about fifteen hours away from Brisbane. This is pure speculation on my part, but en route, he must have encountered a quick-moving pocket of the wildfire that's been burning through the Australian bush over the last few weeks."

Nora squeezed her eyes tight. She knew firsthand how dangerous and destructive a fire could be. When she was eight, during one of the hottest Mediterranean summers on record, a wildfire ravaged just over half the vineyards on Isola Nostrum in a matter of hours. The consequences had been devastating.

Not only were homes destroyed, but so many people were injured. Nonno and Papa both aged overnight. She'd never recalled seeing either of them appear so helpless and broken.

"Have there been any search teams sent out to try and locate him?" Her voice wobbled. She fought to keep a building bubble of dread at bay.

"I've been informed that right now, it's too dangerous to send anyone out. The fire service captain I spoke to was hopeful the conditions would be more favorable in ten to twelve hours when the winds die down." Matthew's voice sounded exhausted. "They have a team on standby in case a window of opportunity opens before then."

Nora's eyes flashed. "What kind of an answer is that?" Anger surged through her veins, and she jumped to her feet. "I will not idly sit by and wait! Lucas is out there somewhere, stranded with no supplies, in one of the most unforgiving landscapes in the world—the Australian outback!" She paced the room. "Give me thirty minutes. I'll put in a few phone calls and have a plane chartered to Brisbane with a squadron of Isola Nostrum's elite navy search and rescue teams."

"Nora, your heart is in the right place, but as difficult as it might be, in this instance, stepping back and letting the professionals do their job *is* going to be the best means of finding Lucas."

"But I have to do something." She picked the phone up off her bed and sucked in a steadying breath. "If I'm left here waiting to hear any news about Lucas, I'm going to go mad."

Was this how Nonno and Papa had felt?

She heard Matthew rustling through several sheets of paper in the background. "If you'd like something to do, it would be immensely helpful to me if I were able to have you get in contact with Lucas's parents."

"Of course. I'll ring them at first light." She dug her nails into the tender flesh of her palm. "Is there anything else that I can do?"

"You can stay positive. Remember, Lucas is a resourceful man. He's much stronger than the world thinks he is. Don't dwell on the infinite number of worst-case scenarios. You'll only end up driving yourself mad."

Like Mrs. Bennet and her nerves in *Pride in Prejudice.*

After she made Matthew promise that he'd contact her with any updates, they disconnected the call. Nora's mind was overloaded. It was as if she were looking at the world through a saltwater aquarium.

She felt so helpless sitting there waiting to hear about Lucas. Her hands shook. Her chest ached, and her breath grew short. Every time she closed her eyes, her mind conjured one horrible image after the other of what-if scenarios. What was Lucas doing now? Was he lying unconscious in a field? Wandering aimlessly through a vast desert? Or was he safe and sound and just had no means of contacting anyone?

She walked over to her window and opened it, breathing in the cool, fresh air. Although she couldn't see the water, she could hear the sound of the waves crashing against the coast of the island below. Her gaze traveled up to the bright orange full moon. Thousands of blue-and-gold stars littered the sky as if someone had sprinkled a can of glitter on a piece of navy-blue velvet. The scene should have calmed her. Yet instead, it ignited a sense of guilt.

I have to occupy myself. Anything will do.

Nora padded over to her desk and sat down. She clicked on her small desk lamp. Opening her laptop, she turned it on and waited for the icons to load. Her eyes took a moment to adjust to the blue tint of the screen. With a few clicks of her mouse, a blank Word document opened. She took a few deep, steadying breaths.

Writing Austen fan fiction always transported her to a safe haven. She had full control over her characters and the plot. Certainly, there was the age-old proven plot formula where Jane Austen's heroine developed feelings for the story's rake or rogue. The villain caused a scandal, and just as it seemed all was lost for the heroine, Mr. Right swooped in and saved the day. However, she could adapt the formula as she saw fit.

The cursor blinked. Nora started typing the first stream of words that entered her mind.

Catherine "Kitty" Bennet squeezed her younger sister Lydia's hand. "You will write to me? Won't you?"

"You shall have to wait and see. Married ladies rarely have time to worry about such droll tasks as writing to one's family." Lydia removed her hands from Kitty's and slipped a pair of white kid gloves over her fingers. "To think that of all my sisters, *I* shall be the first to marry!" she proclaimed gleefully.

Kitty's face fell. Out of all her siblings, Lydia had always been her closest companion. Once Lydia said goodbye to Longbourn, to whom would she be able to turn? Jane had Lizzy, and Mary . . . well, she had her music.

I'll be all alone.

Kitty Bennet was so often overlooked. There weren't enough stories about her or Mary. Opening up a second blank Word document, Nora started to outline her plans for the plot. She swallowed hard and forced herself to block out everything except Kitty's world.

"Kitty Bennet, speak to me. Removed from the influence of your horrid younger sister, who are you?" Nora mused aloud as she rubbed her eyes. "I want to give you the happy ending you deserve, like my Lord Malcolm."

Four hours later, she covered a yawn with her hand. She had written the first four chapters of her story. Her body ached—it felt as if she'd run a long marathon.

Ten thousand words. Not bad. She'd call that a productive session. She wondered what her beta readers on the Never Far From Netherfield forum, like Sabrina Hill, might say. She was one of the most reliable readers and always took the time to provide Nora with useful, constructive feedback.

She checked the time on the lower right hand of her screen. It was six-thirty in the morning. Saving the document, Nora stretched, then went to shower and dress. An hour later, she returned to her desk. She'd thought the shower would help to rejuvenate her mind and body, but she still felt numb. She still hoped against all odds that Lucas might pop into her room and tell her this was all an awful hoax.

With clammy hands, she picked up her phone and dialed the phone number for Lucas's mother. She took a deep breath as a monotone female voice answered. "This is the office of the Duchess of Trent. Ms. Percy speaking. How may I direct your call?"

"Good morning, Ms. Percy. This is Princess Leonora. It's urgent that I speak to the duchess at her first available moment regarding her son." Nora was proud of how calm her voice sounded.

"Your Serene Highness, of course. The duchess will ring you straightaway. She has an opening in her agenda at one this afternoon. Will that be sufficient?"

Nora's mouth formed the shape of an O. One p.m. was considered urgent?

Nora's private secretary would put a call through directly to her if someone close to her didn't have her private mobile number and said it was urgent.

"Actually no, it will not." Nora breathed sharply. "Perhaps I wasn't clear when I said the call was urgent—it's an emergency."

She heard typing in the background. "If that is the case, I can rearrange the duchess's schedule for a ten a.m. call?"

Her eyelids twitched. What type of person was Ms. Percy? Did she not understand the word emergency? She slammed her fist onto her desktop. "Let me be crystal clear, Ms. Percy. Lucas, Lord Merrick, the *heir* to the dukedom of Trent, is missing. *I've* been tasked with informing the duke and duchess about the situation. If you could provide me with their personal mobile numbers, I'll ring them directly myself."

Ms. Percy's answer was curt. "Unfortunately, Princess Leonora, Lord Merrick being merely missing does not constitute enough of an emergency to rearrange the duchess's schedule. I also regret to inform you that neither the duke nor the duchess has a private mobile phone. All calls to them are routed through this office or the office of the Duke of Trent."

Nora didn't have time to play games.

"Fine. Schedule me for ten. In the meantime, since you don't seem to have any empathy or regard for Lord Merrick, I'll have my father, *King Lorenzo,* ring the personal mobile phone of *King Reginald,* your British king, and get the duke's number from him. Grazie."

Without waiting for a response, Nora ended the call. Fuming, she muttered under her breath in Italian as she stormed out of her room for the rooftop pool in search of her papa.

In the words of Mr. Darcy, my good opinion once lost, is lost forever.

"Leonora. I understand how upset you are, but you simply can't drop everything, and fly halfway across the world without a plan of action." Papa crossed his arms. "This is where I draw the line."

She didn't care what he said. She was still going to do whatever it took to get herself to Australia.

"But Papa…" Nora's eyes glistened with unshed tears. She'd used the last of her energy reserves to plead her case to him.

"Every time someone has a problem, no matter its size, you jump at the opportunity to try and fix it." Papa's face softened. "When you were a child, it was releasing the salt-water aquarium fish back into the sea. When you were a teenager, it was trying to self-fund the building of a new roof for the library in Ananostrum because you didn't like how long it would take for my government to approve the funding to fix the old leaky one."

"I was a child then. It's different now." She stamped her foot in frustration. "I'm an adult. I *have* to be there to help—"

"Leonora, right now you are throwing a child's tantrum." Papa scooted his chair away from the kitchen table. Its legs scratched against the hardwood floors. "As rough as it might be to hear this, not every problem or situation is fixable."

She was wasting her time being here. She could be on her way to Brisbane. Why did she feel as if she had to do things the "proper" way and ask for Papa's leave?

"But it's Lucas," she sputtered.

"Si, and he *is* a part of this family." Papa pinched the bridge of his nose. "Leonora… how can I get through to you?" He placed his hands on her shoulders. "Let me ask you this: What would you going to Australia accomplish? Is there something you offer the search and rescue teams that isn't already being done?"

What good would her presence do? She felt as if she were an animal that had been locked in its kennel for the evening.

"I don't know, Papa." Her body shook. "I just… I feel so lost. So helpless. I'm terrified I'm going to lose one of my best friends. He could be grievously injured and lying somewhere, lost in the outback. What if he isn't found in time. What if…"

"Leonora, take a deep breath." Papa hugged her tightly for several seconds. She cried into his shirt. Its linen fabric was light and soft against her eyes. "Know that everything that can be done for your young man right now is being done. As difficult as it is, you have to be able to let go and trust those around you."

"It's not that easy," Nora sobbed.

"It never is." Her father swallowed hard. "If the situation were reversed and it were your mama who was missing, I would be doing all *I* could to become a part of the search effort."

"Then you understand why I have to get to Brisbane." Nora breathed deeply. She released her father.

"I do. I never said I'd forbid you from going to Australia. I merely said I wouldn't allow you to travel without a plan." Papa's facial features tightened. "I still need you to take a step back and examine the situation objectively."

Nora dried her eyes with her wrist. Her tired brain couldn't compute whatever her father was trying to hint at to her. "Papa. Can you tell me what lesson you want me to learn, per favore? I'm stressed. I'm tired, and I haven't had any coffee yet."

"Think back to our conversation from last night." Her father sighed. "Being a king and the head of state is never easy. I have to be an objective leader who rules with my head rather than my heart. My decisions affect many lives."

He thinks I'm doing too much. Her stomach muscles clenched. *He wants me to make the mature decision not to rush to Lucas simply because I can. Because I'm a princess. He wants me to wait it out and trust the process.*

Her body was on fire, as if two velociraptors had sunk their claws into her arms and were each seeking to pull her in opposing directions. One led her to Lucas and Australia. The other toward the throne and Isola Nostrum. She had to make a decision. Her chest ached.

"Capisco. I think I understand now, Papa." Nora's voice was raw. "I am the Principessa dei Fiore now, and I have the responsibility to look at the larger picture rather than just what's in front of me."

"Si. Esattamente." Her father nodded.

She felt physically ill. Her heart pounded in her ears. "Respectfully, if I cannot live up to the weight of the expectations of the job, I must abdicate my place in the line of succession. Lucas is too important to me, and if I am forced to make a choice between him and the crown, I choose him—"

"No. No. No." Papa's face whitened. "Leonora, we are humans. Not robots. We are allowed to have emotions. While I'd like to see you come to terms with the limitations of the scale of help or assistance you offer to others, I don't wish for you to resign. I *want* you to go to Australia as a special envoy."

"You do?" she gasped.

Even if it's doing too much?

"Si. Lucas is your fiancé." Her father's brows knit together. "I've learned from our ambassador to Australia that the people of Queensland are in dire need of any extra supplies and support that we can offer them. In your first official act as the Principessa dei Fiore, you will be escorting a cargo plane full of supplies to Brisbane on behalf of our people."

A wave of relief rushed through her body. "Grazie, Papa."

"You'll be departing from Pisa. Lorenzo will escort you to the mainland." Her father glanced at his watch. "I'd like you to take a nap—I don't like to see you so exhausted—but I'm also aware you will wish to depart as soon as possible."

"Si. I do." Nora hugged him again and raced up the stairs to her room to begin packing.

She'd be the first person to admit doing too much was a fatal flaw of hers. It was what would make her a tragic hero, but she couldn't change who she was. *Lucas, I am coming to you. Just hold on, mi amore. Hold on.*

Nora's mobile phone buzzed later that afternoon as she sat inside the cabin of the Toscani family yacht. Unlocking her screen, she was happy to see that it was a message from Matthew. About time he texted her. She'd been waiting for several hours.

Matthew: I just saw your previous message. Kudos to you for successfully being able to reach Lucas's folks.

Nora: Is that why you tasked me with contacting them in the first place? Because you knew how incompetent their staff is?

Matthew: *Blushing emoji* Can you blame a bloke who is running on fumes?

Nora's facial features softened.

I guess not. Matthew has had a lot to sort through since last night. I know that like me, he hasn't slept.

Nora: I'll give you the benefit of the doubt.

Matthew: Thank you.

Three dots blinked. He was typing.

Matthew: I also saw that you're off to Australia? How long is it going to take you to reach the land Down Under?

Nora: Si. Roughly twenty-two hours. I have to make a stop in Singapore before continuing on to Brisbane.

Matthew: Got it. I'll send a text to my mate Dan. He'll pick you up at the airport and take you straight to Lucas's flat and to Rex.

Nora: Has he had any success in getting Rex to eat or drink anything?

Matthew: Very little, I'm afraid. Rex is still acting as if he's lost his best friend.

Poor Rex.

Nora: I'll make sure he receives the VIP treatment from me.

Matthew: Having you there can only help Rex.

Nora: Thanks for all your help. I'll text you from Singapore, and when I'm in Brisbane.

Matthew: Likewise. I'll keep you apprised of any changes.

Nora tucked her phone away. She closed her eyes to ease the ache of her pounding head. She was both mentally and physically drained. She dreaded the thought of sitting on an airplane for an entire day and night.

Her thoughts turned to Lucas. She pictured him in a tattered shirt and pair of jeans, stumbling blindly through a sandy terrain coated in thorny bushes. His normally bright blue eyes were glassy. Stubble coated his jawline. Perspiration dripped down his forehead. As if speaking to a ghostly apparition, he wheezed, "Nora. I need you." He reached out to her.

Nora lifted her own hand. But no matter how hard she tried, she couldn't touch his. He remained just out of reach. "I'm here."

The skies were covered in thick, dark smoke, obscuring the sun. Was it night? Or was it day? She smelled wood and grass burning. There was no moisture in the air.

"Nora." He coughed, having a difficult time catching his breath. "Where are you? I can hear you, but I can't see you."

"I'm coming. I promise."

"So hot. So thirsty."

Her pulse raced. "Listen to me, Lord Malcolm, you have a very important job to do. I need you to stay safe until I arrive. I will find you. I promise."

Suddenly, there was a rustling sound. They both looked behind them. Hundreds of indigenous animals scampered in their direction. She spotted snakes, dingoes, flying foxes, crocodiles, red kangaroos, wallabies, echidnas, wombats, and koalas fleeing a black hole swallowing everything in its path.

Lucas's eyes widened. "We have to get out of here. Run."

Her body was too heavy. She stood frozen in place. There wasn't time to run. The black was approaching too quickly.

Extending her hands toward him in desperation, she screamed, "Lucas… I love you!" The ground started to shake. The darkness swallowed her.

She gasped, and her eyes opened. Ice-cold water drenched her body. She gasped deeply again and saw Lorenzo's chalk-white face. In one hand, he held an empty cup. With the other, he squeezed her shoulder.

"You were having some type of night terror. I'm sorry for getting you wet, but I couldn't wake you up. You kept shaking and screaming for Lucas."

She rested her palm on her forehead. "It was a dream? But it was so real. There was a fire, a massive black hole, and an earthquake."

"It was all a terrible dream," Lorenzo confirmed. His warm cinnamon-brown eyes roved her body. "You're safe and sitting on the royal yacht in the harbor of Port Livorno."

A high-pitched whistle screamed. "The kettle!" Lorenzo rushed over to the kitchenette and turned off the stove. From a stainless-steel kettle, he poured piping-hot water into a white ceramic teapot for one.

She must have fallen asleep without realizing it. She never wanted to see Lucas in such a state ever again.

"Here is a towel for you to dry off with." Lorenzo set a silver tray down on the edge of the kitchen's bar area. "And some tea for your nerves."

"You made me tea?"

"You always say a hot cup of tea is the best rejuvenator." Lorenzo shrugged. "Before your nightmare, you looked dead on your feet. Like a vampire or a werewolf."

Nora stood, walked over to the island, and flipped one of the teacups over. She lifted the pot and poured. "Not the most flattering comparison."

"I just call it like I see it." Lorenzo started opening cabinet drawers. "Anyhow, some chocolate might give you a boost of energy too."

"There isn't any chocolate on board. Lu and I ate all of it last time. I haven't had time to replenish it. There are, however, some toffee-covered biscuits in the cabinet above the sink."

Lorenzo retrieved the blue-and-white package and passed it to Nora. She placed one on her tea saucer and offered one to him. They ate in silence. She savored the combination of her Earl Grey with the semisweet flavor of the toffee.

Lucas was the one who opened her eyes to the world of tea. When she first arrived at uni, she was a strict coffee drinker. Nora recalled how disappointing it had been to not be able to find what she deemed a suitable cup of coffee. Growing up under the influence of Italian cooking and confections had spoiled her. British coffee could simply not be compared to a cup of Italian coffee.

While he was waiting one night for Siobhan to finish getting ready to go out to dinner and the cinema, Nora and Lucas had a long, extended debate over the merits of tea versus coffee. Both of them refused to give in to the other.

She thought it was the end of it, but the next thing she knew, a special delivery from Fortnum and Mason was sitting on her desk from him. He refused to end the debate until she had sampled a "proper" cup of tea. He patiently taught her step-by-step how to boil the water to the right temperature, strain the tea leaves, let it steep, and even how to drink it.

The smirk on his face when she grudgingly admitted she was wrong was priceless. From then on, he made sure she was always stocked with a ready supply of Irish breakfast tea, Royal Blend, and Earl Grey from F and M, even after they had graduated. She still received a delivery from them once every three months.

Lorenzo finished his biscuit and helped himself to another. "Leonora, I don't think you should travel alone. Lucia or I could accompany you to Australia."

Nora shook her head. "No. I'll be fine. Lu has final exams, and Papa has a special project for you to take charge of. He'll tell you more about it, but you are to spearhead our efforts of selling wines at the Cinque Terre's farmers' markets."

What she didn't tell him was that she and her father had agreed it was a brilliant cover to keep her brother busy, and to get him off the island and near people again.

Papa might not know it, but some of the stall vendors like Tonia would also keep an eye on him. They'd watched Nora and her siblings grow up. They viewed Lorenzo as an extension of their families, like a son or grandson. Italian mamas and nonnas were fierce. They wouldn't let any harm come to him.

Lorenzo crossed his arms. "Leonora. You're the only bossy older sister I have. If you had a fatal flaw, it would be that you always take on too much."

There were those words again. Nora inclined her head.

"You need someone to look after you," Lorenzo emphasized.

"I appreciate the concern, but I will be fine. It's just the stress that has me out of sorts. Lucas is lost out there all alone." Nora stood and rested her hands on her brother's shoulders, "I'm just worried. I want to see him home safely. I love him." The words tumbled out of her mouth. It was the first time she'd said them aloud.

Her subconscious was telling her all along that Lucas was so much more than a fake fiancé. She didn't know when she first fell in love with him, but she thought she'd always known he was a very special man.

"Love knows no bounds," Lorenzo muttered to himself. "It's more trouble than it's worth." He grimaced, then ran a hand through his hair. "There are exceptions to every rule, I suppose."

Lorenzo was wrong. Love was worth it. She wished he'd see that, but he needed time to be able to reach that conclusion on his own. Her telling him that wouldn't help.

She finished her tea. Her brother wouldn't be satisfied until she was on the plane, and it had taken off. He was too protective at times. She fluttered her eyelashes at Lorenzo. "Maybe I am more tired than I thought I was. Can I trouble you to drive me to the airport in Pisa? I don't fully trust myself."

Lorenzo lifted his chin. "Of course. I'd insist on doing it even if you hadn't asked me."

"Grazie." Nora smiled at him.

Lucas, I am on my way. Wherever you are, as I said to you in my nightmare—I will find you.

CHAPTER 13

Arrival in Brisbane

Nora's legs wobbled as she moved to exit the plane. Three pilots in crisp navy uniforms removed their caps and saluted her. "Your Serene Highness, it was an honor to be able to fly you today, Principessa."

Hiding any signs of discomfort, she forced a smile onto her face. "It's I who should be thanking all of you. Captain Alessando. Captain Mattias. Captain Niccolo." She locked eyes with each member of the crew to acknowledge them. "You are three of the most skilled pilots in the world. Isola Nostrum is so lucky to have you as distinguished members of our Air Force."

Let the diplomatic duties begin. As usual, Papa was right. As resentful as she was about it, by taking an additional four hours to get here rather than traveling on her own, they had the opportunity, even if it was a small one, to help more people than just Lucas, and animals as well. In fact, he would be the first person to say they should be rendering aid to whomever they could.

142

Walking down a set of steps off the plane, her smile fell. She was greeted by a man with salt-and-pepper hair and a neat beard. He wore a blue-and-white-pinstriped suit. A woman with blonde hair in a black-and-white-striped dress stood to his right.

"Your Highness." The man bowed. "All will be well, Principessa," he added softly in Italian.

Clearing her throat, Nora responded in English. "Ambassador Zucheretti, a pleasure as always to see you." They exchanged handshakes. Her gaze turned to the woman.

"May I present the governor of Queensland, Her Excellency, Mrs. Ashleigh Kaplan," the ambassador said.

The governor curtsied. "Welcome to Queensland, Princess Leonora. We are honored you've chosen to visit us during our hour of need. I only wish it were under better circumstances."

"Indeed." Nora shook her hand.

"Is this the first time you've visited Queensland? I understand you've been to the states of New South Wales and Western Australia on a previous occasion."

"No, I have been here before. I was lucky enough to travel privately for a holiday to Sydney, Brisbane, and the Sunshine Coast last year."

"Did you now?" The governor asked a few additional questions about Nora's plans and offered a few of her own recommendations.

Nora attempted to maintain a polite demeanor. Internally, she was fighting her exhaustion and her anxiety. More than anything, she wanted to change out of her pink dress, remove her heels, and meet Matthew's mate.

Sensing her shift in mood, Ambassador Zucheretti

stepped in. "Apologies, Your Excellency, but I believe we have some photographers and news crews waiting to speak with you both."

The governor's cheeks colored. "Yes, yes, of course." Her assistant signaled for the cameras and media teams to step forward. A pair of microphones was placed in front of them.

Practiced in the art of official appearances, Nora placed her public relations mask on. "G'day to everyone," she said. The cameramen laughed. "Isola Nostrum and Australia have always enjoyed a close working relationship with one another. Our two countries have been trade partners and allies for more than one hundred years. It is vital that in times of crisis, friends are able to count upon other friends to offer them aid."

She took a deep breath. Camera shutters clicked. An airplane landed in the background.

"On behalf of my father, King Lorenzo III, and the people of Isola Nostrum, I, Princess Leonora, the Principessa dei Fiori, am here today to present the people and the government of Queensland with a cargo plane packed full of fire supplies and also offer the assistance of our firefighters from Isola Nostrum's armed services in the hopes that we will be able to help the Queensland Fire and Emergency Services teams stop the bushfire that is raging through your beautiful state."

The governor applauded. "Thank you, Princess Leonora. We welcome these supplies and the extra help with open arms. The past few weeks have extended our emergency response teams to the maximum."

Nora and Her Excellency fielded a few questions and posed for several photos. By the end, the muscles in her face had grown tight from all the smiling.

Three hours after Nora had arrived, she sat in an unmarked white sedan double-parked in front of the baggage claim area of Brisbane Airport's international terminal.

Angelo, a bald man with broad shoulders who was the longtime head of Nora's security detail, turned around from the front seat. "Principessa, per your wishes, I will remain at as discreet a distance as possible from you. Ricardo will be on duty when I'm asleep or otherwise engaged. You have your panic button on you?"

"Si. I always do." Nora tapped her black Longchamp backpack.

"Brava."

"I'm being picked up by a man named Dan Wakefield. He drives a black Highlander and is taking me directly to Lucas's flat. I'll check in with you tonight. As far as my plans go for the rest of the day, I'll only leave the flat if Rex shows any desire to go for a walk."

Angelo nodded. "Mr. Wakefield's background check and driving record both came back clean. Ricardo and I will be staying in a holiday let on the second floor of Lord Merrick's apartment building. As always, you will only see one of us if there is a situation that requires intervention or if you ring or message one of us."

Nora kissed him on the cheek. "Grazie. You are my favorite spy. Don't tell Ricardo, though."

"That is our secret, Principessa." He winked.

Over the years, Nora had grown to appreciate that Angelo gave her such a wide leash when it came to her privacy and her freedom of movement. He was so good at being stealthy that there were many times when Nora forgot he was present, lurking in her shadow. As an adult, she only tended to have a security detail when she was on an official engagement or traveling to a crowded destination.

Nora slid out and looked for door number four. She sent Dan a text.

Nora: I'm just arriving at baggage claim. Looking for you now near door four.

Dan: I'm on my way from the car park.

She took a selfie of herself.

Nora: Brilliant. I'm wearing a baby-blue maxi dress, oversized mirrored sunglasses, and a white bucket hat.

Dan: Lucas has shown me your gorgeous picture before. I'm the bloke with the vibrant ginger hair, in a white button-up shirt and jeans.

Nora placed her hand on her sunglasses and tilted them down. "Dan!" she called out, waving her hand.

A tall man waved back and jogged toward her. "Nora," he said with a thick Aussie twang, slightly out of breath. "G'day." He raised an eyebrow. "No luggage?"

She gestured to her backpack. "Everything I need is in here." Angelo had her three suitcases if she needed anything else.

"I always admire a gal who packs light. Let's get a move on, Princess."

"You know…" she said slowly.

"I do," he confirmed.

Nora pulled the brim of her hat down lower.

"Just act as you normally would. I don't think you're likely to be recognized. It's a busy airport, and no offense, but you aren't a major royal around here like the British royals."

"None taken." She breathed a little easier. "Who told you? Matthew or Lucas?"

Dan shrugged. "Neither. I was aware that Lucas had a

fiancée named Nora and that she was from Isola Nostrum. When I saw you on the news, it didn't take me long to connect the dots."

She wondered if he was aware Lucas was an earl and the future Duke of Trent.

They stopped in front of a valet booth. He retrieved a parking ticket from his pocket and handed it to the man.

"We'll be back with the vehicle straightaway. Give me two shakes," the valet said, taking a key off the hook.

Dan slid his hands into his pockets and casually leaned against the wall of the valet booth. Nora could see the fine lines of stress on his forehead and telltale purple shadows under his eyes. "Rex will be happy to see a friendly face. The poor dog is in a soddy state."

Her face fell. Although she wasn't in the mood to chat, good manners dictated she should be polite and converse with her host. "Any changes this morning?"

"He took some bone broth and rice for brekkie."

They exchanged a few more notes on Rex, then the valet returned with the Highlander. Nora slid into the passenger seat as Dan drove them from the airport to the suburb of St. Lucia, near the university.

Brisbane was just as she'd remembered—a sprawling, hilly metropolis built upon the serene Moreton Bay, packed full of lovely pockets of green spaces. She'd fallen in love with the trumpet-like flowers produced by the Jacaranda trees, tranquil walks along the Brisbane River, and the ease of access to hidden oases like the picturesque Curtis Falls on Mount Tambourine, and perfect golden sand and azure water of Cylinder Beach. Today, however, the sky was darkened with an unnaturally thick gray haze, matching her mood.

"Thank you again for picking me up."

"No problem at all. I consider Matty and Lucas good mates."

Trying her best to keep the flow of the conversation on neutral territory, Nora said, "If you don't mind me asking, how did you become acquainted with Matthew?"

"We met during our gap year in Thailand." Dan shook his head. "I'd just arrived in Bangkok from Sydney and had an overnight layover before an early morning flight to Phuket. Being a brilliant eighteen-year-old, I thought I would pass the time by seeing what the nightlife was like in Bangkok."

"I can sense where this story is going." Nora sighed, then bit back a yawn. "You enjoyed yourself a little too much, didn't you?"

"Guilty as charged." Dan glanced over his shoulder and changed lanes. "I ended up missing my flight and was told I had to buy a new ticket if I still wanted to travel to Phuket. I was so angry with myself. The only way I'd be able to afford a new ticket was if I rang my mum."

Nora nodded in understanding. The last situation any teenager would've wanted to be in the middle of was having to ring their parents to ask for money.

"When I was pleading my case with the ticketing agent, Matty happened to be checking in for his own flight. He overheard my story, and for some reason, took pity on me. He booked me a new ticket using his credit card's airline points. We've been good mates ever since."

"I never would've guessed Matthew was such a softie."

"He's a good bloke, just like Lucas." The car stopped at a red light. Dan glanced at Nora. "Matty changed my life. I ended up meeting my wife on the flight he booked for me. She's been the best thing that has ever happened to me. We've been together five years next month."

Her eyes widened. "Congratulations."

"Thank you."

The signal changed, and Dan shifted gears and maneuvered the car forward. "Life always has a funny way of working out."

Nora looked out the window. The landscape was changing. The suburb of Saint Lucia was packed full of residential homes situated on the river, shaded by trees. "I dearly want to believe that."

Dan's voice grew quieter still. "The fire service and emergency rescue teams are all top-notch. They will locate Lucas and bring him home."

Nora's stomach muscles clenched. "I just hate being stuck in limbo waiting for news."

Dan agreed and opted to change to a safer topic. He and Nora chatted about his wife and her job as a vet. "Georgia spends four days a week at a wildlife sanctuary, and on Fridays, she makes the rounds to various zoos and veterinary clinics that require a specialist. As an exotic and indigenous species specialist, she's in high demand."

"That must make for some interesting dinnertime conversations."

"It does. Just yesterday, she was telling me about how she had to use glue to help heal tears in the wings of several flying fox bats. The membrane might heal on its own, but sometimes it needs a helping hand."

"Are those the bats I've seen photos of that are as large as a human?"

Dan's lips curved. "You're thinking of the golden-crowned variety. Those mega bats are native to the Philippines. In Australia, we have the grey-headed flying foxes. Fully extended, their wingspan is only a meter long."

"As opposed to…"

"One and a half meters."

Nora's eyes widened. "That's taller than me!"

Five minutes later, Dan parked the car, and opened the passenger-side door for her. She followed him into the white stucco apartment building and ascended the stairs to the first floor. Stopping in front of apartment 7D, he inserted the flat's key into the lock.

As the door opened, they heard the sound of Rex's nails rubbing across the hardwood floors as he bounded like an excited puppy into the entry hallway. Barking, Rex wagged his tail wildly and planted his front paws on Nora. She fell to her bum, and he took advantage of the opportunity to lick her face.

"Rexie. It's so good to see you, boy." She scratched his ears and buried her own face into his coarse black-and-white fur.

"Well, would you look at that." Dan shook his head. "If I hadn't seen it with my own eyes, I never would've believed that this is the same dog I left here an hour ago."

"Rex. Are you hungry? We have some delicious and nutritious food for you," Nora said.

The border collie barked and padded down the hall. She stood and followed him into the kitchen. Rex pawed his stainless-steel bowl and looked expectantly at Nora, as if he were saying, *I thought you'd never ask. Where's my meal? I'm ready.*

Dan laughed. "I'll prep some more broth and a little food. I think it's best if we reintroduce food to him slowly."

Nora thanked him for the help.

After Dan left for the afternoon to pick up his daughter from day care, Nora stood in the living room with Rex by her side, surveying the scene. Goosebumps formed on her arm. The silence, aside from Rex's panting, was eerie. She swallowed hard. She was alone for the first time that day.

Two framed poster-sized black-and-white photographs of the border collie were displayed on the white wall behind a stone-gray couch. In the center of the room, a square walnut coffee table held the remote control for the television, a large stack of notebooks, a circular glass jar of Cadbury caramel-chocolate eggs—Lucas's favorite candy— and a few stray wrappers.

Her eyes were suddenly drawn up to a silver picture frame on the fireplace mantel below the television mounted to the wall. "This wasn't here last time," she said to herself. Her fingers brushed the glass as she picked up the frame.

I'd know this image anywhere.

In the photo, both their faces held goofy grins. Lucas had one arm draped around Nora's shoulder while the other proudly held her hand up to the camera lens, displaying her engagement ring for all to see. She hugged the frame to her chest, then replaced it.

One of the waiters from the Ampersand Hotel took the photo at the Jurassic Afternoon tea the day Lucas proposed. She thought the hotel had forgotten to send it to them, but Lucas must have had it the entire time.

Her emotions began to swell. She felt as if a dark, gloomy rain cloud had descended overhead. Everything felt heavy and lifeless. Her heart began to ache as if someone were jabbing it with pins. A few tears ran down her cheek. She'd do anything to be able to have a simple conversation with him. She missed the arch of his eyebrow when he was intrigued, and of course, watching his glorious rosy-red lips when he was in Professor Malcolm mode.

She moved on to the room adjacent to the living room —the spare bedroom Lucas used as his makeshift office. Standing in the doorway, she spotted a full laundry basket, and two piles of folded clothing atop the white futon. As in the living room, piles of books, highlighted notes, and unopened mail lay scattered atop an antique writing desk. She shivered and rubbed her forearms against her chest.

In the corner of the room, by an open window, Nora observed two houseplants with yellowing leaves, and unexpectedly, noticed another framed photograph. In the image taken during her visit the previous fall, Nora had her head resting on Lucas's shoulder. They both wore wet suits and had red-rimmed eyes. Lucas took the selfie after they spent the day surfing on Bribie Island.

Her eyes began to sting. Everywhere she went in the flat, she was reminded of the man she'd entered into a fake relationship with. Lucas cared enough to have these pictures printed and framed for a reason. Was it because he had feelings for her? Or was she reading too much into this, and the photos were all a part of his cover?

Turning around, Nora's eyes traveled to the built-in bookcase. Every available crevice was jammed full of books. Some were stacked vertically, others lined up horizontally. She ran her fingers over their spines, staring at the academic-sounding titles, and stirring up a thin layer of ash. She watched it rise and settle back onto the shelf. Lucas's books were among his most prized possessions. He'd never stand for them to be left in a condition like this.

She stared blankly at the gray substance on her finger. Here was undeniable evidence that Lucas was missing. Her throat constricted, and she had trouble breathing. She sank to the floor on her hands and knees. *There is a real chance I may not ever see Lucas again.* Her body shook with silent sobs.

"Come back, please come back…" she choked out.

Nails scratched against the wooden floor. Rex butted his head against her arm and licked her face. He let out a high-pitched whimper.

Nora raised her head, meeting the dog's sad chocolate eyes. "I know you miss him more than anyone." Rex barked in confirmation.

Lowering her walls, Nora felt for the first time she could finally stop pretending to the world that she was fine. Internally, she felt as if her emotions were a giant, chaotic, tangled mess. She sat on her knees and hugged the dog, burying her face in his fur. As she listened to the sound of his rhythmic panting and heartbeat, her own breathing evened out.

Releasing her canine companion, she breathed in, counted to five, and exhaled. Rex's gaze stayed trained on Nora, surveying her every movement.

Being in here was like sitting inside that black hole she dreamed of. It sucked all of the energy and life out of her. Nora blinked twice. *Lucas and I have a strong bond and connection with one another. I'd know if he…* She refused to finish the thought. *I'd just know.*

She stood and brushed some of Rex's stray white hairs off her skirt. "We need to get out of our heads and change the vibe I'm getting from this flat." The dog barked in agreement, his tail wagging wildly. "Here is the plan, Rexie. I'll send Angelo a message, and have him escort us while we go for a walk. Then, we're going to go to the market and get as many fresh flowers and green plants as we can find.

Before I sleep tonight, this flat is getting a thorough cleaning from top to bottom."

Rex barked again and padded over to the door. Nora read his response as, *"This is the best idea you've had all day, you silly human. I've been waiting to go out for a walk since you arrived. While you're at it, how about we also buy some new tennis balls? I fancy a game of fetch."*

It was a truth universally acknowledged that dogs truly were man's best friend.

CHAPTER 14

The Wildlife Sanctuary

Two days passed without any updates. Nora remained anxious. She was unable to sleep much or eat, but tried her best to hold herself together by keeping her mind occupied and away from grim thoughts. She worked on Kitty Bennet's story, went on long outings with Rex, and did stress cooking. Soon, Lucas's freezer was bursting with enough containers of lasagna, fettuccini, gnocchi, and spaghetti to last him at least six months.

On the third day, a concerned Dan managed to convince her to leave the flat for a visit to the wildlife sanctuary where his wife worked, about an hour outside Brisbane. She wrestled with her decision through yet another sleepless night, questioning the appropriateness of going out with Lucas missing.

Dan made the case that it would help pass the time quicker. He promised that at the first inkling of any news, they would head back to the flat. She just hoped she was doing the right thing. It felt utterly wrong to go out. However, at the same time, she felt that if she spent another day in the apartment locked inside, she might go mad. Lucas would tell her that she needed a change of scenery. She'd do it for him.

The car traveled up a long gravel drive. Dan entered a makeshift car park and turned off the engine. As she climbed out, Nora felt like she had entered a forest. Everywhere she looked, she was surrounded by dense layers of trees and green foliage. The air was humid. She heard a symphony of insects humming and the laughter of one of Australia's famed kookaburra birds.

How did that nursery rhyme go? *Kookaburra sits in the old gum tree. Merry, merry king of the bush is he.* She couldn't remember the remainder of the lyrics.

"Are these all gum trees?" she asked, wincing at how dull and flat her voice sounded.

Dan removed his sunglasses. "Not all of them, but heaps of them are."

"What about eucalyptus trees?" She pulled her hair into a low ponytail.

"A gum tree *is* a eucalyptus tree. Gum tree is just the nickname we Aussies have given to them."

Nora's cheeks warmed. "Oh."

Dan clicked the alarm on the car and led them up a dirt path to a rustic wooden cabin-like structure that served as the sanctuary's visitors' center. "It's pretty incredible, but everything from the timber used for the decking to the windows came from a skip and has been repurposed."

Hearing that made Nora appreciate the building even more. The animals that lived here weren't the only ones receiving a second chance.

Dan opened the glass entry door. A strawberry-blonde woman in a green polo shirt and a green baseball cap was recording notes on a clipboard. She glanced up, and her round face broke into a wide grin. "Right on time."

Dan leaned over the countertop and kissed the woman on the cheek. "Nora, this is Georgia, my better half." He beamed with pride as he spoke.

"How ya' going?" The petite woman waved and returned the clipboard to the wall. "I hope Dan hasn't given you too much of a hard time."

Nora shook her head. "Not at all," she answered quietly.

"Come on through, you two." Georgia opened the gate dividing the office from the check-in area. "If you are up for it, I was just about ready to head on over and feed our youngest resident her brekkie. Would you like to tag along and meet Daisy?"

"Yes please," she said.

Brekkie? She heard Dan say that word a few days ago at the airport. She was pretty sure it meant breakfast. Aussies had so many shortened slang words. Macca for McDonald's. Arvo for the afternoon. Barbie for a barbecue. She thought about Lucas and how he'd adopted a hybrid Aussie slash UK slang. She'd had to ask him to clarify what he was saying half the time. English was already tricky enough without trying to figure out new words.

After they exchanged their shoes for Wellie boots, Georgia led Nora and Dan out the back of the visitors' center. The trees thinned and the dirt path widened. She smelled the scent of hay and mud. Volunteers rolled wheelbarrows filled with fruits, vegetables, grains, tree branches, and other assorted items past them toward two of the largest barns in the facility.

"How big is your property?" Nora asked. Her questions

and answers were short. She was trying hard to engage Dan and Georgia, but it was challenging.

"Thanks to the collaboration between the Queensland government and a generous anonymous donor, we have roughly five hundred acres of pristine grassland and forest that our animals are free to explore."

"That's a lot of land." Nora let out a long whistle.

"It isn't as much as you might think." Dan rubbed the back of his neck.

"Indeed. In the wild, elephants and giraffes can travel upward of eighty kilometers per day. We have a herd of ten Asian elephants, and three giraffes, and they require every inch we can give them," Georgia said.

Nora had expected to see native Australian animals, not exotic ones like elephants and giraffes.

Georgia scanned her badge at an entry door. It buzzed and granted them access to the most modern facility on the property. The interior reminded Nora of the stables on Isola Nostrum. There were two rectangular stalls, three stacks of hay bales, cleaning tools on the wall, and a set of wide doors that opened to a grassy field.

However, where Nora had expected to see horses, she saw a one-and-a-half-meter-tall baby elephant staying close by its mother's side. Her eyes immediately softened upon seeing the wrinkly skin of the baby and its tiny trunk and ears. The baby's tail wagged from side to side.

Lord Malcolm would undoubtedly just happen to know everything there is to know about elephants too. I can hear him saying now that the baby elephant reminded him of Rex, then jump into some explanation about the dino ancestors they evolved from.

She resisted the urge to stick her fingers into her pocket to check her mobile phone for an update. At lunchtime, she'd ring the rescue center again to see if they'd had any leads or follow-ups to share. Although had the number memorized, she had quickly programmed the number into her contacts.

Focus, Nora.

She heard Georgia's voice speaking. She shook her head. "I'm sorry. Can you repeat that, please?"

"The larger elephant is called Maisie, and the baby we've named Daisy," Georgia said. Maisie fanned her ears, let out a high-pitched trumpet noise, and entered the barn to greet her guests. Georgia lowered her voice. "Any babies born to the herd are kept here for the first few months of life. For your safety, I'm going to ask that you and Dan remain behind the fence while I check on mum and baby. Elephants are shy, intelligent creatures, but they can spook easily. Please try to keep any talking to a low volume."

Nora watched as Georgia entered the stall with her own wheelbarrow of pineapples and one of the largest baby bottles she had ever seen. Maisie lifted her trunk and sniffed Georgia with interest. Daisy stayed firmly tucked behind her.

"G'day to you, too, Mama Maisie. And how is your little one getting on?"

They were so precious. It was like Maisie thought Georgia was a member of their herd. Nora watched Georgia offer Maisie a whole pineapple as an enticing treat to let her give the elephant mum a checkup. Baby Daisy, meanwhile, slowly inched forward, her curiosity getting the better of her.

"Oi, Daisy. Look at what I have for you, baby girl. Are you hungry?"

Daisy coyly used her trunk to investigate the bottle of formula offered to her by Georgia. Realizing it was full of milk, she came directly up to Georgia, butted her head against her lap, and greedily started drinking from the bottle. It didn't take long for the formula to disappear entirely. Satisfied with her charges, Georgia gave the girls a rubdown, then bid the mum and calf a good morning. Nora and Dan met her outside.

"That was amazing! How long did it take you to gain Maisie's trust?" Nora shook her head in disbelief.

"I've worked with Maisie since the day she arrived at the sanctuary from Thailand. So about three years?" Georgia removed her jacket and tied it around her waist. "It's been a long journey. Maisie is a slightly older mum at forty years old. She hasn't been able to produce quite enough milk for Daisy, and we've had to intervene and supplement her meals with bottle feedings."

Nora's eyes widened. Forty years old? "And how old is Daisy?"

"Daisy is about six months old. She's smaller than average, but doing well. She's hit every milestone a little elephant baby should. We'll start introducing her to the other members of the herd next week."

Dan glanced at his watch. "Do you have other rounds to make? I can take Nora on a grand tour of the grounds, then meet you for lunch at half twelve?"

Georgia scratched the back of her neck. "I always have patients to see. Half twelve is brill. I'll meet you back in the visitors' center. I'd like to get some lunch at the pub near Karana Downs today."

"It's a date." Dan nodded, and Georgia waved goodbye.

Turning to Nora, Dan pointed to an electric golf cart charging across from the baby elephant enclosure. "Our chariot awaits."

The small patch of lightness she'd experienced a few

minutes earlier disappeared. She fought to suppress the dread and emptiness in her chest.

"Or if you'd rather, there are a couple of camels in the paddock over there." Dan crossed his arms. "I should warn you, however, that Lloyd, the two-humped camel, is spoiled rotten, and he never listens to the keepers."

Nora tried to picture Dan sitting on the back of the camel. She imagined him wiggling the reins on Lloyd, trying to make the camel walk forward, only to have the stubborn animal sit on the ground and tuck its legs in.

"The golf cart is perfetto."

As Dan unplugged the vehicle, Nora's face fell. They climbed into the front seat, and she sat quietly with her hands on her lap, staring at her feet.

"Would you rather try to find the elephant herd first, or some of the other occupants at the sanctuary? There are a mob of roos and wallabies, koalas, two lions, some snakes, and Lucas's personal favorite, saltwater crocs."

Dan hesitated, realizing too late his blunder.

Nora's head rose. "Is Lucas a frequent visitor?"

"He's been working here part-time with the educational outreach department since moving to Brisbane. Once every two weeks, Lucas gives lectures to the public and visiting schools about dinosaurs and how closely related they are to today's reptiles."

Dan glanced over his shoulder and backed the golf cart up. "Every time he's here, he'll spend hours working on his computer while the crocs stare at him through the glass. Their keeper, Colin, jokes that Lucas has become the favored live entertainment for the reptiles."

Lucas had been working here for two years? She always wondered how he'd been supplementing his income. He tended to skirt around the issue of money when she brought it up with him. She knew that the studentship offered to him by the university didn't cover all his bills and expenses.

Nora sighed. When his father cut him off financially, it was such a blow to him. Being the stubborn man that he was, Lucas refused to take any help from her, saying he'd manage just fine. *Look at you now, Lord M. You not only managed to find the perfect part-time job for yourself, but you've managed to keep it under wraps.*

"I'd like to see the crocs, but if you don't mind, I have a quick call to make first." She couldn't wait any longer. She grew concerned that if they were out in a more remote area of the property, there was a chance she'd lose her cell service.

She excused herself, stepping out to the side. With shaking hands, she dialed the direct number to Tilly Green, the agent in charge of Lucas's search.

On the third ring, Tilly's calm voice answered, "How you going, Nora?"

"So-so. I'm sorry to bother you. I just wanted to check if . . ."

"I'm sorry, dear, but there is still no news. The search crews are still grounded until winds die down," the older woman said slowly.

"And you'll ring me with *any* update?"

"Yes. You're the person at the very top of my list." Tilly recited Nora's mobile number back to her.

Her throat constricted. "Thank you," she croaked out.

Dan didn't say anything as Nora shuffled over. He patted her hand and slowly drove the cart through the facility to the reptiles.

❧

The morning of her fourth day in Australia, Nora was sitting on Lucas's living room couch sending out updates to both of their families when she heard the news anchor's report: "In other news this morning… the weather conditions have improved for the Queensland fire service teams fighting the bushfires near Carnarvon National Park."

She dropped her phone onto the cushion beside her and reached for the remote, turning up the volume. "Dramatic progress has been made in containing the blaze on the eastern and western fronts. The fire has burned through hundreds of kilometers of remote, rugged terrain since its inception roughly two weeks ago. There have been some reports of property damage in the municipalities of…"

From his oversized plush dog bed by the sliding door, Rex lifted his head and appraised Nora with interest.

"It might be good news, Rexie." His tail wagged slowly. "We just have to find out what this means for Lord M." He lowered his head, resuming his nap.

Forty minutes later, Nora received her answer in the form of a video chat request from Matthew. She clicked the green "accept" button. Matthew's face appeared on the screen. His skin was dull, and there were dark purple rings under his eyes.

"Grazie for ringing me back, Matthew. I know it's late where you are. I haven't been able to get a hold of Tilly."

"It's no bother at all. Tilly is out in the field. I just got off the line with her assistant. I was told that their agency will start conducting a thorough search for him beginning this morning. The assistant mentioned that they've identified three areas as probable locations where Lucas might have sought refuge."

"Brilliant." Nora smiled for the first time in days. "I have some good news too. Captain Alberto has advised me that Papa has loaned the Queensland government use of Isola Nostrum's new thermal-imaging helicopter. It arrived last night and is ready to be put to use today. I feel more hopeful than I've felt in a long time."

"Me too." Matthew's green orbs glowed with excited energy. "I mean, I know it's still like searching for a needle in a haystack with how large the area is, but I think with the helicopter and Tilly's people out there, we are giving Lucas a real fighting chance." He ran a hand through his hair. "How have you been holding up?"

"I've been trying to stay occupied, but I'm almost out of chores. I need something else to stress bake or clean. Lucas's flat is spotless, and his refrigerator is overflowing with food."

"It's a shame you aren't close to Gloucester. I could use your help tidying up and cooking." He held up a flattened red-and-white Chinese takeaway container. "I've been living off these guys for the past week."

"Really?" she chided him, crossing her legs and sitting up taller.

"Between my running around meeting clients for my regular nine-to-five job and ringing my contacts Down Under for any updates after hours, it's been easier to order meals than to pick up groceries. My body is confused. It hasn't been easy keeping track of time here and where you are."

She hadn't realized just how involved Matthew had been. She owed him a large debt. "When Lucas is found and the dust has settled, I'll be at your doorstep with cleaning supplies to make your flat sparkle. You'll receive the full Nora-rella service. By the time I leave, you will have to purchase a second refrigerator to store all the meals I'll make you."

She'd also see if she could tempt him with a holiday in the Cinque Terre or on Isola Nostrum for a little rest and relaxation.

He rubbed his stomach. "I'm very much looking forward to it."

They exchanged tired glances.

"Did meeting Georgia and seeing where she works help distract you at all? Dan mentioned he might take you when we last spoke."

Nora pictured the blonde-haired vet, who was among one of the most energetic people she'd ever encountered. "Yes and no. Georgia is so passionate about what she does. I enjoyed meeting her and seeing her work in her element, but I'm afraid I couldn't fully appreciate it all. My mind was elsewhere. I have plans to go back in the future."

Matthew nodded. "She's a real firecracker. Did Dan tell you the story about how they met?"

"I think he said they met on an airplane."

"That's part of the story." The corners of his eyes crinkled. "It was love at first sight on his part. Georgia wanted nothing to do with him. Stubborn Dan, however, followed her to the elephant sanctuary she was visiting and wouldn't leave until she finally gave him her name and mobile number. She was a serious vet student back then and wanted nothing to do with a bloke taking a uni gap year. He had a penchant for clubbing." He rubbed his chin. "They're a real-life example of opposites attract. Georgia's been a real lifesaver. She's the one who has been keeping a close eye on Rex."

Nora's mouth opened. "I didn't know." She hadn't connected the dots.

Matthew hid a yawn with his hand. "I had better turn in. I'm having a difficult time keeping my eyes open. I have to be in London by eight tomorrow morning. My company has some retreat we're supposed to attend every other year. Something or other about the best practices for showing properties to potential buyers."

"Fun," Nora said in a sarcastic tone.

"Exactly. I don't need a refresher class for it. But it's a free night at the posh Saint George Hotel in Mayfair and a Michelin-star dinner on the boss." He shrugged. "I'll try to check my phone when I can."

They said their farewells and ended the call.

Nora stretched and stood. Her pulse hammered against her ribs. Today could be the day they found Lucas! "Rex, are you ready for your walk?"

Rex didn't need to be told twice and rushed over to the peg where Lucas kept his harness and leash. She slipped a purple University of Queensland hoodie belonging to Lucas over her black T-shirt and leggings and headed out the door.

CHAPTER 15

All Roads Lead to Roma

Later that same morning, Nora received a text message from Lucas's father.

Duke of Trent: Dear Princess Leonora, I hope this text message finds you well. I wanted to advise you that the mobile number this message is being sent from is my new personal mobile number. I am not quite sure how to pull up what it is at this end, but I am hoping you will be able to figure it out. However, be forewarned that I am still acclimating to how this device operates. Sadly, it has taken me nearly three-quarters of an hour to type this message to you. Thank you for continuing to relay all the updates to me via my private secretary. However, I'd much rather find out about my son directly from you, instead of an intermediary. You may ring me at any time day or night. I still have a pilot on standby to fly me to Australia should you require my services. Regards, Bill.

Nora: Your Grace, a hearty congratulations on your new mobile phone. Just a note… text messages are generally more informal than traditional letters and email messages. In case you need your mobile number, I can see that it is +

44 7 62 578 8924. Please don't hesitate to text or ring me if you require assistance figuring out how to use your mobile phone. I will ring you straightaway with any updates.

Duke of Trent: Dear Princess Leonora, I'm afraid formalities are ingrained in the very fabric of my DNA, yet I shall endeavor to be a bit more informal with you. Regards, Bill.

Nora: Your Grace, I've just been informed that search teams are heading out as we speak. I'll be heading out myself to the search-and-rescue base camp, and will ring you with an update as soon as I can.

Duke of Trent: Dear Princess Leonora, thank you for all that you've done. I am proud to be able to call myself your future father-in-law. I only hope when Lucas is found, he'll be willing to speak to a foolish old man. Regards, Bill.

Nora: Your Grace, he will. But it may take some time.

Duke of Trent: Dear Princess Leonora, I trust you. Regards, Bill.

Nora closed the back window of the car. Rex, however, continued to press his nose to the glass. Once they headed from Brisbane on the A2 National Highway toward Carnarvon National Park, the skies grew from a rusty orange to a murky brown, obscuring the sun. Pinhead-sized pieces of ash rained down upon the windshield.

As Angelo drove the car closer to where the bushfire was burning, she was reminded more of the deserts of Tatooine from *Star Wars: A New Hope*, one of Lorenzo's favorite films, than of a tropical paradise. This was how she'd imagine a post-apocalyptic world to look.

She remembered the endless expanse of the cobalt-blue

sky. The sparkling turquoise water of the beach and the rich, lush green of the forest scape around Queensland.

Thinking about last year took her back to the hiking trip she and Lucas took through the Daintree Rainforest. He was so excited to share a place with her that was older than the dinosaurs. To think it was one hundred sixty million years old. It was like walking through a living museum. A place untouched by time.

They saw so many towering, cascading waterfalls and plants and trees of every size and shape. She hoped it managed to withstand the bushfires. It would be devastating for it to survive for so long, only to see it destroyed by flames.

Nora squinted. It was difficult for her to see beyond the other side of the road. "It doesn't feel as if we're in the same area we visited last year."

"Unfortunately, Principessa, it is only going to grow worse the farther inland we drive," Angelo said with a frown.

Nora sighed. "I know you disapprove of my entering the danger zone, but I have to be here. I've had this nagging feeling all day that Lucas is so close and waiting for us to find him. With every hour that passes, this feeling has only grown stronger. It's like a magnetic pull. I can't exactly describe it. I just instinctively know this is where I need to be."

"Will you at the very least promise me to wear a respirator mask when we step outside?"

If that was what it took to satisfy Angelo and get him to refrain from telling Papa where she was until they were back in Brisbane, of course she would.

"Si."

Angelo continued to drive along the A2 highway. Many

of the tiny rural towns they'd passed had populations of less than one hundred. She saw small clusters of buildings, followed by large stretches of open grassland. In Europe, it was rare to drive fifteen minutes without encountering anything.

"We must be close to the outback by now," she whispered.

About four hours into their drive, Angelo pulled into the largest town they'd passed in for over one hundred kilometers.

"The name of the town is Roma? How fitting."

"All roads lead to Roma, Principessa." He was signaling to turn into a petrol stand when Nora felt a jolt in her tailbone, causing her to jump in her seat. "Principessa?"

"Don't stop for petrol. Keep driving." Her voice was tight. She couldn't explain what was happening to her, but she inherently knew it was related to the search for Lucas.

Angelo hesitated and reluctantly did as she asked. "Where shall I go?"

"For now, follow the main road." They drove for another five minutes until they encountered an airfield. A premonition told her this was where she was supposed to be. "If you could turn in here, please." She heard the roar of an airplane revving its engines in preparation for takeoff. Angelo followed through with her request. "This is it."

He rolled down his window to speak with a security guard at the airport's entrance. A moment later, they were waved through the gates of Roma's airport. Angelo parked the car, turned off the engine, and made his way around the vehicle to open the doors for Rex and Nora. Both human and canine climbed out and stretched.

Angelo removed his sunglasses. "Principessa, I'll see to

the dog. Your mask, per favore." He slipped the cotton mask into her hands.

"Principessa Leonora," a man in an army-green camo flight suit called out to her. Tucked under his arm was a white helmet and mirrored sunglasses. He saluted.

"Captain Alberto." Nora returned the salute. "Please, stand at ease." Her cheeks warmed. "What are you doing out here? I thought you were stationed outside Brisbane."

Captain Alberto relaxed his posture slightly, tucking one hand behind his back. "We are, Your Highness, but the sudden shift in weather conditions forced me to land our bird"—he gestured to a sleek helicopter painted with the royal standard of Isola Nostrum—"at the nearest available airport, and that so happened to be in Roma. We just received clearance to take her back up to resume our search."

Angelo fought to restrain Rex. He pulled the security guard toward the pair, barking. "Is that…?" Angelo started to ask.

"The newest helicopter in the Isola Nostrum arsenal?" Nora replied. "Yes… yes it is."

Angelo let out a long whistle. "Impressive."

She glanced at the helicopter, then back to its pilot. "Captain Alberto… do you have room for one more person to join you?"

Rex whined.

"Apologies, one human and one canine."

Rex barked and wagged his tail. He focused his large brown eyes on Captain Alberto.

"Principessa, what will your father say if he finds out?" Angelo planted one hand on his hip.

"He won't say anything"—Nora glanced over her shoulder—"because if he does, I'll be the first person to refresh his memory that *he's* the one who insisted I complete a military training course as his heir and the next commander in chief of the Isola Nostrum armed forces."

Angelo closed his mouth and dropped Rex's leash. The border collie started toward the helicopter and barked, as if to say, *"You humans are always keeping me waiting. Let's crack on with it already."*

"The principessa was at the top of her class." Captain Alberto chuckled. "There is a spare flight suit in the helicopter. Commander Chiara stayed behind at Amberely to receive the drones King Lorenzo has sent along. You two are about the same height and build."

"I'm in good hands, I promise," Nora reassured Angelo. She pecked him on the cheek and jogged after Rex.

When a young lady is to be a heroine, nothing will prevent her from seeing the task through to the end.

Captain Alberto expertly maneuvered the helicopter out of Roma to commence a search of the area northwest of the A2. Visibility was low and prompted him to stay within a few hundred meters off the ground. Amid the mountains, pockets of greenery and copper desert that comprised Queensland's diverse landscape were smoldering black scars where the fire had burned.

Nora's voice echoed over the headset as she spoke to the captain. "Lucas could be anywhere. How far are we from the area where his car was found?"

"Approximately sixty kilometers."

Assuming he wasn't too injured, Lucas could have reasonably walked that far. He had been missing for five days, but before that, he was in peak physical shape and had just completed another triathlon last month.

"How wide is the search radius?" she asked.

"Tilly Green and I thought about two hundred kilometers would be sufficient." The captain's eyes stayed focused on the thermal imaging screen in front of him. It was filled with pink, orange, and blue hues. They were searching for any shapes that were yellow. "According to my Aussie colleagues, this was one of the best places for your young man to become lost if it had to happen. There is ready access to water and food sources."

Rex rested his head on her lap, and she absently stroked it. What type of condition would Lucas be in when they found him? Had he been able to find food? Water? Shelter? Did he have any injuries?

She was so frustrated that it had taken so long to get a team out to search for him. Had she been allowed, she would've spent every possible waking hour searching for Lord Malcolm herself! But Nora understood that there were safety rules in place for a reason. Fires as large as this one created their own unique and unpredictable weather patterns. If they tossed aside the rules, more than one life could be lost.

She shuddered in her seat. *Come on, Lucas, you have to be okay. Where are you?* Her eyes were glued to the screen. They were itchy and heavy from lack of sleep, but still they searched. She had been positive that everything was aligning, and they would find him straightaway. But as more time elapsed, her heart began to sink.

Three hours later, there still wasn't a trace of Lucas. Tears threatened to fall.

"Principessa, we are going to have to turn back and return to Roma to refuel in ten minutes' time. The daylight is also beginning to fade. We may have to curtail our search efforts until tomorrow."

Her lips trembled. Her muscles clenched. "Of course, Captain. I appreciate all the effort. Do whatever you think is best."

Five more minutes passed. Then, like magic, a medium-sized yellow thermal-energy signature appeared. "Captain!" she exclaimed. Her body jolted upright in its seat. Her heart pounded, and her muscles tensed. Rex whined.

"I see it too! I'm going lower now. It's difficult to gauge how large the signature is. It could be another kangaroo, for all we know."

It's not a kangaroo. It can't be. It has to be Lucas. I can't stand to wait another day to see him.

The helicopter descended rapidly, and her ears popped. The shape on the screen grew larger. Her euphoria surged. The signature unquestionably belonged to a human. It appeared to wave its arms, but neither Nora nor the captain could hear if the person was shouting over the noise of the helicopter.

"Principessa, this may or may not be your Signore Lucas. Regardless of the outcome, please remember that our first duty is to help whomever we have found."

"I understand."

The captain nodded. "There is an emergency supply kit under your seat. While I radio in our position and call for a secondary team, your job will be to take the thermal blanket and to treat any injuries that are affecting this person's ability to breathe."

She located the first-aid kit. "I remember my training. Airway, breathing, circulation. Everything else comes secondary."

"Exactly."

CHAPTER 16

Rescued

They were only a few kilometers from the base of Mount Kellar. Rocks jutted from the ground like the sharp teeth of a dinosaur. Towering eucalyptus trees were packed together in tight clumps. Captain Alberto searched for a clearing to land.

"It looks like there is some type of access road over there." Nora pointed to a dirt road.

"Good observation, Principessa."

The helicopter seemed to float as it landed, stirring up a whirlwind of dust. Nora braced herself and waited for the signal from Captain Alberto that the propellers had stopped rotating and it was safe to open the door. Time seemed to move in slow motion. Her nails dug into the tender flesh of her palm. She was on high alert, adrenaline pumping through her body.

Captain Alberto gave her a thumbs-up. Nora opened the door, and like a gazelle, leaped out of her seat and sprinted through the forest with Rex leading the way. Dry leaves crunched. She heard the buzzing of insects and loud bellows of koala bears warning off intruders to their territory. The air smelled like a mixture of medicine and campfire.

She breathed hard, her pulse pounding in her ears. The metal first-aid kit rattled. The hairs stood up on the back of her neck. She stopped and placed her hand on her forehead to shade the sun, looking for any signs of where Rex had gone. Cupping her hands to her mouth, she yelled, "Rex!"

He barked, crashed through a thicket, and ran toward her. Nora met him halfway. "Is it Lucas? Where is he, boy? Take me to him." His tail wagged like the rudder of a boat.

He barked and led her into a small clearing. Her breath hitched. Sitting on the ground against the back of a eucalyptus tree trunk was Lucas. His chestnut-brown hair was matted, making it appear a muddy brown; his jaw was lined with scruff, and his clothing in tatters. Yet other than appearing pale, she didn't spot any obvious signs of injury.

Nora exhaled a deep sigh of relief. Her heart leapt. In that moment, she felt an overwhelming sense of joy. She'd never been happier in her life to see him. She wanted to jump into his arms and kiss him with wild abandon, but all that would have to wait.

Rex returned to Lucas's side. He licked his master on the face with unbounded excitement. Lucas scratched his ears and wrapped his arms around the dog.

Nora slowed her pace. Hearing the sound of sticks snapping and leaves crunching, Lucas's head moved up. His agate-blue eyes met hers, shimmering like diamonds. "I knew you would find me," he whispered, his voice hoarse. "I can always count on you, my Lady Nora."

His voice broke the spell. A few stray tears leaked from the corners of her eyes down her cheeks. "Lucas! I've been so worried. Are you all right?"

"I've been better." He breathed heavily. "I ran when I

heard the sound of the helicopter, hoping to flag you down."

Grazie for the foresight, Papa.

"It worked. We saw your heat signature inside." She quickly closed the space between them and knelt by his side. Ripping open the thermal blanket, she draped it across his body. His hand stroked her cheek.

"Please don't cry. I'll be okay. This Lord Malcolm is built to last."

A ghost of a smile appeared on her lips. Even now, he was trying hard to be upbeat.

"Wrap yourself in this; you must be freezing." She noted his parched lips, dry and cracked. "And thirsty— would you like some water?"

"Some water would be nice." He nodded weakly. "I've had to rely on chewing on tree leaves and wild berries. It took me the better part of two and a half days to realize that I was walking in the wrong direction. By the time I realized my mistake, my body couldn't move as fast. I had to focus on finding enough liquid to stay hydrated."

Nora grimaced. From the first-aid kit, she retrieved a packet of emergency drinking water. Lifting his arm from under the blanket, he reached for the packet. His hand touched hers. It was cold and clammy and coated in mud and angry red scratches, but she found its weight comforting. She sniffled.

"I found some water in the forest, but then I thought to myself that if I had a hard time seeing the sky through the trees, then help wouldn't find me too easily." Lucas met her gaze. "I always knew help would arrive. Did you know that mud acts as a natural sunscreen? It's a handy trick I learned from watching elephants. As a physical barrier against the powerful UV rays, it…"

She was deeply engaged in everything Lucas said. Listening with rapt attention. She'd never complain about hearing him ramble on ever again. She also owed a large debt of gratitude to the elephants at the wildlife center.

"Drink slowly," she instructed.

Lucas grunted his thanks. He tipped the packet back and let out a contented sigh.

"Do you have any injuries that I should be aware of?" Nora sterilized her hands with alcohol and slipped on a pair of latex gloves.

Lucas's jaw clenched. "Nothing major. A few cuts, scratches, and a few blisters."

Nora furrowed his brow. "Lord Malcolm, you had better *not* be hiding anything from me. So help me, I will take both your Xbox and PlayStation back to Isola Nostrum with me."

He winced. "You wouldn't do that to a bloke who's been lost in the wild for a couple days, now would you?"

She crossed her arms. "Try me."

"There isn't much you can do about it out here," he muttered.

Nora fought to maintain her glare.

Lucas sighed. Wordlessly, he peeled back the silver foil blanket to reveal a long, angry patch of burned skin that traveled up his shin, disappearing under his pant leg.

Nora inhaled sharply. She instantly wanted to kiss it better. It looked so painful. But at least it appeared as if Lucas had tried to keep it clean. She didn't see any outward signs of infection.

She cleared her throat. "I'm going to cover the exposed bits with a clean dressing. It might sting a bit. I can give you some minor pain relievers, but I'm hesitant to do so in case it might interfere with whatever the doctor gives you when you're transported to a hospital."

"No meds. It can't be any worse than when it first happened." He grimaced as he shifted his body and straightened his leg.

Her head shot up. "What else hurts?"

"Ribs." He squeezed his eyes shut and took a few shallow breaths. "I think I cracked one jumping out of the car. The fire came out of nowhere…"

Nora shivered. "Like a black hole."

His eyes opened. "Exactly."

They exchanged glances.

"Did you happen to experience any, um, strange dreams?" Her voice trailed off.

"Yes."

Her pulse raced. He leaned forward, as if to reach for her hand. But a wave of pain stopped him. "Gah. Bugger off." His hand went to his midsection. He collapsed back against the tree trunk.

Nora wished she could help bear the brunt of his pain. She placed her hand on his, and he squeezed it hard. For a moment, they sat together in silence. "I can wrap them after I see to the burn," she said in a hushed tone.

"Okay."

"I, um . . . also need my hand back too." Reluctantly, he released it.

Quickly, she located a few supplies in the first-aid kit and started cleaning and dressing the edges of the burn. Her hands trembled. Now that she could see him with her own eyes and touch his hands, she could finally start to breathe again. He'd become a part of her that she didn't know she needed or was missing until he was taken from her.

I love you, Lucas. I think I always have. I've worked hard to try and suppress it, but can't. I love you. I love you. I love you.

She wanted more than anything to shout it at the top of her lungs. To bellow as loud as the koala that greeted her. But what if he rejected her? She couldn't risk losing him when she'd just found him. That was a conversation she'd have to have with him at another point in time. Right now, they needed to get him to a hospital.

Lucas stroked Rex, who sat by his side loyally. "Thank you for taking care of Rex. I'm sorry for causing all the trouble."

"You're never any trouble, Lord Malcolm." She stared at the metal case as more tears threatened to fall.

"I disagree. Your being here means you put your life on hold for me and flew halfway around the world." He lowered his gaze. "I was foolish and should never have attempted to take a shortcut to Winton." He pinched the bridge of his nose. "I could see the thick plumes of smoke as I drove inland. I'd heard reports that the fire was in the opposite direction. The wind picked up, and the next thing I knew, when I checked the rearview mirror, the fire was traveling toward me."

"Lucas, don't beat yourself up. There is honestly no way of knowing how a fire is going to behave. Not only is it a primordial force, but the science behind fire weather is only just beginning to be understood," she said softly. She looked up from his leg to him. "It's easy to sit here in hindsight and say that you should or should not have done something. But it's all in the past. No matter how much you might want to change it, it's too late. We can only look to what's ahead."

"You're right, of course." He scratched Rex's chin. "You always are."

"As for my coming out to Australia… you're one of the most important people in my life. You're—" She hesitated and carefully chose her words. "One of my best friends. I'd do anything for you."

A moment later, they were interrupted by the roar of a second helicopter coming in for a landing. Nora leaned over Lucas's body in an effort to protect it from any flying debris.

"Principessa?" the voice of Captain Alberto called out.

"We're over here," she replied in English.

Their moment of privacy was over. A team of paramedics arrived from the air ambulance and took over Lucas's treatment. Nora stepped back and watched helplessly with Rex from a distance as they loaded him onto the helicopter and flew away.

She should have felt calm and at peace. Lucas had been found and was already on the road to recovery. Yet she felt just as confused and worried as before. What if she missed something? Should she have taken care of his ribs first? The burn appeared to be the more serious of his two major injuries.

As they made their way back to their helicopter, Captain Alberto said, "You did well today, Principessa. You demonstrated all the true hallmarks of a leader. You were calm, cool, and collected. The paramedics were praising your treatment of Signore Lucas. Your father would be proud."

"Thank you, Captain. It means a lot to me to hear you say that. I felt like a green rookie."

"The first mission is the most difficult. It will become easier with more experience."

Captain Alberto started up the engine and took off into the darkened sky. Seeing Rex asleep by her feet, Nora closed her own eyes. Her lids were heavy. Her body was achy. The exhaustion of the last few days had finally caught up with her. She felt weary to the bone, but content.

"Sleep, Principessa; I'll wake you when we arrive at Amberley air base."

But Nora couldn't hear him. She was already fast asleep and lost to the world of dreams.

Lucas was kept in the hospital for three days before being released to Nora's care with strict orders to take it easy while his body recovered. He had come away from his adventure in the wilderness with a series of relatively minor cuts and scrapes, two cracked ribs, a fractured left fibula, and a second-degree burn on the same leg. His injuries would heal in six to twelve weeks.

On a Wednesday afternoon, three weeks into her stay in Brisbane, Nora shook Lucas's pill bottle and poked her head into the living room.

"Lucas, it's time for you to take your afternoon meds. Do you need me to refill your water glass?"

Lucas reclined on the couch, fully engrossed in working on his computer. He had regained his coloring and was looking healthier by the day.

"Huh?" He glanced over the top of the screen.

"A refill on your water?" Her gaze traveled to the empty glass on the coffee table.

"Oh. No. It's full."

Nora breathed in, counted to ten, and released her breath. "Lucas…"

He was lost to his own world, muttering to himself as he typed. "… as evidenced by the study conducted by Dr.

Scott Hocknull et al. on the discovery of the Diamanti-nasaurus, a sauropod that lived during the late Crustaceous period, ninety-four million years ago, in the Winton Formation…"

"Meds." Nora tapped her foot.

"I just need to finish the methodology section."

"Now."

Finishing a section could take him more than an hour if he was dissatisfied with the wording or had to go back and add in the citation information.

Grumbling, he placed the lap desk with his computer on the couch cushion beside him. Careful not to jostle his leg under the blanket, he reached for the empty glass on the coffee table. His cheeks warmed. "Um… it appears as if I may need some water after all."

Wordlessly, she took the glass from his outstretched hand, filled it in the kitchen, and offered it to him with the pill bottle.

"Lucas. This can't continue."

He furrowed his brow. "I don't know what you're talking about."

"This." She gestured to the computer. "You spending twelve to thirteen hours a day writing up the findings of your research is not rest. When was the last time you went outside for a nice walk? Rex would certainly enjoy the company." The border collie lifted his chin at hearing his name called. "The doctor said some light physical activity is good for you now that you have a walking boot. You don't want the muscles in your leg to atrophy, do you?"

"I'll do it later. Between the time I spent missing and in the hospital, I lost a week and a half of valuable writing time." Lucas returned the cup to the table and resituated the lap desk. "If I want to finish my program on time, I have to stay on track and catch up. I don't have the luxury of taking any more time away."

"I'm certain your advisors would understand and give you an extension if needed." Nora's eyes twitched.

She was under the impression he didn't technically have any hard deadlines for assignments. Everything was supposed to be flexible.

"I don't do excuses." His expression darkened. "I *have* to finish on time."

"A week and a half won't make that much of a difference in the long run, will it?" Nora crossed her arms. "Besides, not everyone finishes in three years. Some people take much more time. Life happens."

"Not an option."

Nora frowned. Her patience was growing thin. "Then tell me, Lord Malcolm—why do you *have* to finish on time?"

He threw his arms up into the air. "Because I'm holding you back!"

"Holding me back?" She opened and closed her mouth. "Is that what you've come to think?"

"Yes!" He rubbed his temples. "Our agreement was that as soon as I finished my program, we would break off this phony engagement and go back to our own lives."

His words cut her deeply. Nora felt as if Lucas had struck her with an arrow. *But I've fallen in love with you. What if I don't want to break this up?*

Lucas continued. "I'm sure you're more than ready, just as I am, to move on from having to live a lie twenty-four-seven, three-sixty-five. So the sooner I finish, the better. I never should've agreed to it in the first place. It was a mistake, and it's going to be an absolute mess to deal with when it comes to revealing the charade to our families."

This was how Lucas had come to see their relationship? As something he was exhausted by and regretted? A mistake? She'd been reading all the signs wrong.

The blood drained from her face. Nora's head began to swim. "I'm going out."

Not staying long enough to see his reaction or hear his reply, she turned on her heel, and blindly walked out of the flat. His words continued to echo in her brain. *"I never should've agreed to it all in the first place. It was a mistake."*

Mr. Knightley

Sliding her hands into her pockets, Nora started walking. Her thoughts, however, were interrupted when she heard the sound of panting behind her. As she turned, Rex's coarse fur brushed against her leg. He whined and pawed at her as if to say, *"Silly human, you can't go anywhere without me. Tell me what's wrong. I know you're upset."*

She knelt down and hugged the faithful border collie. "Did you sneak out when I wasn't looking?" He licked her face. "Your master is an obstinate, headstrong man." A stray tear ran down her face. "He makes me so angry at times. To think that he sees our fake engagement as an engagement of convenience."

She buried her face in his fur. "I can't do it anymore, Rexie. I can't pretend like I don't care about him. About us. Because I do. Deeply. To me, nothing about our relationship is fake anymore. It's real."

She sniffled. "His words just now ripped me apart as if I'd taken the spikes from a stegosaurus's tail to my flesh. I feel so raw and exposed. I love Lucas so much that my heart is ready to burst. But he'll never return my love and affection. To him, I'll always just be a friend."

A flood of salty tears streamed down her face. Rex licked them. "Maybe it's time we do end it once and for all. If I'm not in contact with him anymore, eventually it'll dull the pain and I won't feel so broken." She stood and rubbed her eyes with her hand. "If I ring Angelo and Papa, I could probably leave Australia as early as tomorrow. I've put off starting a new life in Florence for him. Having a fresh start in a new city with my new job might be the best thing for me right now."

Rex barked.

"I know, boy; I don't want to leave you either." She fanned herself with her hands. "Look at me. I'm one giant, walking mess. I've smeared all my makeup." She took a few deep, settling breaths. "Let's go for a walk around the block. I need some time to make myself presentable. If we're lucky, Lord Malcolm won't even realize that we're missing."

"Of course he will," Lucas said in a low tone.

Nora froze. She squeezed her eyes shut and clenched her fists. Her body grew uncomfortably warm. "How much of my conversation with Rex did you hear?"

"All of it." She heard the thud of Lucas's crutch closing the gap between them. "Did you mean what you said?"

She swallowed hard. Her pulse raced like a jackrabbit bounding across a meadow. "Every. Single. Word."

She felt his left hand touch the exposed skin on the back of her neck and shivered. "Will you turn and face me, please?"

Slowly, she turned, opened her eyes, and stared down at her feet.

She'd never be able to look at him the same again. They needed to get this over with. This was where he'd tell her he'd never be able to love her. That instead of waiting for him to finish his studies, it would be best if they went their separate ways now.

Lucas tenderly placed a hand under her chin and lifted it. "Nora. My beautiful, lovely Lady Nora."

His eyes glowed, full of warmth. The folds of his mouth were extended upward as far as they could rise, revealing his handsome dimples. Reaching for her hand, he brought it up to his lips, kissed it, and positioned it over his heart. "Can you feel that?"

Nora nodded. Underneath the light cotton of his white T-shirt and his hardened chest muscles was an ever-present and steady thump. It reminded her of a metronome, establishing the rhythm for a piece of music.

"It beats for you. And only you. When I was missing, thinking about you and Rex was the only way that I managed to stay sane." He adjusted his weight over his crutch, leaning closer to her. "I've spent the better part of the last year and a half hoping against all odds that I might be able to work up the courage to express to you the three most magical words in the English language. I. Love. You. I never dared to dream that my affections would be returned."

All this time… he's loved me? Have I heard him correctly?

Her eyelids fluttered. There was no mistaking the depth of the emotions flowing through his body. She looked to him again for confirmation.

"I. Love. You," he repeated.

An exhilarating rush of happiness coursed through her body. Fireworks went off inside her mind. *He loves me!*

Then her thoughts returned to their earlier conversation. Her eyes began to sting and water. "Uno momento…

if you love me, then why did you try to push me away earlier? Why did you say that you wanted to move on with your life?"

"It's no secret that I'm not very good at expressing myself. I'm a scientist. We deal with hard facts and figures. I'll never be a man who is able to rattle off a sonnet or poetry." His Adam's apple bobbed up and down. "If I loved you less, I might be able to properly talk about it more. It took me all of ten seconds after you had walked out the door to realize that I had muddled up my words and been an idiot."

Spoken like Emma's Mr. George Knightley.

Lucas winced. "Please don't ever think it's gone unnoticed by me how much of yourself you've had to sacrifice and give up." He shook his head. "Nora, I foolishly thought if I were to let you go, that it would be my way of repaying the gargantuan debt I've amassed from you. Released from our fake engagement, I thought would free you to follow your heart and find love."

"Then when you said you were holding me back, you meant…" Nora choked out.

"I meant that I was being selfish toward you. Your happiness means more to me than just about anything. There is not a single person who knows me better than you. You are the woman that has captured my heart. You are the woman I love. The *only* woman I will ever love."

Nora couldn't wait a moment longer. "And you are the only man I will love."

They leaned toward one another. His left hand traced the outline of her lips. She carefully looped her arms around his neck, feeling the heat come off his body. Their noses nuzzled, and they kissed. His lips were as soft as satin. She soaked in the scent of his fresh, woodsy, and vanilla cologne. They were like two swans performing a delicate dance with one another over a moonlit pond.

Nora's mind exploded with the music of maestro Ludwig von Beethoven's "Ode to Joy." Being held in Lucas's warm embrace, she felt as if she were home. He was the missing piece of the puzzle that she'd longed to find. He was the man who she could spend a lifetime searching for, only to realize he'd been right beside her the entire time. Her Knightley. Her best friend. Her soulmate.

They broke apart, and she felt Lucas's breath hot upon her skin as he whispered into her ear, "You are so beautiful. You are that rare fossil a man searches for and waits his entire career to discover. I love you so much, my Lady Nora. If I am ever so inclined to name a fossil after someone, it will be named in your honor."

"A Leonorasaurus?" Her heart fluttered. Her stomach swarmed with butterflies.

"Perhaps. I rather fancy the idea of a Noraceratops or a Noradactyl." His lips twisted. "It would, of course, depend on the species, genius, location of the discovery—"

Nora silenced him with another kiss.

Rex barked, demanding their attention. Nora and Lucas released one another and laughed.

"I think someone is telling us that he doesn't want to miss out on the lovefest," Lucas said.

"Oh, he's asking you to name a fossil after him too," Nora giggled.

"I seem to have a lot of work ahead of me." Lucas ran a hand through his hair. "But there will be plenty of time for that in the near future. For now, what do you say to the three of us going inside, spending some time together on the couch cuddling while watching all four parts of your favorite adaptation of *Emma*?"

"Not *Pride and Prejudice*?" she said with mock seriousness.

"If you'd rather. I'm not adverse to it. I merely thought *Emma* was your favorite Austen film."

"It is." She walked her fingers up his arm. "*Emma* sounds perfect."

"a." He breathed a fake sigh of relief. "It seems that I have quite a few lessons to learn from both your Misters Knightley and Darcy."

Lucas didn't need to take lessons from anyone. He was Mr. Knightley incarnate—a dashing and witty earl with a heart of gold.

Reluctantly, they separated and slowly retreated down the hallway toward flat 7D, Rex leading the parade.

Lucas was so stiff. They'd have to stretch his leg before watching *Emma*. It must have taken a lot of strength and effort for him to get up off the couch and come find her. He had been living on that couch when he wasn't in the bedroom or bathroom.

They walked through the front door and entered the living room.

"If you'll take charge of getting the DVD queued up, I'll see to getting you a heating pad and making us some snacks. A few dog biscuits for Rex and popcorn for you and me."

"Sounds ace." Lucas nodded. "You know, in the UK we have ice cream at the cinema."

He gripped the arm of the couch and slowly lowered himself onto it. Stretching out, he grunted and absently rubbed his thigh.

Nora was instantly by his side. She spent several moments expertly kneading the area of overworked muscles and still-healing skin. "We prefer pizza or mini calzones on

Isola Nostrum, but ice cream sounds just as good. I just so happened to have picked up a pint of Cadbury chocolate ice cream on Monday in case you were feeling up to it."

"Cadbury, you said?" Lucas perked up.

"Si." She laughed. "I recently discovered you have an affinity for all things coated in Cadbury chocolate."

"Oh, how well you know me, Lady Nora." He sighed in relief, the muscles in his leg relaxing. "That feels much better. Thank you."

She kissed his forehead. "That's what girlfriends are for."

Lucas reached for the remote control. "Is that how you would label us? Are we officially boyfriend and girlfriend now?"

Nora blinked slowly and brushed a lock of hair behind her ear. "I don't know what else we would be."

Lucas grinned. "So long as I have the chance to *properly* sweep you off your feet before I propose to you a second time, girlfriend and boyfriend is fine by me."

Nora's cheeks seared with heat. "Propose?"

"Of course. You are the only woman I will ever love. Give me time, and I'll prove to you how ardently I love and admire you." He winked. "You have bewitched me body and soul. I love you."

She wanted to melt like a piece of fine dark chocolate.

Lord Malcolm, your words are so incredibly sexy to me. Sonnets and Shakespeare, move over. You have no idea the power you have over me when you quote an Austen man.

Nora swallowed hard. "I'll… get the popcorn."

Leaving the room, she popped into the kitchen and leaned against the doorway.

He sees a future for us. Together. I'm living a real-life fairy tale right now.

In the late hours of the night, the end credits of *Emma* had long since finished playing. The title menu was displayed on the television's screen, its sound muted. Rex lay on his back in his fluffy bed by the window, no doubt dreaming of herding sheep and chasing and retrieving tennis balls thrown by his two favorite humans. Nora rested her head on Lucas's chest. His arms were draped across her body.

As he played with the curly ends of her hair, he said, "In the end, Emma gained everything she ever wanted. She became Mrs. George Knightley, she was able to continue to reside at Hartfield and care for her father, and presumably she'd remain the center of Highbury society. What is it that you want, my Lady Nora?" He kissed the exposed skin of her neck. "Tell me, and I, your Lord Malcolm, shall make it happen."

"I want us to be like Emma, for everything and nothing to change." She burrowed under the blanket.

"Nora, I asked you an important question, and you didn't answer it. I want to know what *you* want." He chuckled. Reaching under the blanket, he started tickling her. "Think long and hard about it before you give me your answer. You are constantly considerate of others, but for once, your obstinate, headstrong man wants you to give him a selfish response."

Nora squirmed. Lucas had found her weak spot—the soft, tender skin below her rib cage. "Si. Si. Enough. I relent."

"Good."

She poked her head back above the blanket, her sides aching from laughing so hard. She took a moment to catch her breath. "For at least the next year, I'd wish to finally start living in my own flat in Florence."

Nora explained to Lucas that she'd recently been hired as an assistant curator at the Tuscan Museum of Music in Florence. It would be her job to see to the upkeep and care of their violin and stringed-instrument collection. After putting herself through countless disappointing failed orchestral auditions, she'd finally come to the realization that she couldn't stand another rejection.

"When one door closes, another opens. I never thought about any job prospects outside of playing in a symphony until I saw the advert online. I've already made a new connection at the museum. Its director is head of the Florentine Musicians' Guild. If I play my cards right, he said he might be able to book me as a guest artist at a few gigs he's overseeing during the summer concert season."

"That sounds like a perfect fit for you." Lucas stroked his jaw. His forehead creased. "I must have put a terrible wrench in your plans. If it weren't for me, you would've already moved and been settled in Florence by now. Instead, you've spent the last three weeks in Australia."

"The museum's management team has been very understanding and sympathetic to the situation. They've kindly pushed my start date back one month. You"—Nora poked his pectoral muscle with her pointer finger—"are my priority in life. Everything else will always come second."

"Not everything."

"Oh?" She raised an eyebrow.

"Isola Nostrum," he gently reminded her.

"I've been doing a lot of thinking about that lately." She drew circles on the silky ribbon at the top of the blanket. "Not too long ago, I had a discussion with my father about how important it is to me to bring a modern outlook to the monarchy."

"And what has that brilliant mind of yours concluded?" Lucas kissed her forehead.

"The monarch, no matter if it's a king or queen, can't rule alone. It has to be a team effort. Just as a person evolves and learns from the lessons of life, so must the crown." She breathed deeply. "If my brother and sister agree to it, I'd like them to become more involved in the running of the country. I want them to know that as long as they wish it, I'll always have a job for them as working royals."

"You three would be a real dream team."

"Not just the three of us… the four of us." Nora took hold of his hand and squeezed it. "I'd like you to take on a role too."

"Me?" Lucas sputtered.

"Si… that is my selfish desire. I want *us* to be a power couple, like Emma and Knightley combining the estates of Hartwood and Donwell Abbey. I want *us* to oversee and shape not only the future of Isola Nostrum, but also Rose-wood Hall. Besides… where else would you be?"

He squeezed her hand back. "Digging up old bones in some remote corner of the world?"

"I don't want you to change who you are; I just want to sprinkle in a few new layers to it." Nora rolled her eyes. "I fully expect you to continue to go on fossil digs, write papers, and run a rescue-dog charity, just as I will continue to pen Austen-inspired stories and play my violin."

"I, Lord Malcolm, am a man of my word. As the Lady Nora requests, her will be done."

They shared a rousing laugh.

Nora hid a yawn with her hand. "The Lady Nora

commands us to go to bed. By the time I clear off the futon, it'll be two in the morning."

"You can take my bed tonight. I'm more than happy sleeping on the couch."

Nora furrowed her brow. "Are you certain?"

"Positive. I'm happy to sleep right here. I'm already falling asleep."

Nora wiggled out from under the blanket. "As you wish, Lord Malcolm, but I better not hear you complain in the morning about having a sore back."

"Good night, my lady."

"G'nite, m'lord." Nora saluted him and sauntered out of the living room.

CHAPTER 18

A Day Out

Nora stared at the cursor on her screen and pondered how she should block the final scenes of Kitty's story.

"Lydia, you've ruined any chance *I* might have had at future happiness. How could your husband have accumulated two thousand pounds in gambling debts? Did Mr. Darcy not go to extreme pains to procure Mr. Wickham an officer's position in Newcastle *and* settle all his previous debts?" Kitty clenched her fists.

Her younger sister bit into an apple and chewed slowly. She reclined against the couch inside Longbourn's sitting room as if she had not a care in the world. "La. I don't see why you should care. Papa will see to Wickie's debts and all shall be fine."

Her face turned crimson red. "And how, *dear* sister, do you suppose Papa shall be able to raise such a sum?"

Lydia rolled her eyes.

"From *my* dowry," Kitty said. "I am the only

Bennet sister remaining who has not yet married or become engaged, and now I likely never shall."

Kitty watched in disgust as Lydia tossed the core of the apple behind her and wiped her hands on her dress. "No doubt Darcy and Bingley will—"

Kitty held up her hand. "Darcy and Bingley have both cut Wickham off. I was present when our two brothers had the conversation."

"They are not *our* brothers. If they had been, they never would have banished us to Newcastle. Life is so droll. There are so few balls and gatherings."

Lydia was blinded by her husband's faults. She would never understand the pain he inflicted upon others or have any care for the consequences. Was Kitty such a foolish young lady as she only a year ago?

"Lydia, it's clear as day to me now that the only person you have ever cared about is yourself. You may be married and the mistress of your own home, but you are still very much a child. I pity you."

Without a care for her stunned sister, Kitty left the room with as much dignity as she could muster. Keeping her facial expression calm, she gathered her spencer, bonnet, and gloves and stepped outside into the warm afternoon sun.

Her feet carried her past the soon-to-be harvested golden fields, over the Netherfield fence stile, to the top of Oakham Mount. Alone and surrounded by the rocks, trees, and a few game birds, she shouted out her frustrations at the top of her lungs. Her bonnet flew off her head and blonde curls came tumbling down. She dropped to her knees and covered her eyes with her hands.

"Mr. Bernstein will never have me now. He will

never wish to associate himself with a woman with such lowly connections and a pittance of a dowry."

Tears flowed down Kitty's cheeks. Suddenly, a twig snapped, and she turned around to see the wide eyes of her would-be suitor.

Her hand flew to her chest. "Mr. Bernstein!"

He removed his hat from his head and knelt to assist her to a standing position. "Miss Catherine, nothing on this Earth could deter me from coming to make an offer for you."

She closed her eyes and hung her head. "I fear you shall change your mind after you hear what my youngest sister's husband has done."

"I have spoken with your father and with Mr. Darcy, my dear Miss Catherine. All shall be well." His eyes twinkled with mirth.

Nora stretched her fingers and rolled her head from side to side.

Lucas entered the room with his hair still damp from the shower and a fluffy white towel draped over his shoulders. "How is your writing coming along?"

"I always seem to stumble when I'm trying to wrap up the story." Nora stuck out her tongue. "At first, I was going to have Kitty make a match with her art master in London, but then I decided I wanted her to marry as well as Elizabeth and Jane."

"Uh-huh." Lucas leaned over the arm of the sofa and skimmed the contents of her Word document. "I assume Mr. Bernstein is going to announce he's been keeping a secret from Kitty."

Nora nodded. "Si."

Lucas sat on the edge of the couch and dried his hair. "Let me make a wild guess. Mr. Bernstein is not the second son of the earl that he's been pretending to be. He's actually a viscount and heir to the earldom, or a wealthy baronet."

Nora groaned. "Is it that obvious?"

"I know how your mind works, and Regency romance. I'm just surprised you didn't decide to make him a duke."

"That thought did cross my mind." She clicked "Save" and closed her computer. "Having a woman fall for a duke is in vogue right now."

Little did Lucas know that she had that particular storyline earmarked for another manuscript.

Nora stood. Her leg and back muscles protested. "Ugh… I'm so stiff."

Lucas patted the couch. "Let Lord Malcolm offer you his services." Nora sighed and sat down once more in front of her boyfriend. He placed his hands on her neck and began to knead her tense muscles.

"Mmm… that feels nice." He worked his thumbs into the tender spot between her neck and shoulder blade. She arched her head backward.

"I know all the trigger spots," he boasted. "Here. Here. And oh, here."

She shivered. "My body is putty under your hands."

"You, my dear Lady Nora, require a distraction before you fly home on Monday. How would you like to take a trip to see the uni and its surrounding area today?"

Nora's eyes fluttered open. "Can you manage to walk that far?"

"No, but that's why you insisted we pick up the knee scooter."

Nora grinned. "I did. It's much safer than renting a tandem bicycle built for two."

She sighed and put her right hand on top of his. "I'd love to see the place where you spend most of your time."

"Brilliant." Lucas stood and removed his cotton T-shirt. "I just need a few minutes to change."

Nora admired the impressive cut and definition of his abs. "You don't want to go out like that?" she joked.

Lucas tossed the T-shirt at her, but Rex spoiled his shot by getting up from his bed and catching the shirt in his mouth, his tail wagging.

"If it were only you, yes. But around the university, I have a semi-professional reputation to retain around my students and advisor."

She shook her head. "Capisco. I understand."

Lucas left the room. Rex dropped the T-shirt by her feet. "Would you like to come along, Rexie? You could pull Lucas on his knee scooter."

Rex huffed, as if to say, *"I'm not a sled dog."*

He left the room in search of his master. Nora shrugged.

"This is the South Bank Parklands. It's one of my favorite places to come and relax." Like a skateboarder, Lucas pushed off the ground on his right leg, gliding along on his knee scooter under the shade of a walkway covered in lilac bougainvillea. Nora walked beside him.

Earlier, they'd stopped for a light lunch and munched on sushi while watching families swim in the man-made pools designed to resemble a beach and romp on the large playground.

"I can see why. There are heaps of things to do. You could spend all day sampling food, walking through the botanical gardens, or visiting that modern art museum we passed on the way in," Nora mused.

"Heaps… brekkie…" Lucas laughed. "You're picking up the local lingo."

Nora's eyes crinkled. "I had you as a teacher."

"We'll take the left pathway when it forks." Lucas turned the handles of the knee scooter.

As the trees cleared, Nora set her gaze on a white steel Ferris wheel that was similar to the size of the London Eye. It had about fifty pods that appeared large enough to hold five to ten people at a time.

"Oh, that looks like fun. I bet the views up there are stunning." Just as she was about to suggest they check it out, her eyes traveled to Lucas's scooter. A surge of disappointment took hold. Too bad they wouldn't be able to ride it. Nora sighed. Maybe next time.

"That's the Wheel of Brisbane. It's better at night, but during the day it still provides a spectacular panoramic view." Lucas pressed the hand brake and leaned onto his elbows. "If you'd rather not have a go on it, I understand. We can skip it and take a taxi over to the koala sanctuary now instead of later if you'd rather."

"I'd *love* to ride it with you," she sputtered. "I didn't know if you'd be able to."

"Why wouldn't I be able to?" He stared quizzically at her.

Her cheeks warmed. "I don't know. I just thought the standing, or the space the knee scooter takes up…" Her voice trailed off.

Lucas scratched his chin. "I can stand for ten or fifteen minutes. But if I needed to sit, there *are* seats inside."

"Oh." Her neck and ears burned.

"Come on. You're adorable when you're embarrassed." He grinned. "I have the tickets arranged on my mobile phone. Race you there." Lucas sped off ahead of her.

"Lucas, not fair! You have wheels!" She jogged after him.

Panting and slightly out of breath, Nora met Lucas at the entrance, where he sat casually on the knee scooter with his arms crossed. Smugly, he stood and offered her his arm. "My lady."

She frowned. "A gentleman would never have rolled off ahead of his lady."

An impish smirk crossed his face. "Perhaps I'm not a gentleman. Maybe I'm a rake."

A worker greeted them and scanned the QR code on Lucas's phone. They waited a moment for the wheel to come to a stop, then entered the air-conditioned pod. After walking around the humid city, the cool air was a welcome relief for both of them.

"Have fun." The attendant winked and closed the door.

The pod shifted. Nora and Lucas fell back onto the bench and shared a laugh. Through the tinted windows, Nora looked out over the Brisbane River. A water taxi sailed up toward the city center. A couple paddled downstream in a canoe. A flock of black swans glided near the footing of the wheel.

"Come here." Lucas placed Nora on his lap. She wrapped her arms around him, sighing in contentment and resting her head against his shoulder.

"We have the entire pod to ourselves! I can't believe our luck."

Lucas puffed out his chest. "It's all a part of my devious plan as a rake to seduce you."

She walked her fingers up the length of his neck. "If you'd like to seduce me, Lord M, I'm all yours."

They kissed greedily, like teenagers who'd just been

handed the keys to a Porsche and their father's credit card with no spending limit.

Once the pod had reached its apex, they broke apart.

"Tell me what you know about the skyline," Nora urged, returning her head to Lucas's shoulder.

He cleared his throat. "The tall black building is the Brisbane Skytower, and the white one over there is called The One." He shook his head. "Other than that, I have no idea what the rest of the buildings are. All I know is that in Brisbane, the high-rise buildings are either residential or places of business."

"Don't *all* high-rise buildings fall into one of those two categories?" Nora asked, playing devil's advocate.

"I suppose."

Lucas pointed to some of the many bridges they could see spanning the river. Their modern architecture reminded her of London.

"That one almost looks like the Sydney Harbor Bridge, except it's got two towers instead of curving at the top," she said.

"That's the Story Bridge."

"And what's its *story*?" Nora's body shook with laughter. She couldn't resist a bad pun.

"Very punny… I think you can scale it like we did in Sydney." He scratched the back of his head. "There's a lot I don't know about Brisbane."

Nora sat up and removed her arms from around him. "You have been busy."

"It's not an excuse." Lucas sighed. "I should be getting out more and making the most of my time in Brisbane. Not just waiting for you to visit to explore. I won't be living here forever. Having you around and taking the time to work a normal schedule has been a breath of fresh air and a real eye-opener. I never realized how stressed and alone I've been." She scooted off his lap and Lucas stood and walked over to the rim of the pod. He looked out over the river. "Did I mention to you that my father rang me this morning?"

Nora's countenance sobered. "He did? I didn't hear your phone ring."

"I didn't want to wake you. It was early, and Father forgot about the time change." He shoved his hands into his pockets.

"What did the duke have to say to you?"

Did he follow through on his promise to tell Lucas he was proud of him?

Lucas let out a dry laugh. "It was strange. He was very… er… I suppose emotional is the best way to describe it. He told me that he and mum have been horrid parents and that they realized it was high time they made an effort to make amends with me."

"Uh-huh." She wanted to pry for more details, but understood the contentious relationship Lucas had with his family was fragile. She considered her next words. "While you were missing, I spent quite a bit of time speaking to your papa."

Lucas turned and stared at her with wide, curious eyes. "Father spoke to you?" he asked slowly.

"Si. You can read through the text thread if you'd like. Some of them are quite amusing, but others are more telling." She took a deep breath. "In his own way, he cares about you. He wanted to come out here the moment he heard you were missing, but we decided it wouldn't do any good. He even kept a pilot on standby just in case."

"He's a difficult, complex man." Lucas nodded stiffly. "Just as I think I've started to understand him, he does something to confuse me. This morning, he offered me an apology for every hurtful remark he's ever said to me." Lucas sank back onto the bench. "Then there's the fact that he told me he's been reading up a bit on paleontology. He even made a concerted effort to engage me in conversation about it.

"There are so many emotional scars I've carried with me since childhood. I've tried to push them out of my mind and forget about them, but when Father does something like…" He pinched the bridge of his nose. "I explained to my father that if he intends to build up a relationship with me, we would have to do so in small pieces. I need time to process this newfound attitude. To come to terms with the past and the present."

An olive branch had been extended. The duke had shown that he could and was willing to change. It was never too late to rekindle and reconnect with family, especially since Lucas was his only son.

"I can only imagine all the emotions you're going through with him and with your mum." Nora reached for his hand. "Just know that no matter what, I am always here for you, to listen and be your biggest advocate."

Lucas returned the squeeze of her hand. "I know," he said softly. "And that's why I love you, my Lady Nora."

They sat in contemplative silence with one another until the pod returned to its starting point. Nora wondered whether, now that they were "officially" together, their dynamics as a couple would change. And how would they ever put an end to the elaborate fake wedding their families were eagerly planning?

Part Three

CHAPTER 19

Treasure Hunt

ONE YEAR LATER

Lucas focused intently on using a bristle brush to remove as much debris as possible from a roughly two-and-a-half-centimeter long, angular, milk-chocolate-colored fossil. He stood hunched over a portable table and tray of soap and water.

"Well? Have I done all right? Is it a fossil? Or is it a rock?" Nora asked, frustrated by his silence. A warm breeze blew through the open tent, causing the ends to flap up and down.

Lucas's mouth opened and closed. He set the brush down and washed the fossil in the water before drying it. He turned the item over in his hands again, shaking his head. "I don't believe it. There are so few places in Australia where Cretaceous or Jurassic rocks are exposed to the surface. The odds of finding this are a million to one."

Nora moved from her stool to Lucas's side and stared at her discovery over his shoulder. "So it's a fossil."

He jerked in surprise, as if he'd forgotten she was

present. "Nora. I'm so sorry, I was lost to science." His cheeks flamed red. "Yes, this is a fossil. But it's not just any fossil… It's a sauropod tooth!" The corners of his lips turned up into one of the widest smiles she'd ever seen.

Nora raised an eyebrow. "Brava! Not a rock."

"No." Lucas chuckled. "This is so incredibly rare. Sauropod teeth are notoriously difficult to discover on this continent. Normally, the sediment layer they would be found within is buried too deep to be accessible. It's only by happenstance that we're even working on this dig site."

Lucas had said something about the farmers who owned the land wanting to know what the large earthen mound in the middle of their grazing pasture came from. It was odd that the rest of the land was so flat.

Lucas held the fossil so she could take a better look at the indentations and grooves embedded in it. "Sauropods didn't have molars and couldn't chew food. All their teeth were semi-conical, meaning they were curved, with a sharp bit at the end. Their jaws and tongue mashed the food enough for it to be swallowed. Then their gut digested it over two to three weeks."

She really didn't need to hear about dinosaur digestion. "And you can tell all that by studying one tooth?"

"Yes and no. It's all hypothetical. We'll never know for certain, but based on this and other teeth that have been discovered on other continents, we can make fairly educated guesses."

One of Lucas's colleagues, Phil, a short man with flaming red hair, entered the tent. "Is it true? Did you find a tooth?" His eyes looked longingly at the fossil Lucas held.

"Check it out, mate!"

"Wow! Look at the size of this baby," Phil said with the enthusiasm of a child opening gifts on Christmas morning.

"Must be from the lower Cretaceous. Do you reckon it may have belonged to a Savannasaurus or an Australotitan?"

Lucas shrugged. "If we were closer to Winton, I'd wager it's an Australotitan tooth, but with the range of the Savannasaurus…"

Nora stepped outside to let the men have their time to marvel over the discovery. A group of ten students and two professors carefully chiseled and sifted through dirt close to where she had found the tooth. She had been amazed to discover how long it took to get to the actual digging. The team had to lay out a matrix, dig trenches, and choreograph the individual task each person was performing.

If it were me, I'd just dig anywhere and have no notion of what layer whatever I'd dug up came out of.

She heard the sound of plastic being pushed aside and the crunching of dirt. "Your first day on the dig, and within an hour, you discover a hidden treasure! You are the good luck I needed!" Lucas joined her and kissed her cheek.

Nora stretched her arms up. Her shoulders were stiff and unused to hunching over and digging. "And to think I almost stayed behind at your flat."

Lucas used the moment to tickle her stomach. "Should we see if your lucky streak continues to hold?"

"Lucas!" She laughed as her hands moved to protect her ticklish spot.

He relented, took hold of her hand, and guided her under the shade of an old oak tree. "Lord Malcolm, we're going in the opposite direction of the dig site."

"I know." From the largest pocket of his khaki-colored cargo shorts, he handed her a small trowel shovel. "Lightning never strikes in the same place twice. Call it a premonition, but let's see how you do over here."

Nora removed her sunglasses and gave herself a moment for her eyes to adjust to the dimmer lighting.

"What do you notice about the dirt?" Lucas crossed his arms and leaned against a wooden fence.

"It has tree roots on top?"

"And?" he prompted.

"The patch where we are standing has all this loose gravel. It's not smooth like the patches in the sun." She crouched down. "If I didn't know any better, I'd say something—or better yet, someone—has disturbed this patch of earth recently."

Lucas schooled his face into a puzzled expression. "Shall we test your theory?"

Nora grumbled in Italian and stabbed her trowel into the dirt. It was soft—the dirt felt like sand. The shovel shouldn't go into the soil so easily. Since Lucas didn't seem concerned about supervising everything she was doing, he must be up to something. *What are you hiding, Lord M?*

She set to work at a furious pace, tossing dirt behind her. When her hole was about fifteen centimeters deep, the tip of her shovel made contact with something metallic.

Lucas bent down. "What do we have here?" Reaching into the hole Nora had dug, he pulled out a shiny sterling-silver box.

"It's too clean to have been buried long. It looks brand-new." She cringed. "You really shouldn't bury silver. It'll oxidize it much quicker than normal."

You're the scientist; you should know this.

Lucas ignored her and blew on the top of it and frowned. "Well, look at this"—he passed the box to Nora—"it has your name on it."

It was her turn to frown. Her fingers touched the cool surface of the box. Engraved over the top in a swirly cursive script was the name "Lady Nora." She turned the box over in her hands. Discovering a latch on the front panel, she flipped it and lifted the lid. Inside was a crumpled ball of lined white paper.

"Hold this please." She handed Lucas the box and reached for the paper. Carefully, she unwrinkled it and smoothed it out to reveal a pair of stick figures and four spots marked with an X.

"Well? What does it say?"

Nora's eyes traveled to the top of the paper. "Lady Nora's Treasure Map," she read aloud.

"A treasure map, you say?" Lucas chewed on his bottom lip. "How curious."

"Lucas"—Nora held up the paper and waved it in his direction—"this is your handwriting and clearly has been ripped out of your field journal notebook."

"I beg to differ, my Lady Nora. Based on the fine lines of the paper, this map has been buried for a few million years," Lucas said with mock seriousness.

Nora rolled her eyes. "Perhaps the person that buried it should have taken the care not to use a paper that has his initials and student ID number printed at the top of the page."

"It does?" Lucas's eyes widened. "Huh, I never noticed that." He glanced at his watch. "By my calculations, you have about an hour and a half before the team will break for lunch. You'd better get cracking if you want to complete your treasure hunt before then." He tucked her box under his arm. "I'll see about getting this cleaned up while you have fun."

Nora reached for his shirt collar before he could leave. She pulled with such force that the top button came undone, revealing a patch of pale skin and a hint of the defined pectoral muscles underneath. "Oh no, you don't. You, Lord M, are coming with me. A lady never knows what dangers she might encounter on the search for buried treasure. What if there are pirates or a rogue dinosaur?"

"Nora…" Lucas whined.

"That's *Principessa* Lady Nora, and it isn't a request. It's an order," she challenged.

"It's going to take all afternoon," he groaned.

You should've thought about that before you made the buried treasure areas so far apart.

Nora smirked. "All the more reason for me to have some company on the adventure."

Lucas sighed. "As the lady wishes." He kissed her cheek.

The first X was easy enough for Nora to decipher. Following the map, she walked the perimeter of the fence and uncovered her buried "treasure" about twenty feet from where she'd discovered the box.

"What should I be looking for?" she asked.

Lucas shook his head. "You'll know it when you see it."

She sighed and studied the ground, searching for a patch of dirt that didn't blend into its surroundings. She knelt and began to dig until she uncovered a clutch of three pink, yellow, and blue plastic children's Easter eggs.

"Is this it, or are there more items here?"

"That's it for this hole. Each one should have three." Lucas opened the box. "If you put it inside, we'll open all the eggs at the end."

Her eyes twitched. "Is all your buried treasure in plastic Easter eggs?"

Lucas's eyes narrowed as he corrected her. "They are plastic dino eggs, thank you very much."

"Capisco."

They shared a laugh.

"To the next spot."

All went well until Lucas and Nora reached the final X on his map.

"Lucas, you should *never* have buried your passport. What were you thinking?" Nora crinkled her nose and held up the sopping-wet document.

"The water from the drinking trough must have leaked down into the hole. It was dry when I buried it. Why didn't I use a plastic bag?" He held his head in his hands and groaned. "It's going to be a nightmare to try and replace."

"Again, *why* Lucas?"

Sheepishly, he removed the passport from her possession. "At the time, I thought it would be romantic for you to discover our passports with—"

She splayed a hand on her chest. "You didn't bury mine, too, did you?"

"No. No. I couldn't find it."

Thank goodness, or else she would've had to travel to Sydney or ask Papa to issue her a special travel visa. Lucas's heart was in the right place, but sometimes she wondered about his brilliant brain.

"I'll have to change our plane tickets and hotel reservations." Lucas kicked at the dirt. "I wanted to surprise you for your birthday with a special trip—our first together as a couple. We were going to spend the two weeks of my spring break in Japan. All the eggs have Japanese candies inside of them."

His disappointment reminded her of Rex and his sad puppy-dog eyes.

Japan? He planned an entire trip during his spring break for her? For them?

"Oh, Lucas… that's so sweet." She rose onto the tips of her toes and kissed him. "I thought we'd be digging up bones, and that's why you wanted to train me up on excavation techniques."

"Nora, I made a commitment to you last year that we would spend more time together. That *your* every wish was going to be my command." Lucas took hold of both her hands. "Last summer, you spoke about how sad you were to have just missed out on exploring Japan during cherry blossom season. This time, when I realized that your visit was going to coincide perfectly with the expected bloom dates, I knew we had to go."

Nora's stomach erupted with butterflies.

"Lucas…" she said in a hushed tone.

"You have always taken care of me, and now it's my turn to take care of you. As soon as I get this"—he flailed his now useless passport in his hand—"replaced, we'll leave for Japan."

Nora's eyes fluttered. She pictured herself and Lucas sitting on a picnic blanket in one another's embrace under the shade of a cherry blossom tree. Thousands of soft pink flowers would shower upon them, with a picturesque snow-capped Mount Fuji in the background.

"Where did you book us into?"

"Tokyo, Kyoto, and Osaka. Three of the cities with the best reputation for blossom viewing. I did my research."

Nora's heart warmed. "That sounds magical."

"Only the best for my principessa."

CHAPTER 20

The Cherry Blossoms of Kyoto

A week later, Nora and Lucas exited a taxi dropping them off at the entrance of the Arashiyama Bamboo Grove in Kyoto.

"The locations of the temples and shrines are much further apart than I expected. We grew spoiled when we were in Tokyo with the easy access to the train and subway systems," Nora mused.

"We could've taken a train here too; the grove *is* open twenty-four hours a day. But I read online that unless you visit first thing in the morning or late in the evening, it is too crowded to properly enjoy."

Nora nodded in agreement. They'd learned from their mistakes the day before not to visit the more popular tourist sites in Kyoto after eleven in the morning unless they wished to shuffle shoulder-to-shoulder with other tourists.

"You don't think we'll encounter any deer here as we did in Nara, do you?" Nora grimaced. "They were adorable, but a little too friendly and aggressive for my liking."

They were like walking rubbish bins. She couldn't

believe they were bold enough to eat the map and ice cream cone right out of her hands.

Lucas chuckled. "No deer. Only monkeys. We should be safe."

"Monkeys?" Nora cocked her head to the side. "You know what, forget I ever asked."

As they climbed a set of steps and were enveloped by the dense bamboo trees, it was as if they'd left the modern world behind and entered an enchanted forest. The thick green trunks of the trees climbed endlessly toward the sky. They heard the chirping of birds, the eerie creak of the twisting bamboo trunks, and rustling of leaves. Only a small amount of sun penetrated through the treetops.

"It's so magical," Nora said in a hushed tone.

Lucas removed a large DSLR camera from around his neck and snapped a few test photographs. "Brilliant. Just brilliant." He revealed the digital camera's screen to Nora. "Look at that juxtaposition between the lightness of the green treetops and the darkness of the brown hue of the tree trunks."

"It doesn't appear real."

Lucas played with a few of the settings on the menu screen. "What do you think? Have we found the perfect spot for us to take out first anniversary photos together?"

Nora cocked her head to the side. "It's not *quite* been a year yet."

Lucas waved his hand. "Eleven months is close enough."

The sun had risen a little higher in the sky. The canopy of leaves now had a golden-yellow hue added to it. The lanterns lining the pathway were still illuminated.

"Let's do it."

"That's ace." Lucas rubbed his hands together. "There is only one other thing you're missing."

She propped her hands on her hips. "And what would that be?"

Lucas set his camera on the ground and untied the belt of his camel-colored overcoat.

She licked her lips. Underneath the trench coat, Lucas wore the black-and-white trousered kimono traditionally favored by men, with a black haori overcoat. "A kimono."

Nora covered her giggle with a hand. *How did you manage to dress yourself in that?*

Lucas turned in a circle, modeling the garment for her. "What do you think?"

"It looks nice on you."

"I'm glad you agree. Akemi is behind you, and she'll help you dress while I finish playing with the DSLR."

Nora's breath hitched. She spun around to see a petite woman bowing in a red-and-white cotton kimono. "Ohaiyogozaimasu. Good morning. I am Akemi."

"Ohaiyo, Akemi. I'm Nora." She inclined her head. "Forgive me. I didn't hear you sneak up on us."

"I am trained to walk with the stealth of a ninja." The corners of her eyes crinkled in mirth. "Please, come with me."

Lucas has gone to so much effort every step of the way for this trip. Her heart fluttered. When she thought back, a year ago, they were still dancing around one another. She was constantly questioning if he would ever return the feelings that she had for him. They were both so terrified of rejection, yet here they stood.

A few minutes later, Nora's fingers self-consciously brushed over the cotton fabric of her purple-and-white yukata kimono adorned in a traditional motif of cranes and flowers. She had learned that a yukata was a casual type of kimono worn in summer months and often favored by tourists. A more traditional kimono was much heavier and, as Akemi mentioned, could be uncomfortable to those not accustomed to wearing it.

"Here is a parasol for you. Now you are ready."

Nora's lips curved up. "Arigatou, Akemi."

Lucas slid in next to her. Nora smelled the sage and lemon notes of his cologne. "You look like a beautiful principessa in the purple," he whispered into her ear. She felt a tingle radiate through her spine.

Lucas pointed to his camera on the ground, positioned about ten feet from them. "I'll take a few of us together, then we'll do some individual shots of you on the bridge by the river with the cherry blossoms in the background. The timer is set for ten seconds."

They scooted close to one another. Nora twirled her parasol in her hands and positioned it behind her shoulder. "We could ask Akemi to take a photo for us."

"I have it all worked out, trust me." Lucas opened a folding fan slightly. "Ready? One, two, and three." The shutter clicked. Lucas jogged over to the camera to check on his handiwork.

"How did it turn out?"

Lucas returned with deep patches of red appearing on his cheeks. He rubbed the back of his neck. "I've accidentally managed to chop our heads out of the picture," he said sheepishly.

Nora snorted. *Oh, Lucas.*

He cleared his throat. "I'll ask Akemi."

～

Later that afternoon, after a stop at the hotel to change out of their kimonos, Nora and Lucas stopped for a snack at a café located inside a two-hundred-year-old converted farmhouse with a thatched roof. Like the majority of the restaurants in Japan, its windows displayed lifelike colorful plastic replicas of the dishes and drinks they offered. Despite being fake, it made Nora hungry every time she set eyes upon them.

After ordering coffees and desserts, they settled at a table next to a window overlooking the river.

"Don't let me walk out of here without my shoes." Lucas lowered himself onto the tatami mat and tucked his long legs under him.

Nora's body shook with laughter. "I'll try."

One might think that shoes would be the first thing that came to mind to put on if you were going for a walk outside, but Lucas had already forgotten his shoes twice.

"Do you have enough room?" she asked. None of the furniture was built for his lanky frame. On the other hand, it was just the right size for her.

He grunted. "I'll manage."

She knew he was also hangry. They'd need to stop for lunch soon. His sweet roll wouldn't hold him for long.

Nora bit into the matcha green tea sponge cake. "Mmm. So creamy."

Lucas made a face.

She slid her plate toward him. "Try some?"

"No thank you." He shook his head. "I don't care much for the flavor. It's too sweet."

"More for me." She shrugged. "You are missing out. My lord the tea purist."

"And don't you forget it." He grinned cheekily, devouring his roll in two bites.

Nora sipped from her coffee. "What's next on the agenda for today?"

Lucas patted his mouth clean with a napkin. "At five, the hotel receptionist booked us into a tour of Kinkaku-ji—the Temple of the Golden Pavilion—and a tea ceremony near the Gion district."

Nora sat up straighter. "Oh, that sounds amazing."

"In the meantime…" Lucas reached under the table. From the cognac-colored leather messenger bag he had been carrying, he retrieved a thin notebook-sized package wrapped in metallic gold paper. "Happy birthday."

Nora's hands shook. She placed her coffee down and accepted the parcel from his hands. "Grazie, Lucas. You didn't have to get me anything. Being here with you is more than enough for me."

"You *never* ask for anything. That's precisely why I wanted to give you something."

Her fingers brushed over the smooth paper. Turning it over, she noted the uneven folds at the ends and a messy tape job. She smiled at the thought of Lucas personally wrapping the gift. Carefully, she peeled back the layer of tape. Lucas watched her with an unreadable expression on his face.

Inside the package was a manila file folder containing five individual sheets of paper. Nora inspected them closely. "It's sheet music for a violin . . . written in the key of D major, in three-four time—a waltz, if we're being more precise." Her fingers tapped out the notes on the table as she sight-read and hummed the melody of the first three pages. "This is beautiful. I don't think I've ever heard this song before."

She lifted her chin, glancing at Lucas.

"I hope you haven't." He smiled coyly.

"The melody is really sweet and romantic, like music for a film." She turned the pages back to the front page. "I don't recognize the composer." Then she noticed the title of the piece: "Leonora's Waltz."

Her head snapped up. Lucas was staring out the window. She swallowed hard. He must have had this piece of music written just for her. He knew how much she loved music and her violin.

"Lord M… Lucas, this is so much more than any gift I've ever received." Nora stood and walked around the table. She knelt beside her boyfriend, wrapping her arms tightly around him and kissing his scratchy, defined cheek. "Thank you so much. I don't know what to say."

He pulled her into his lap. "I'm happy you like it. I had a friend in the music department at UQ write it for me. I don't know anything about music. *I* liked the way it sounded when she played it back to me, and I hoped that you would too."

"I love it, and I can't wait to play it on my violin the moment I arrive home." She sighed and rested her head on his chest. "This has been hands down one of the best birthdays yet, and the best *almost* one-year-anniversary celebration. Thank you for making it so special."

"You're not going to let go of the fact that we're still a month away from it, are you?"

"Of course not. You're the scientist. You people prefer accuracy."

"As do musicians." Lucas cupped Nora's cheeks. "And the day is still young. I still have one more surprise for you, my Lady Nora."

How are you going to top this?

~

Nora didn't have to wait long for her answer. As the day turned into night, Lucas surprised her with a moonlit stroll down Shinbashi-Dori, a flagstone street near the Shirakawa River. On either side of the street, cherry blossom trees laden with the delicate, cloudlike white-and-pink blossoms were illuminated to create a glowing tunnel.

"The traditional wooden buildings make it seem as if we've been transported back in time to a bygone era." Nora squeezed Lucas's hand.

They paused on a red wooden bridge. Lanterns flickered. Tourists mulled over the window displays of the restaurants lining the street, debating on what to eat. Suddenly, three geishas came out of a teahouse. Their faces were painted white, and each one wore a colorful and elaborate kimono. Nora found herself transfixed with how they managed to shuffle and walk so gracefully.

"Come on." Lucas pulled her in their direction.

They followed the geishas down the street, with the women attracting the attention of the many tourists. Some stopped and tried to chase them to ask for a photo, but were disappointed when the geishas didn't stop. Others simply stared. Lucas and Nora maintained a discreet distance, matching their pace. They watched as the women entered the side door of a wooden building.

They'd reached the end of the street. An English-language sign identified the building as the Gion Corner Theatre. Like the other buildings in the area, it was built from wood and had a green roof. Its entrance was adorned with red-and-white lanterns.

"They must be performing inside. It would be amazing to see a show like that," Nora mused.

Lucas bowed. "As the Lady Nora commands."

"You have tickets to the theatre?" She stared quizzically at him.

He puffed out his chest.

"Of course you would." She shook her head. "You have to be one of the most connected men in the world. Even more than my father, and he's a king."

"As it so happens, yes. Thanks to Akemi, we'll be treated to an evening of traditional ikebana flower arranging, Noh, koto, and a performance of the geisha dancing." Lucas laughed. "Her brother was educated at Harrow. We were in the same class together."

They entered the theatre. Lucas gave his name and a uniformed attendant led them inside to the center of the front row. The stage was an open wooden platform with an auspicious pine tree painted on a gold background. The four rows of seats were all empty.

Nora frowned. "We must be early. They haven't let anyone else inside yet."

"Everyone is here. Happy birthday, Lady Nora." Lucas grinned from ear to ear, his agate-blue eyes sparkling with amusement. "As another birthday surprise, tonight we're being treated to a private performance."

Nora covered her mouth with her hand. "You're the most amazing man. How did I ever get lucky enough to have you for a boyfriend?"

"Let's not forget the bit about being a fake fiancé too."

Leaning over the armrest of her seat, she smashed her lips into his. They parted slightly, granting her access to his mouth, like a thousand cherry blossoms opening their petals for the first time on the first warm day of spring. Nora had never felt more loved.

I love you so much, Lord M. He had done so much to

make this entire trip special, and she wanted to show him exactly how much she appreciated it.

When they eventually broke apart, Nora said, "I just wish I could thank Akemi too."

Lucas pulled at the collar of his jumper, fanning himself, his cheeks a rosy shade of red. "You can after the show."

"Does she work here?" Nora asked.

Lucas let out a raspy laugh. "She's a geisha."

"Oh."

A performer entered the stage and bowed. Lucas and Nora focused their attention on the show.

Lucas's birthday wasn't for another four months. How was she going to be able to top this? She'd better start planning now if she wished to have any chance at succeeding.

Part Four

CHAPTER 21

Operation Bath

ONE YEAR LATER

Nora: Are you free to chat this evening? Or do you need to postpone it?

Lucas: I'm more than happy to break from my presentation prep to see your gorgeous face.

Nora: *blushing emoji*

Lucas: As a scientist, I'm only stating the facts as I see them.

Nora: Shall we say seven p.m. your time?

Lucas: Whatever the lady wishes.

Nora: Perfecto. I shall pencil you in, Lord M. I have some news to share with you about Lorenzo!

Lucas: If you're referring to one Miss Sabrina Hill, I am already in the know about your brother's girlfriend.

Nora wracked her brain. Did she ever mention to Lucas that she knew Sabrina before her brother through the Jane Austen forum, or that Sabrina was staying with her until she was able to figure out what she wanted to do with her life?

Nora: ????

Lucas: You are not the only member of the Toscani family I'm on friendly terms with.

Ah… Lorenzo had spoken to him about her.

Nora: Spoilsport.

Lucas: *smiling emoji*

Nora: I shall see you at seven.

Lucas: Until then, my heart.

The bells of Florence's Santa Maria del Fiore cathedral sounded ten times. Nora opened her window, welcoming the relief of the fresh morning air. On the street below, other Florentine citizens were slowly beginning to wake up. In the café across the street, she spied the regular patrons sitting at the circular tables, scrolling through their phones while enjoying their morning cup of coffee and a jam-coated croissant.

She moved from her bedroom to the spare room she used as a catchall—a practice room, writing room, and dressing room. Her black IKEA desk was covered by two piles of sheet music, a notebook containing plot points for future stories, a garnet necklace, and her laptop. Opening the room's sole window, she was treated to a view of boats lazily drifting along the Arno River.

She hoped Sabrina would use this morning to sleep in. They were up late after the excitement of last night. Lorenzo was asleep on her couch as well, and they'd be lucky if he was up before three this afternoon.

The ringtone on her phone chimed. Lucas's tanned face appeared on her screen. She swiped to answer the call. "Good morning, Lord M."

"Don't you mean good evening?" he countered. He placed his tablet on a stand and proceeded to wash a head of green lettuce in his kitchen sink.

"I should've just said ciao." Nora removed her camel overcoat, scarf, and pink chiffon dress from her desk chair and unceremoniously tossed them onto the daybed. As she sat, the chair squeaked. She leaned the phone on its PopSocket.

He squinted at the screen. "Your practice room is a mess. It's as if we've reversed roles. My flat is spotless right now. It's the only way I can keep myself focused on my final project."

"How's that going, by the way?"

"It's going," he chuckled. "But now isn't the time for me to ramble on. I want to hear about you. Tell me, Lady Nora, why the disarray? Did you host a wild party last night?" He reached for a packet of cherry tomatoes.

"It would be a resounding 'no' on the wild party." Nora leaned her elbows onto her desk. "But last night *was* a bit chaotic. Sabrina and I arrived home late from the Spring Fling benefit performance for the museum. This room is a mess because I didn't have the time or the energy to put everything away. I'm surprised I managed to text you."

"That's right! The largest fundraiser on the museum's calendar." He moved to a cutting board and located his favorite knife. "How could I have forgotten? You were the concert's star performer! How did it go? Are there any videos I can stream of it on the internet?"

"No videos, but it went well. Maestro Umberto, our chairman, calculated that we've received double the amount of donations we'd projected." Nora placed her hands behind her head.

"Brilliant! You are probably the best hire the Museum of Music has ever had!" Lucas gushed.

"Not at all." Nora's cheeks flushed. "I've just been lucky they've taken so many chances on me the last two years. I knew next to nothing about what actually goes on behind the scenes of a museum when I began my job."

"And yet, they saw something special inside you. Look at you now. You're a key member of the museum's staff. The head of the string instrument collection *and* the lead violinist for its public performances." Lucas started to slice a bright orange pepper.

Only because she wanted to be the first violinist so badly that she assured Maestro Umberto she'd willingly add it to her list of duties without asking for any additional pay.

Nora cleared her throat and sat taller in her chair. "So… um… about last night… When Sabrina and I were walking home, we might have found ourselves in a spot of trouble."

"Oh?"

She rubbed the back of her neck and lowered her gaze. "A man attempted to steal my violin."

Lucas's eyes widened. He placed the knife down, wiped his hands on his apron, and approached the screen. "Are you two all right? Where was Angelo? Has the thief been apprehended?"

"We're both unharmed. Sabrina boldly chased the thief and saved the day. The Carabinieri arrested him right after." Her stomach muscles tied themselves in knots as she recalled the scary situation. "Yesterday was Angelo's day off. Gerardo was on duty. I sent him home after the concert. It's a short walk from where the concert was to my flat, and I thought we would be safe."

"Nora, you have your security detail for a reason."

She sighed. "Of that, I'm well aware. It was a foolish mistake, and it won't happen again."

If Angelo had been on duty, he would have still discreetly followed them home even after she'd dismissed him. She made a classic rookie mistake with Gerardo.

"You are one hundred percent certain you and Sabrina are fully fit?" Lucas leaned into the tablet's front-facing camera.

"Si. Lorenzo rang a doctor to give us a wellness check before he fell asleep in my living room."

Lucas scratched his head. "Lorenzo? He doesn't normally attend your concerts. Or did he come down from Isola Nostrum after the incident?"

"To your surprise and mine, he was there in the front row. I think he had hoped to catch a glimpse of Sabrina. Even though they're still at odds with one another, Sabrina confessed to me that she still has feelings for my brother."

It had been about two months since they'd had their fight. In some ways, it felt like so much more time had passed.

Sabrina had just started to fall for my brother when he learned that she knew he was a prince. Most other people would be able to see that Sabrina is nothing like his crazy ex-girlfriend. But not my brother. He had to go and callously break her heart.

I'll never understand why he thought promising himself he would never fall in love with a person who knew about his being a royal was a good idea. You can't choose who you fall in love with. They are so much like Lizzy and Darcy.

Lucas returned to the cutting board. "Is Lorenzo still sending flowers to your flat?"

"No, he's gotten the message and mercifully stopped." Nora chuckled.

At its peak, her flat resembled a greenhouse. Lorenzo sent an expensive bouquet of flowers to Sabrina every day. His idea of a grand gesture was taken to the extreme.

A sudden thought struck Nora. "Lucas…" She stared at the screen, tilting her head sideways. "When Lorenzo was attempting to apologize to Sabrina, one thing that I couldn't seem to figure out was how he managed to gain such a deep knowledge of the Regency era so quickly."

Lucas moved on to slicing a zucchini. "I thought you mentioned something about your brother borrowing your Austen DVD collection."

"He did," she said slowly.

"Well, there's your answer," Lucas said, keeping his focus on the green vegetable. "He must've watched them all and taken detailed notes on Darcy, Tilney, Wentworth, Knightley, Bertram, and Ferrars."

"I don't think so." Standing up, she took hold of her phone and paced the room. "Even with my own intimate knowledge of all of the Austen adaptations, when I began writing Regency stories, I spent hours conducting research. There were a lot of gaps to fill." Nora arched an eyebrow. "Lorenzo is like you. He's a quick study for maths and science, but not at sketching one's character."

"You are too smart for your own good, Lady Nora." Lucas shook his head. "You would make one amazing detective." He tossed his vegetables into a clear salad bowl.

"Have you been assisting Lorenzo the entirety of the time he's known Sabrina?"

"Did I mention the fascinating paper I was reading earlier? Dr. Roger Seymour of the University of Adelaide has theorized that the skeletal structure and nutrient foramen uncovered from the femurs of sauropod fossils directly correlate to high arterial blood pressure," Lucas sputtered.

"Huh?"

"That's what I was originally thinking too. But after I read through his journal article, it makes perfect sense that sauropods likely had four-chambered hearts. With their sheer size, it would have taken a large cardiovascular system to be able to support—"

Nora pinched her nose. "Lucas, please stop deflecting. I haven't had my morning coffee yet."

A sheepish expression crossed his face. "What's the phrasing that Americans always seem to use? I plead the fifth?"

"I knew it!" Nora smirked.

Lucas was one of her most trusted beta readers. His own knowledge of the Regency was second only to her own. She wondered what he would say when he read the draft of her first original novel. Would he enjoy that she'd named and modeled the lead character of *Entering the Marriage Mart* after him?

She set the mobile device back down on her desk. Opening her story notebook to a blank page, she located a pencil and wrote "Operation Bath" at the top. She folded her hands on her desk.

Lucas placed his hands on his hips. "What are you thinking, Principessa? You have a gleam in your eye that tells me, you are up to something."

"I am thinking that Sabrina is like Elizabeth Bennet and Lorenzo is a Mr. Darcy. They clearly want to rekindle their romance, but both are too stubborn to admit it to one another. So we are going to help them along."

Lucas hesitated. "I don't think we should run interference. We should let events unfold in their own time. Let the two of them work their feelings out themselves."

"We don't have the luxury of time." Nora shook her head. "Sabrina is visiting Europe on a holiday visa. It was only good for ninety days. She only has about a month left. When time is up, she'll have to wait another six months to reenter this part of Europe."

"I see."

"Lorenzo and Sabrina are moving their relationship along at a snail's pace." Nora twirled her pen in her hand. "This is the happiest I've seen Lorenzo in a long time. I don't want him to muck this up. Sabrina too. She deserves to be happy after the crap she's had to go through to get here."

"What did you have in mind?" Lucas asked warily.

"The original purpose of Sabrina traveling across the pond from the States was to attend the Jane Austen Festival that's held every June in Bath." Nora rubbed her hands together. "The highlight of the festival is always the Masquerade Ball."

Nora walked over to her bookshelf and retrieved a tattered copy of *Emma*. Holding the book up to the screen, she said, "Mr. Knightley finally came to the realization that he loved Emma when they danced together at the second ball in chapter…" Nora opened her book with a satisfying crack from the spine. "Thirty-eight."

Lucas stared at her with a blank expression. "I'm not following you."

Nora snapped the book closed. "You and I are going to work together to create a magical ah-ha moment at the ball for them." The wheels in her mind began to spin. "You'll continue to drop select hints to Lorenzo about how he can woo his lady. I'll handle Sabrina and any logistical details."

Nora wiggled the pen in her hand. On the paper she wrote down:

- *Alibi for Lorenzo*
- *Air ticket for Lorenzo*
- *Regency costume rental*
- *Regency dance lesson*
- *Carriage rental*

Lucas ran a hand through his hair. "That sounds like an awful lot of work."

She winked. "If we do this right, the rewards it yields will be well worth the effort, and Sabrina will officially become my second sister. Did you know that we've been friends for four years on the Never Far From Netherfield forum? She's another one of my trusted beta readers."

"As long as you think you can handle this, you can count me in."

Nora grinned.

Walking over to the freezer, Lucas removed a frozen steak and located a frying pan from a lower cabinet. Nora enjoyed watching him cook. She found a man who knew his way around the kitchen to be incredibly attractive.

He poured some canola oil and butter into the frying pan and let it sizzle. "Was there anything else you wanted to discuss? I'm going to be at an excavation and out of mobile-phone range for the next week and a half."

"Yes. Our sham wedding."

Lucas groaned.

Nora closed her story notebook. Opening the second desk drawer, she reached for a blue spiral-bound notebook. Flipping past the first twenty pages, she ran her finger down the sheet of paper, then looked up at the phone screen.

"Mama and the wedding planner have started to pick up the pace of their planning now that you are due to finish your program in the next four months. We have to make a decision on how we're going to break it to my parents and yours that it isn't going to happen. At least, not in the time frame they're expecting."

She and Lucas had been officially dating long-distance for two years. When he moved back to the UK or to Isola Nostrum, they'd finally be able to move in together and decide what their next step was going to be.

Lucas placed a slab of meat into the pan and turned down the heat. "I might not be finishing my program this spring. It might be another two years at least."

Nora dropped her pen. "Scussi?"

"My advisor mentioned during our check-in last week that my department is considering offering me a post-doc position. It's a two-year fully paid position that comes with a research stipend and a few other bells and whistles."

Nora couldn't believe what she was hearing. "Have you already decided you'll accept it?" she sputtered.

"Not exactly."

She crossed her arms. The happiness she'd experienced just ten minutes ago dissipated, replaced with resentment. "Well, it's either a yes or a no."

Lucas frowned. "You sound as if you are angry with me. I thought you'd be excited."

Nora wanted to smack her palm into her forehead. "Lucas, I don't know how you'd think I'd be happy for you. It's two more years you'll be in Australia."

"Two years isn't that long of a time. Look at how quickly the past three years have passed."

"No, Lucas. It *is* a long time. But that's not the part that angers me."

He used a spatula to flip the meat over. "What are you upset by? I didn't think—"

She cut him off. "Exactly. You *didn't* think. I'm your girlfriend. I've been waiting for you to finish your program and your studies so that we can finally be together! I want you to be more than just a long-distance boyfriend. Your future plans also affect *my* future plans."

She slammed her fist on her desktop. From her desk drawer, she pulled out two white envelopes. "This is a letter of resignation for my job at the museum, and this one was an advertisement I was going to submit to the property-rental agency to let my flat."

With shaking hands, she tore the envelopes up, piece by piece, and tossed them into the air. Lucas watched in silence. "It seems that I won't be needing them anytime soon. *You* can be the one to tell *both* of our families of your plans."

"Nora, I'm sorry. I'll let my advisor know that I won't accept it."

"You did it again!" Her eyes flashed. "You just made yet another decision without us talking about it."

Lucas turned off the stove and leaned his hands on the countertop. The muscles in his eyes twitched. "What do you want from me? To take the post doc? Or not take the post doc?"

"Do whatever you want. My opinion doesn't seem to matter. Have a *great* night."

Nora disconnected the call and tossed her mobile phone onto the day bed, fuming.

Could she not have been any clearer? Any plans about the future needed to take both of them into consideration. Lucas had repeatedly done whatever he wanted. She was tired of being the one who constantly compromised. She'd gone to Australia three times. He'd never come out to visit her even once. She was the one who was willing to quit her job and close up her flat. Yet Lucas wanted to stay in school forever.

When they became a couple, Lucas was adamant that he would do whatever she wanted. Up until this point, it hadn't mattered what she wanted. She just wanted him to be happy. Had he ever cared about her happiness? Or had it been all talk? She loved Lucas, but if he couldn't follow through on his promises, maybe they didn't have a future together.

You have said over and over again that you love me. Prove it to me.

CHAPTER 22

Appeasing Mama

As spring arrived in Florence, the days steadily grew longer. Nora increasingly found herself spending her rare free moments outdoors. Watching butterflies floating from flower to flower, hearing the trickle of water flow from her fountain, and having the warm, gentle breeze greet her face relaxed her.

Two weeks after her argument with Lucas, sitting on the bench in her garden enjoying the quiet of the morning, Nora balanced her laptop on her lap and wrote the climax of *Entering the Marriage Mart*.

"I should have known better than to blindly trust a man of the Ton like you, Lord Malcolm," Miss Kennington shouted, not caring who heard her. "As a woman, my reputation is all that I had. And now you have sullied my good name, along with any chance I had of obtaining future happiness." A stray tear rolled down her cheek. "I shall endeavor never to darken your doorstep again. I shall leave via the next post chaise to Greenbrooke. This is goodbye."

Lord Malcolm kept his back turned to the woman who had become the dearest friend of his sister.

A door opened and closed.

Goodbye, Miss Kennington.

The grandfather clock in his study chimed. The fire crackled. Lord Malcolm stood, his hands tucked behind his back.

Nothing else could have been done. Miss Kennington was a thief. He could not in good conscience have a woman like that stay under his roof and influence his most beloved sister.

He began to pace the room, recalling their first encounter at the Norwich ball. Miss Kennington's eyes had glistened like green emeralds. She'd cut a fine figure on the dance floor, her tiny hands fitting perfectly in his. As they danced the supper set, he remembered how Miss Kennington had taken the pains of ensuring that their conversation remained amusing to him.

His thoughts were broken by the thud of footsteps running down the stairs. The doorknob to his study turned. "Brother! What have you done? Miss Kennington is gone!" Alice's face was stained with tear tracks. She appeared so much younger than her six and ten years. "I cannot lose her like I lost Mother! You must do something." She sniffled.

Alice's companion, Mrs. Lisle, entered the room slightly out of breath. "Apologies, my lord."

To his sister, she raised her voice and declared, "Lady Malcolm, you cannot barge into your brother's study like that just because you are upset that penniless country chit—"

Lord Malcolm found his temper rising. He waved

his hand and interrupted her in a curt tone. "Mrs. Lisle. That is quite enough. I shall see to my sister. Leave us."

Mrs. Lisle's face reddened. She inclined her head and fled the room, closing the door behind her.

Lord Malcolm swallowed hard. How could he explain to Alice that Miss Kennington had stolen pieces of their mother's jewelry? He hoped the words would magically come to him. With a twelve-year gap in their ages, Lord Malcolm understood that Alice viewed him as more of a father figure than a brother.

Their mother had been gone these ten years. Alice was but six then, and had a difficult time coming to terms with her passing.

In a soft, calm voice, he urged her to sit in his wingback chair. He offered her tea, but she declined.

"Poppet, Miss Kennington may be a gentlewoman, but some information has recently come to light that calls into question the nature of her character . . ."

"But, brother, Miss Kennington was the most amiable, gentlest woman of my acquaintance. That must be why she left. To protect us from the whisper of scandal. She's even nobler than I realized. You must do something to help so she may return to us."

This was going to be more difficult than he ever imagined.

"Nora…" Sabrina called out from the living room.

"In the garden," she responded.

She heard footsteps. Sabrina walked through the open bifold doors in a cream-colored empire-waist Regency day dress and twirled.

"Bellissima!" Nora placed her laptop beside her and clapped her hands together in delight.

Sabrina's face lit up in a big goofy grin. "This dress is so comfortable. I'm ready for a morning constitutional, Miss Nora."

The two friends laughed. "You're missing your bonnet, Miss Hill."

"It's upstairs in my trunk with my kid gloves."

Nora grinned. "Is it trimmed with bright ribbons and feathers? According to the latest gossip, feathers are all the rage this Season."

Sabrina made a face. "I'll take a hard pass on the feathers." She rubbed her hands over the skirt of the dress. "Do you think this dress will pass for the country assembly and ball we are to attend?" she asked in a soft voice.

That answered Nora's question. Sabrina didn't own a ball gown. *Well, my dear Miss Hill, your fairy godmother will ensure that you are dressed to impress.* Sabrina would make every woman at the masquerade ball envious. Nora mused that blue would work best with her coloring. Or maybe a green. And Lorenzo must have a Regency gentleman's suit of blue or green to match.

Nora placed her hand behind her back and crossed her fingers. "Si. Si. You will see men and women wearing all types of clothing. A mishmash of modern and Regency. Maybe even the odd Victorian garb or two. The important thing is that we are going to have a wicked good time, indeed."

"I'm so happy to hear you say that." Sabrina let out a sigh of relief. "I was so worried. I really wanted to dress up, but I didn't want to appear out of place."

"Miss Hill, my bosom friend, you would *never* be out of place."

A door opened and closed. Lorenzo's singsong voice called out, "Sabrina? Leonora?"

"In the garden," they both responded simultaneously, then looked at one another and giggled.

"Go change. I'll stall my brother." Nora raised an eyebrow. "That is unless you'd like to wear your lovely day dress to Rome."

Sabrina made a face. "I wouldn't wear this to one of the world's most fashionable cities."

Nora schooled the features of her face to appear with mock seriousness. "I would."

Sabrina waved her off. "You, my dear Miss Nora, can get away with making *any* ensemble work. Me, on the other hand—I'm too self-conscious."

Nora scooped up her computer, saved the document, and closed the top. She tucked the device under her arm, and the two women reentered the flat. "Sabrina, I wish you'd have more confidence in yourself. You are an *amazing* woman and friend. You can pull off anything you set your mind to; otherwise you wouldn't be here in Italy, and be my most trusted critique partner."

Lorenzo removed a pair of aviator sunglasses and let out a wolf whistle. "Bellissima."

Nora shot Sabrina an "I told you so" smirk.

Sabrina's cheeks flushed candy-apple red. "I just need to change. I'll be right out." She rushed off to the guest room, leaving the two siblings alone.

Lorenzo slid his hands into his pockets. They spoke to one another in Italian. "Leonora, I was just speaking to Luc —a friend, and I… he's been busy, but extends his sincerest…"

She pursed her lips together. "What did Lucas want you to pass on to me this time? That he's sorry?" She crossed her arms. "If he wants to apologize, all he has to do is pick up the phone and ring me himself. I haven't had a single call or text from *that* man in two weeks!"

Lorenzo stiffened. "No. No. It wasn't anything like that." He lowered his voice and abruptly changed tactics. "I was going to ask if you and I might be able to practice the dances for the you-know-what sometime this week. The quadrille and whatever else I'm supposed to know for the ball."

"Oh. Si." Nora lit up. "How about Friday? Or when I come home for brunch on Sunday? We could use the grand ballroom."

"Sunday would be best. I have other plans Friday."

Nora made a mental note to add it to her calendar. "Are you free any other days this week? I have one other task you need to take care of."

Lorenzo retrieved his mobile phone from his back pocket and scrolled through his calendar app. "I'm at the market most of this coming week. Lucia is taking over for me beginning the week after that."

Nora tucked a piece of hair behind her ear. "Is it time to start preparing for the summer harvest already?"

Lorenzo clicked the phone's screen off and returned it to his pocket. "Si. Papa and I are scheduled to do our walk through the vineyard next week to assess how the vines are doing. We're on schedule to begin hiring the seasonal staff."

"This makes things more difficult. I need to have you fitted for a suit for the you-know-what."

"I own a dozen suits. You can peruse my closet Sunday and find one that'll work for the you-know-what."

"Suit was probably the wrong choice of word." She covered her mouth with her hand for a moment before continuing. "You're going to be attending the you-know-what as a Regency gentleman. I wanted you to meet with a tailor to have a waistcoat, trousers, tailcoat, and great coat constructed for you."

Lorenzo frowned. "That'll take too long. I'll just rent a set."

"We have more than a month before the festival."

"Leonora"—Lorenzo shook his head—"bespoke menswear takes much longer to commission and fit than a lady's gown. The turnaround time is usually a minimum of three months. *And* that is if the tailor isn't booked with clients weeks ahead of time," he emphasized.

"That, I have a hard time believing." She rubbed the back of her neck. "Menswear is so simple. It's one shape. Womenswear, on the other hand, has to be fit to accommodate different-sized busts, hips, waists, and other attributes."

Lorenzo challenged her with an amused look on his face. "Ask Papa. He'll tell you the same line."

"That's so sad."

"What's sad?" Sabrina emerged from her room and slipped on a light outercoat. "That's an Italian phrase I actually recognize."

Nora shook her head and said in English, "That bespoke menswear takes longer to commission than womenswear."

"Really?" She stared at Lorenzo's chest. "No wonder all your shirts and trousers always perfectly contour to your body." Her face flushed bright red. "Uh…" She averted her eyes.

I can't help you out of this jam.

Lorenzo took pity on Sabrina. "What opera did you ladies see last evening? Did you enjoy it?"

"We saw *The Magic Flute.* It was masterful. I'm sure Sabrina will tell you all about it en route to Rome."

Sabrina cleared her throat. "I will."

These two wouldn't be able to dance around one another much longer. Nora predicted that by the time they returned from the Eternal City, they'd officially be together again. There wasn't a couple more perfectly built for one another than them.

"Andare! If you hope to catch the eight-ten train, you'll have to leave now." Nora ushered them out the door. "Have fun! Take lots of photos for me."

As she shut the door behind them, her mobile phone began to ring. Recognizing the number, she groaned, and swiped to unlock the screen. "Ciao, Mama."

"Ciao, Leonora. I expected to get your voicemail, but this is much better."

Nora walked over to her kitchen and opened the cabinet to remove a coffee cup. "I was up early to see Lorenzo and Sabrina off. They are heading to Rome today."

"Brava. Has Lorenzo dropped any hints to you about his plans with her?"

"They're doing a tour of the Colosseum, the Pantheon, the Trevi Fountain—"

"No, no. Not those kinds of plans. His *future* plans."

Nora inclined her head. "Mama. They are not officially a couple yet."

"I'm only asking," her mother said. "Weddings take at least a year to plan. Look at your own wedding. We only have nineteen months of time left! There are so many details to take into consideration for a winter wedding like…"

Interesting. Lucas obviously hadn't said anything to his mum or to hers about a change in plans.

"Sorry, Mama. I was woolgathering. Can you repeat what you said a moment ago?"

Her mother huffed. "I asked you if you had given any thought to the reception venue. The duchess is keen that at least a part of the festivities be held in England. I told her that wasn't a viable option. You've always dreamed about using the Greek temple ruins as a backdrop. You spent so many hours playing there as a child. She had concerns about the weather, but we're on a Mediterranean island. It doesn't get as cold here as it does in England in December."

Mama must be cross with Lucas's mum if she was referring to her by her title right now and not by Susan, her given name.

"Um… I'll defer to Lucas. He is the one who seems to be making all the decisions about where we stand."

Besides, it's not as if this wedding is going to be the real thing.

"He said the same thing last night," her mother muttered. "You are the bride. This is your call."

Mama spoke to Lucas last night? He was taking her mother's calls and not hers? You know what… she didn't even want to know. Why did she even care? What mattered right now, however, was that she really didn't want to talk to Lucas's mum. She'd find a way into guilting Nora to her side if she didn't get her way.

"Can we have two receptions? The one right after the wedding can be at the Greek temple, and at a date to be determined, we'll have a separate reception at Rosewood Hall?"

"If that's your desire."

"It is." Putting a coffee pod into her espresso machine, she closed the lid, positioned the cup, and pressed the green "Brew" button.

Her doorbell rang. She ignored it.

"I have a meeting in town in about twenty minutes. On Sunday, when you meet with the wedding planner, there are some sketches by your favored designer, Clarissa Lee, to look over. Since she also designed a wedding gown for the Duchess of Leeds, it might be difficult to commission a…"

Her doorbell rang several more times. The espresso machine chimed. The doorbell turned to insistent knocking.

Lucas's voice yelled, "Leonora. I know you are home. I am going to keep ringing this bell and knocking until you answer it!"

She dropped her phone with so much force, the screen cracked.

"Leonora?" Mama's voice questioned.

"Leonora!" Lucas repeated.

She rubbed her temples and took a moment to compose herself. *Too many voices and people calling for me at once.*

Picking up her mobile phone, she said quickly, "Mama, I have a slight emergency. I'll ring you later."

Now to deal with the wayward fake fiancé.

Leaving her mobile phone on the kitchen counter, Nora squared her shoulders, marched to her front door, and ripped it open.

"Two weeks! Two weeks and not a single text or call from you! You made time for Lorenzo and my mama, but not for me! What do you wa—"

Lucas wasted no time in silencing Nora by crashing his lips into hers.

CHAPTER 23

Lord Malcolm's Timely Arrival

For several moments, all Nora was aware of was the urgent, flaming energy and passion erupting out of Lucas. It was like the spark that ignited the universe's Big Bang. She'd been mentally prepared to lash out in anger at her boyfriend, yet the moment his warm, soft lips planted themselves on hers, her mind and body turned to putty.

She'd missed the man more than she would ever admit. Enveloped in his strong arms, she fit perfectly. She was safe. She was home.

A minute later, they broke apart, both breathing heavily. Lucas dropped his arms to his sides. He bowed to her. "Lady Nora, I am here to atone for my mistakes."

Catching her first full glimpse of Lucas, she realized that he was dressed in men's Regency attire. He wore a crisp white cravat with a gold stick pin, a white-and-cream-striped waistcoat, green velvet tailcoat, tight breeches, and knee-high boots.

Her pulse raced. Gently tugging on his cravat, Nora led him inside the flat and kicked the door closed behind her.

"Lord Malcolm, you are in so much trouble with me, but seeing you dressed like *this*"—she gestured to his ensemble—"has softened my mood toward you enough for me to invite you inside and hear what you have to say."

"Lady Nora, I have been a fool." He inclined his head. "I was upset with you the last time we talked. But by the time I had cooled off and sorted through what I'd done wrong, I was in a tent in the middle of a remote region of Australia's Northern Territory, on a fossil excavation." He lifted his chin. His sapphire-blue eyes locked onto hers. "Every day for the last twelve days, I've been kicking myself for not being man enough to ring you back and reconcile." Lucas cupped her cheeks. "Will you forgive this inconsiderate, obstinate, foolish man?"

Nora wracked her brain. She was an idiot. She was so annoyed with him about the post-doc that she completely tuned out the part about his being out of mobile range this week. He wasn't solely to blame for their misunderstanding. They were both at fault.

"I've flown all the way from Brisbane and come direct from the airport to beg for you to give me a chance to prove myself to you." Lucas started to lower himself to his knees, but she stopped him.

"I can't concentrate when you're like this." Nora swallowed hard. "I've dreamed about you wearing an outfit just like this one." She toyed with the gold buttons on his tailcoat. "I need you to convince me exactly *why* I should forgive you. Less talking. More kissing."

She threw her arms around his neck, soaking in the scent of grass and fresh earth. Nora's eyelids fluttered and her mouth opened, granting him access. Lucas kissed her a second time, matching the same level of heat and intensity as before.

Her body felt like a shooting star. Lucas had managed to melt her icy exterior, and now her core was reaching its boiling point. As it reached its maximum sustainable temperature, Nora would launch herself into space at light speed. Flying across the night sky, she would dazzle onlookers by twinkling as radiantly as Polaris.

Much later, in dire need of food, Nora and Lucas settled themselves in the kitchen. As she cracked two eggs over the rim of her frying pan, she said, "*I* love this clothing so much on you, but are you seriously telling me that you sat on a plane for twenty-two hours wearing a Regency gentleman's kit the entire time? Didn't you find it to be a bit restrictive and confining?"

Nora preferred to travel on planes in a long flowing maxi dress or in a loose top and leggings. Comfort was always one of her top priorities.

Tailcoat and cravat removed, Lucas sat in his white shirt, waistcoat, breeches, and boots at the kitchen island, enjoying the bold flavor of an Italian espresso. "It was twenty-six hours of total flying time on three airplanes, plus the hour and twenty-minute train ride from Rome to Florence. I was comfortable enough. Once I removed my boots, tailcoat, and the cravat, it felt a lot like I was wearing a T-shirt and shorts."

He stroked his jaw. "My original plan called for me to show up to your flat and re-create the ending scene from *Austenland*, where Mr. Nobley had such an easy time convincing Miss Jane Erstwhile that his affections for her were indeed genuine. In my mind, if I followed his example by wearing Regency attire when I suddenly appeared at your flat, I hoped I might shock you long enough for me to declare that I'd messed up and I wanted to reconcile."

"The guise worked. But it wasn't the clothing that shocked me. It was that kiss." She touched her still-swollen lips, thinking about the sweet nothings he'd whispered in her ear as they'd made out on the couch.

Lucas took a drink from his cup. "What are you thinking?" he asked in a silky voice, "You're smiling. Are you daydreaming about *me* again?"

Nora appraised him with an expression of mock seriousness. "I'm wondering what you are wearing under your boots. Socks? Men's stockings? Or is your foot naked?"

He snorted. "I can't wear shoes without socks. I'm a baby when it comes to blisters." He placed his cup down, shimmied one of his boots off his leg, and rolled up the trouser cuff. "I have above-the-calf men's dress socks on. The short ones slip. I can't be bothered to constantly have to pull them up."

Nora snickered to herself. They made men's dress socks with tiny dinosaurs on them? Leave it to Lucas to find a pair of those.

She folded a green pepper, mushrooms, onion, tomatoes, cheese, and chicken into the eggs. The vegetables and meat sizzled, filling the room with a decadent aroma. "Another question… why didn't you change clothing on the train or once you arrived?"

His ears and neck flushed rosy red. He removed his other boot and set them by the front door before returning to his seat. "Because I bought the cheapest last-minute plane ticket available, and that meant that I couldn't bring any luggage with me. Are you aware some airlines charge for carry-on baggage?"

She scooped the omelet out of the pan and plated it for Lucas. She scoffed. "You didn't bring *anything*?"

"Thank you." He accepted the plate from her hands. "No. I didn't. It was an extra three hundred quid. I only brought what I could carry in my pockets—my mobile phone, my passport, my earbuds, and a credit card."

She grinned and snapped her fingers together. "Darn, you're going to have to wear this the entire time you're here."

"If that's what my Lady Nora wishes." He winked.

She shook her head and laughed. "We'll pop out and pick up a few essentials for you after we eat."

"There isn't any need."

"Lucas, be serious." She placed one hand on her hip.

"I'll only be here for one night. It'll be fine." Lucas sprinkled some salt and pepper on the omelet.

Her face fell as she cracked another egg. "Only one night?"

"Yes. I have plans for us elsewhere for the next two days. That is . . . er . . . if you agree to them. I know you're cross with me for making decisions without consulting you and I just realized I've done it again, but everything I do for you is out of love and—"

"It's okay, Lord M. I know you mean well."

She sighed. Lucas wore his heart on his sleeve. He always reached for the sky with his grand gestures. Although it irked her to no end when he made plans without her, in cases such as these, she'd forgive the man. Just as Lucas said, his decisions came from a place of love. She had to remember that he was used to living on his own and not having to take another person's opinion into consideration.

When all is said and done, Lucas is a scientist. It's their job day in and day out to come up with a hypothesis based on the information they have at the time and run with it. He has a one-track mind that's focused on reaching the end result.

Her shoulders hunched. "As much as I would love to spend time with you, I have work. I can't miss two days," she muttered.

"I've reached out to your boss, Maestro Umberto. He said that you had quite a few vacation days available. There is no pressure, but if you decide to take the time off, he said he'd grant it to you."

Her eyes widened. "You rang Maestro Umberto?"

"I know it was presumptuous of me, but there were a few surprises I had planned that required some advance notice. They can all be rearranged or canceled, of course," he added quickly, his cheeks coloring. "Ah bollocks, what I meant to say is that I wanted to let you make the decision as to—"

She held up her hand. "Lucas. Enjoy your meal. You don't have to explain your line of thinking to me. Half the time you lose me mid-thought." She laughed. "I'll take the time off. I haven't taken any time off in over a year. The museum can function without me."

He took hold of his fork and knife. "This smells brilliant." He shoveled a bite of the food into his mouth, eating with gusto.

She prepared her own omelet. "What should I pack for whatever activity you have planned?"

Lucas patted his mouth with a napkin. "Your passport, your mobile phone, a charger, a credit card, and maybe one change of clothing."

It might be easy for him to travel with just the barest of

the bare essentials, but not for her. "Is it an overnight stint?"

He stuffed his mouth full again.

"Lucas. Not helping." She plated her omelet and sat across from him at the kitchen island. "If we're going on an overnight trip, my outfit and accessories choices will depend on the climate and how casual or how formal wherever we're going is. I'll need my flats and a pair of heels. My makeup. A pair of pajamas. A—"

He held up his hands in defeat. "We're going to England. We'll stay overnight at my flat in the Midlands. Happy?"

"Grazie." She leaned over and pecked him on the cheek. "That helps."

"Dress for comfort and the English spring."

"Capisco. Layers."

I just hope our plane tickets allow for carry-on baggage. If not, no matter what he says, I'm going to pay the fare difference. There are some things this principessa cannot do without.

Nora adjusted the ribbons on the bonnet atop her head. As she entered the living room, Lucas stood up from the sofa and bowed to her. "Lady Nora. You are a vision in scarlet."

She blushed.

He pulled at the intricately knotted fabric of his cravat. "We might attract quite a few stares strolling the streets of Florence with you and me in our Regency finest."

She'd never been more impressed that A, Lucas knew how to tie a cravat, and B, he could manage to tie it in more than one style. She remembered that he often struggled tying ties.

"Let them stare. You and I will be the most handsome couple in any room we enter." She rose up to the tips of her toes and pecked him on the cheek. "If you are coming shopping with me as a Regency gentleman, it's only fair you're accompanied by a Regency gentlewoman."

Lucas walked over to the front door and opened it. "My lady."

Nora curtsied, slipped on a pair of white kid gloves, and exited the room first. Lucas followed, closing the front door behind her.

They left the private courtyard for the main street, passing a series of tightly packed restaurants, trendy cafes, and artisan workshops. "I never realized there were so many places to explore a few yards from your front doorstep." He offered his arm to Nora. "This is the first time I've visited Florence. I've seen it in photos numerous times, but they don't do the city justice."

Nora facepalmed and muttered in Italian.

His first trip to Florence, the birthplace of the Renaissance, and he was only telling her now? If she had known that two hours ago, she would've insisted on going out and exploring. Not wasting time catching up with one another inside her flat.

"In English, please," Lucas requested.

"I'm sorry, it's just that there are so many places I want to take you to see. It's difficult enough to squeeze in a trip to all of the main touristy sites in the city with a visitor who is here for at least four or five days, but you are only here for a single day." She sighed. "It's nearly two in the afternoon now. We'll spend at least an hour and a half queuing for the Uffizi or the Accademia. They both close at five."

Lucas patted her hand. "Today doesn't have to turn into a sightseeing extravaganza. I am here to see *you*. All of the scenery, while majestic, comes second. There will be other trips to Florence in my future."

The butterflies in Nora's stomach fluttered. "I appreciate you saying that, but I still want to expose you to some of the sites here. After we pick up the list of items I wrote down, how about I introduce you to David?"

Lucas raised an eyebrow. "Do you mean Michelangelo's David?"

"Si. Who else?"

"I thought you didn't want to 'waste my time' queuing." He put his fingers into quotes.

She held a hand to her mouth and giggled. "The original David lives in the Galleria dell'Accademia. There is a marvelous replica of it, however, where the original statue once stood in the Piazza della Signoria."

"Ah."

"The Piazza is one of my favorite places to eat lunch. It's a lovely open-air square that was built for public meetings and ceremonies by the powerful Medici family, the rulers of the city during medieval times."

Turning down a narrow alley, they walked single file past shops selling leather goods and gold jewelry and emerged on a street brimming with tourists clutching designer shopping bags and expensive DSLR cameras and cell phones.

"Is it always this busy?" Lucas scratched his head as he glanced at the bustling outdoor cafés and restaurants. Every available table was occupied. Waiters rushed from party to party, scribbling down orders and carrying large platters of drinks and meals. The scent of fresh garlic bread, cheese, pesto, and wine wafted through the air.

"Si, always." She laughed at Lucas's large doe-like eyes. "It will calm down after three, when the lunch rush is over."

Crossing the road, they paused in front of a line of red, yellow, and green motorbikes. She pointed to a converted two-story palazzo displaying a large banner with a violin, cello, and trumpet. "This is where I work, but the shop I wanted to visit just happens to be across the street from it. Most of the Farmacias in Italy are family owned and operated. I like to give the Zucheretti family as much of my business as possible. They're old family friends."

But Lucas wasn't paying attention to Nora. Like an eager child, his eyes darted to the museum. "Can we have a peek inside?"

"You wish to see the museum? You know we don't have any fossils inside, just musical instruments dating from the seventeenth and eighteenth centuries."

"Of course." He bobbed his head up and down. "Music is an important part of your life. I want to see and experience the same joy and happiness as you when you see a violin."

She glowed, as if her body had been kissed by a ray of golden sunlight. She could tell from his demeanor that his interest was genuine.

"You're in luck, Lord Malcolm. *I* just so happen to boast my own set of keys to every room and display case in the museum. You'll be getting a *private* tour only our most generous donors receive."

He beamed. "That sounds epic." He rubbed his hands together. "What are we waiting for?"

CHAPTER 24

The Museum of Music

Inside, the entire interior of the museum had been converted into a contemporary space. A circular information desk stood in the center of the atrium. Sleek floor-to-ceiling temperature-controlled cases housed the museum's displays, and LED television screens played short informational videos on various composers. Visitors to the museum held audio guides up to their ears.

Nora stopped by the information desk to introduce Lucas to a few of her coworkers. They exchanged handshakes with him and said a few words to Nora in Italian.

"What are they saying to you?" Lucas asked as he removed his jacket.

Her coworker Bella stared at his sculpted shoulders and the way the clothing contoured his body, showing off his lean and defined physique. Two other women gossiped in a low tone, glancing in his direction when his back was turned.

"Bella is asking if I could order Regency men's attire for her boyfriend. And those two are comparing you to some of the statues by the Palazzo Vecchio." Nora stored her bonnet, clutch, and shopping bag of sundries in the cubby beneath the ticket printer.

"To David?"

"Si."

"Gracias." Lucas grinned cheekily and bowed to the ladies.

The women all giggled. Nora covered her smile. "Wrong language. That's Spanish. It's grazie."

"Grazie," he attempted a second time, and offered them another sweeping gentleman's bow.

All three women sighed and rested their heads on their hands. "You are very welcome, Signore Lucas." Bella waved.

"You speak English?"

"Si. All our employees speak some English." Nora pulled his arm. "Andiamo. Come with me." She ignored her coworkers.

"Maybe you should start referring to me as Lord David," Lucas mused once they were out of the atrium.

She punched his arm. "You are an obstinate, headstrong man. That's a much more fitting name for you."

Nora directed him to a set of cases displaying some of the earliest examples of Italian-crafted violins from the Lombardy region of Northern Italy.

Lucas crossed his arms. "And what's your opinion on the matter? Do I have some sort of resemblance to David?"

Physically, she thought Lorenzo looked more like David than Lucas did, but she'd never tell him that. Her ideal man was the one who was a walking textbook of information on geology and dinosaurs. He was the one who put so much thought into how he might apologize to her. Her perfect man was standing right beside her.

She ignored the question. "I thought we could start here and go through the history of violin making. You know my mama comes from a violin-, viola-, and cello-making family in Cremona."

"Nora…" he whined. "That wasn't what I meant."

She sighed. "I think your ego doesn't need to be inflated anymore."

He raised an eyebrow in challenge.

"The perfect or ideal man does not exist. Humans are imperfect beings. But if I had to settle for a human who is the closest living incarnate to David… mentally and emotionally, it would be you. Are you satisfied?"

"Yes." He grinned gleefully, puffing out his chest. "Now we can crack on with it."

Slipping into her own professor mode, Nora took Lucas on a tour of the museum's permanent collection. They spent over an hour moving from case to case before going to the basement to see the museum's off-display and most valuable items.

"Do we need to wear gloves for this?" Lucas asked as Nora unpacked an eighteen-million-euro Stradivarius from a glass storage case.

"Not for the violins. Touching them is good for them. They are played on a constant rotation to keep them in pristine working condition." She carefully placed the blood-orange-colored violin into his hands. "One of the museum's missions is to be able to share our instruments with the public as much as possible. We give public demonstrations every day at noon."

"It's light. I thought the older-model instruments would be much heavier." He turned the violin over and ran a finger over the delicate F curves, noble neck, and ornate scroll. "Beautiful."

Nora sighed. "This is my favorite violin in the collection. I love my Guarneri, but there is nothing purer than the sound of a Stradivarius. It's like red wine versus white wine. A Guarneri has a darker richness than the sweeter, precise Strad."

Lucas handed the violin back to Nora. "Is that what makes a Stradivarius so valuable and sought after?"

"Si. Antonio Stradivari was renowned for being able to craft instruments with unique tones. Countless generations of violin makers have strived to re-create it, but no one has yet been successful. The theory is that the wood he used was somehow affected by Europe's Little Ice Age."

Lucas's gaze met hers. "Will you play for me?"

Her hands itched. She placed the violin down. "Si. I just need a bow."

"Violins don't come with a bow?"

"Less expensive models can and do, but most professionals buy them separately. Just as there are violin makers, there are also specialty bow makers. For example, my bow came from a maker in France."

"Fascinating."

Finding a bow in a separate storage case, she tightened the tension on the hair and added some rosin to it. A moment later, Nora positioned the Strad under her chin and played the first song that popped into her mind: "Spring" from Antonio Vivaldi's *The Four Seasons*.

She always felt a special lightness and warmth move outward from her body as she played the piece. It was such a joyful tune that celebrated the return of life and warmer weather, after the cold bleakness of winter.

Lucas and I are celebrating our own Renaissance, or rebirth. This also represents us.

Her mind filled with her happiest memories with Lucas. Meeting him under Hope at London's Natural History Museum, his fake proposal to her, their weekly video chats, discovering he was safe and sound after the fire, and hearing him say he loved her for the first time. She could still recall the numerous delicate, soft, tender kisses they'd shared, as well as the fiercer and more urgent ones.

As her fingers moved up and down the neck of the violin, she wondered if the music affected Lucas as much as it did her. She played the last note with a vibrato and lifted the bow from the strings, then opened her eyes.

Lucas opened his own eyes. "Otherworldly is the only way I can describe it. It is so hauntingly beautiful. I've never heard anything else like it." He had a thoughtful expression on his face. "You have a gift, Nora. You are my very own angel of music."

He waited until the violin and bow had been put away, then he kissed her. Nora had a new moment to add to her collection.

Atop the museum, Nora and Lucas enjoyed a dramatic panoramic view of Florence. For the first time, she could show him the green valley and hills the city had sprung up from.

"The green copper dome is the Turkish-style synagogue. Notice how its stones are a little pinker than the terracotta stones you see on the medieval buildings? To its left is the Basilica di Santa Croce, where Galileo, Michelangelo, and Machiavelli were all laid to rest." Nora pointed to a gap between two hills. "It's a little hard to make out, but that white bell tower is the Fiesole, or little sister."

Lucas squinted. "I think I see what you're referring to."

"Fiesole is an ancient Etruscan hilltop town. It's about five thousand years older than Florence. The

Romans took it over in zero AD. There are some fun temple ruins and an amphitheater to explore. It has become a posh vacation area for millionaires and billionaires."

Lucas's gaze met hers. "I forget how ancient the city is. We have Roman ruins in Britain, but nothing that's five thousand years old."

Nora chuckled. "It's still millions of years younger than your beloved fossils."

"True."

They settled on a bench under the shade of a wooden pergola wrapped with the tendrils of a pink bougainvillea. Three red brick planter boxes held native Mediterranean plants and flowers. Insects buzzed from plant to plant, collecting pollen and nectar.

"You have the South Bank Parklands in Brisbane, but this is where I come to clear my mind when it's been a rough day, or if I need to find some inspiration." She ran her hand over the blades of ornamental grass. They tickled her skin. "Maestro Umberto was emphatic about having as much greenery as possible up here."

They watched the purple sprigs of lavender dance in the breeze and inhaled their strong, relaxing scent.

"Lucas, when we last spoke, do you understand why I was so bitter?"

"I do. We kind of touched on it earlier. I can't be a man who makes spur-of-the-moment decisions any longer." Lucas focused on a particularly large bumblebee crawling on the lavender plant. "Two weeks ago, I was so damn determined to dive headfirst toward the post-doctoral study opportunity that I let my head rule me instead of my heart. I lost sight of what I promised would always be most important—you and our future. I have to be more aware.

Moving ahead, my choices affect two lives. Not just my own."

Nora nodded. "And I was hotheaded because I wanted you all to myself. I wanted us to start our life together. You caught me off guard. I didn't have enough time to think rationally." She breathed in deeply. "If you are still inclined to do two more years in Australia, then I want you to know that I'm open to it, but I have some conditions."

He switched his focus to her.

She counted on her fingers. "First, I'd like to know why you want to do the post-doc and what happens when it's over. Will you continue to want to stay in Australia? Will you return to Europe?"

Lucas's jaw clenched. "I've been asking myself many of the same questions you're asking me now, and there is no denying that I wanted to do it because I've been so terrified of what comes after the PhD. Having had some time to reflect… the post-doc was going to be my way of delaying making any decisions of what's next. Academia is all I've ever known. It's how I've come to define myself. Removed from it, I don't know who or what I am."

He ran a hand through his hair. "I have struggled with confidence and self-doubt my entire life. Nothing I did ever seemed to please my father. In Argentina, and then in Australia, I finally felt as if I had discovered a place where I belonged. For the first time in my life, I was among like-minded individuals who were interested in hearing what I had to say. My work was valued, and dare I say sought after. I didn't want to lose that."

Nora inhaled sharply. Lucas was a goal-oriented man. He had always had a plan and known how he was going to achieve said plan. She could see how he would consider an uncertain future a frightening prospect. When the post-doc opportunity just presented itself to him, it was the next logical step. But where did it end?

"Taking the first steps outside your comfort zone will always feel clumsy, awkward, and wrong. It is brand-new territory and an uncomfortable place where one has to rely on their instincts." She folded her hands on her lap.

"Four years ago, when I began seeking out auditions, I grew sick to my stomach whenever I had to set foot in a room of people who were going to judge my violin skills based on how I played one measure of music. But by taking the plunge into the icy waters, over time, each audition grew easier. I learned that for all the effort I was putting in, it wasn't worth the disappointment. I widened my net and eventually landed the museum job."

"You are always so confident and self-assured." Lucas shook his head. "I can't picture you hiding in your shell."

"Well, it happened." Nora took hold of his hand and drew small circles on it. "What about when I shared my writing with you for the first time? I was terrified to bits over what you and others might say, but you encouraged me to share it with the members of the Never Far From Netherfield forum. Now, because of your urging, I'm finally at the point in my writing journey where I'm ready to spread my wings and take a gamble by writing stories with my own original characters. That doesn't mean, however, that I'm not nervous about how my readers will react to it."

She kissed his hand. "The point is that you can't stay in your comfort zone forever. Eventually, there will come a point where you will have to leap into the unknown."

Lucas stood. He slowly slid his hands toward his pockets, but realized his trousers lacked them, and settled for placing his hands behind his back. He looked out in the distance. The sun had nearly completed its daily journey across the sky.

"When I moved to Australia, I reasoned with myself that a doctorate was the last qualification I needed to earn in order to give myself a shot at becoming a full-time paleontologist. It's the only goal I've had for as long as I can recall. I wanted to be able to lead my own excavations and uncover secrets that have been lost to time."

He pinched the bridge of his nose. "I was naive. There was so much I didn't know then that I know now. The ugly truth is that academia is a place of endless research and grant proposals. There are more PhD holders out there than jobs available. It comes down to who you know and experience.

"I needed a good kick in the pants to be able to clearly see that it's high time I looked beyond chasing another shiny qualification to add to my CV." He turned and faced Nora. "I don't think I should do the post-doc. I think I should finish my program, move home to the UK, and be with you. What are your thoughts?"

Nora stood and placed her hands on Lucas's shoulders. "Any decision you make, I will fully stand behind. While I had *hoped* that you would choose to return to the UK or somewhere else in Europe, I want you to know that we can still find a way to make it work if your heart is dead set on doing that post-doc. I've been looking into the possibility of moving to Australia for a year. I can't do two years." Lucas's eyes gleamed with emotion at her words. "The bottom line is that *you* have to be at peace with your decision. I don't want you to have any lingering doubts or resentments."

"You're forever giving up your life to cater to mine. Enough. When I graduate and close out my life in

Australia, I'm coming home. To you. Where do *you* want to be this time next year, Lady Nora? What comes after life in Florence?" He picked her up and swung her around in a circle.

Nora laughed wildly, making the muscles in her face spasm. "Lucas." She clenched the fabric of his shirt. "You're making me dizzy."

He stopped spinning. His hair was tussled. Cravat askew. Nora untied it and tossed it to the ground. Walking them over to the bench, he sat down. Nora arranged herself on his lap and rested her head on his chest.

"I've had four glorious years of being Nora Toscani. It's been an epic journey, but like you, I think I'm finally ready to move into the next chapter of my life. When you become Dr. Lord Malcolm…" She paused and made a face. "Lord Dr. Malcolm? Yes, I like the way that sounds better. When you are officially made Lord Dr. Malcolm, I'll finally be ready to become the Principessa Leonora. As you learn how to run an estate, I'm going to learn to run a country as a three-quarter-time working royal."

"And what shall my Lady Principessa be doing the other part of the time? Writing? Playing music?"

"No, silly. Spending time with you!" She tickled the patch of hair previously hidden by the cravat. "I'd like for us to move in together. We've been apart longer than we've been together. Whether we settle in Italy, Isola Nostrum, the UK, or somewhere else, we need time to make the transition from a long-distance couple to a semi-normal couple."

He planted a trail of kisses up her neck. "Where would you be happiest?"

Florence had been a dream. But she couldn't see them living here. For one, he had trouble with the language.

Secondly, she'd like where they lived to have a little bit of separation from their families, where they could just be themselves.

"I'll get back to you with an answer. I don't know yet."

He sighed. "We still have time yet. My final presentation is in twelve weeks. Once everything is accepted and the paperwork has been completed, I'll have to close up my flat and all that jazz." He hesitated.

Nora lifted her head. "Lucas. What are you afraid to ask me?"

He fingered the tips of her hair. "I've always felt indebted to the fire service and rescue teams. The last two years, I've volunteered and given back where I'm able by answering phones, running supplies to their base camps, but with more time on my hands, I'd like to go one step further. The lease on my flat runs through the end of March. What would you say if I used the time to be trained up as a volunteer firefighter and serve for the worst part of the fire season?"

Nora's heart lurched at the thought of him putting himself in danger. "I'd be scared to see you on the front lines, but I'd be proud of you. The fire seasons have grown steadily worse, and I'm well aware that every person who can help make an impact *will* make an enormous difference to their cause."

"Thank you." He kissed the top of her head.

They stayed in one another's arms until the sun fully disappeared and day became night. She wondered if Lucas would be willing to pose in firefighting gear with Rex so she could make her own personal calendar.

Lord Malcolm's Villa

Stepping off the Great Western Railway train at Oxford station the next day, Lucas and Nora grabbed hands and exited the fare gates.

"Oy! Lucas! Nora!" Matthew waved his hands madly, a boyish grin on his face. "Over here, mates."

Matthew still appeared exactly as Nora remembered him, except for the fact that he had exchanged his favored rugby jerseys and trainers for a button-up shirt, slacks, and dress shoes.

"Mate!" Lucas clapped him on the back. "It is so good to see you!"

"Matthew." Nora reached her arms around his burly frame, then they exchanged kisses on both cheeks.

"You're more beautiful than ever." Matthew elbowed Lucas. "You better not do anything to muck up your relationship with her, mate."

"Ow. I won't, trust me. I've already been enrolled in the school of hard knocks, and once was more than enough for me." Lucas rubbed his shoulder. "Thanks for picking us up. We couldn't believe that they aren't sending any trains through toward Cheltenham Spa station. Some type of problem with the signaling system?"

In some respects, Nora felt guilty. She could've easily asked Angelo to find and arrange transportation. But she relished the quiet, intimate moments she was able to spend with Lucas.

Nora nonchalantly scanned the faces within the sea of passengers. She knew the trusted head of her security detail was lurking somewhere in the background.

He was so good at blending in and hiding in plain sight. She had no idea where he was.

"It's been dodgy the last four or five days and cost me several important showings with clients." Matthew rolled his eyes. "But I suppose it can always be worse. It's not like the strikes we had last winter. Blimey. There was a solid two weeks where there was no train service of any kind in these parts." He sighed. "No matter… I am always glad to have an excuse to meet up with you two and to drive through the Cotswolds. It's one of the most magnificent stretches of land in the UK, if I do say so myself."

They followed him to a black sedan. Matthew took charge of settling Nora's backpack into the boot of the car. She reached for the passenger door to the back seat. "Go ahead and sit up front with Matthew. I don't mind, really."

Lucas's brows formed a V-shape. "Matty won't mind if I sit in the back with you."

"He drove all the way to pick us up. He's your best mate. Spend the time catching up with him. Besides, I rather fancy the idea of taking a nap." She covered a yawn with her hand. "I didn't get much sleep last night. It was half past one by the time I finished packing."

"You didn't *have* to bring any luggage."

Nora opened the car door, shot him a dirty look, and slammed it shut.

Matthew slid into the driver's seat and glanced from Lucas to her. "Do I even want to ask? Did you lose a bet, mate, to get stuck wearing that ensemble?" He started the engine. "Never bet against a woman. One of the first lessons I ever learned."

"That's nice of you to say so, Matthew, but Lucas didn't lose a bet. He and I got into a row a few weeks ago, and he had it in his mind that flying to Italy to apologize as a Regency gent was a brilliant plan of action."

"Oh? Is that what you meant by the 'school of hard knocks' comment?" Matthew checked the mirrors and slowly backed the car up. "If you arrived yesterday, why are you still wearing that getup?"

"I bought a ticket that didn't include any luggage," Lucas muttered.

Matthew snorted.

"He declined my buying him any clothing yesterday, declaring that he'd be fine until we arrived at today's intended destination."

"Do you want me to swing by your flat first, then, or go straight to the Pittville Pump Room?"

Nora sat up taller in her seat. Her stomach fluttered. "We're going to a pump room? But I thought we were going to Cheltenham."

The car circled the roundabout, leaving the City of Dreaming Spires and heading toward the A40 motorway.

Lucas ran a hand over his jaw. "Our destination was supposed to be a secret."

"In that case, my lips are sealed," Matthew said.

"The surprise was spoiled when you made me in charge of the train tickets to Cheltenham." Nora crossed her arms. "I *could* perform a Google search to read more about it."

"Or you could wait an hour," Lucas suggested.

The lines around her mouth grew tight. "Fine."

Matthew let out a low, raspy chuckle. "What do you know about Cheltenham, Nora?"

She stared out the windows, enjoying the rolling fields, dry-stone walls, and thick greenery. As Matthew slowed the car to drive through the first of many picturesque rural English villages, she spied thatched roofs and the stone facades of tightly packed cottages clustered near a babbling brook. A thin veil of drizzle rained upon the car window.

"It's in Gloucester."

"Anything else?" Matthew asked.

"Lucas owns a flat there?"

"Matty," Lucas warned.

"Give Nora a little hint. It'll only help your cause." Matthew glanced at him.

"Fine." Lucas clenched his jaw. "Cheltenham has a long-established history as a market town. In fact, it is old enough to be listed in William the Conqueror's Domesday Book. But it wasn't until seventeen sixteen that the town began its rise to prominence when a flock of pigeons was discovered pecking at salt deposits around a well near where today's Cheltenham Ladies' College sits."

"Capisco," Nora said slowly. "What was so special about the salt and pigeons?"

Matthew chuckled. "It was said to have magical healing properties that could cure any ailment."

"Like the water in the city of Bath?"

"Exactly like Bath, except for the bit about the thermal hot springs," Lucas added.

"Now I see. Cheltenham became a spa town."

"Indeed." Matthew nodded. "When the Mad King, George III, and his family stayed in Cheltenham for five weeks in seventeen eighty-eight to take the waters, the town was officially awarded a royal seal of approval. Shortly thereafter, the rich and fashionable began to travel to Cheltenham. Guesthouses and businesses began to pop up, and overnight, it became a leading leisure center of Regency society. Today, Cheltenham is hailed as one of the most complete Regency towns in all of England, if not the most."

Nora pictured the ring of flat-fronted white Georgian-era townhouses that formed Bath's Royal Crescent. She wondered if Cheltenham was similar in appearance.

Bath was a lovely town. She spent more day trips exploring it during uni than she cared to admit. Taking tea in the pump rooms that Jane Austen and the who's who of Regency society frequented was always a highlight. What must the Pittville Pump Room be like? Who had visited it?

"That's enough information for now. Any more will ruin her surprise," Lucas said.

"All right," Matthew relented.

With the mood Lucas was in, it was clear she wouldn't be on the receiving end of any more hints until they'd reached Cheltenham.

Nora closed her eyes. "I'm going to nap. Wake me when we arrive, per favore."

Matthew took the hint to engage Lucas in conversation about the weekend's exciting Premier League football match. "Did you see how the shootout from the Man City match versus Aston Villa went?"

"No. I was otherwise occupied."

"Aw, you missed a match for the ages. Watts, the goalkeeper, saved a shot from Kingsley that bounced off…"

Nora tuned out what the men were saying. Her

breathing evened out, and she fell asleep, dreaming of Lucas leading her into a pump room with a neoclassical facade to sign the registry that they'd arrived on holiday in Cheltenham.

Nora awoke to the view of a town with tree-lined streets and expansive gardens. White period townhomes with sweeping classical terraces and black wrought-iron fences were clustered tightly together among a mixture of shops and boutiques.

"Lord Byron, Jane Austen, the Duke of Wellington, and Queen Victoria have all spent time here." Matthew pointed to the towering white Greek revival building with elongated Corinthian colonnades. Greek architecture had inspired a number of buildings in the city. "The Queen Hotel on the right over there, named for Queen Victoria, is one of the top ten in the country."

While Matthew went on about the thirty-two Caryatid maidens the town's Montpellier district boasted, Nora's attention was stuck on his previous statement.

"You said Jane stayed here?" She wrinkled her brow. "Do we know where? Is it possible to see it? How does it compare to Sydney Place in Bath and Chawton in Hampshire?"

Lucas and Matthew exchanged knowing glances.

Matthew took the lead in answering her questions. "It isn't known which townhome she may have rented, but she took the waters here near the end of her life. It's thought she and her sister Cassandra might have taken quarters near the Royal Crescent, which was within walking distance to the Royal Well."

Nora couldn't wrap her head around it. Matthew changed lanes and slowly drove around the roundabout of Georgian homes, which was much smaller than Bath's, but nonetheless impressive.

"Lucas's flat is in the suburb of the area called Pittville. You'll notice more greenery and that the houses are more varied in style."

Five minutes later, Matthew stopped the car and double-parked in front of a two-story white stucco villa two blocks from the expansive Pittville Park. He turned the hazard lights on.

"This is where I'll leave you two." Matthew winked. "Ring me if you need anything. I'm only a short drive away." He climbed out of the car and retrieved Nora's backpack from the boot.

"We can't thank you enough, Matty. Are you sure you won't stop in for a spot of tea? I think there's an electric kettle and dishes in the mess somewhere." Lucas scratched his chin.

"No. I have a hot date to keep with a lady of my own. But I did make sure your kitchen was stocked and the reception room was presentable. Although, I can't speak for the state of the remainder of the flat."

Lucas cringed. "The boxes."

"They're pretty bad," Matthew admitted.

Nora rubbed her eyes. Was this the property he owned? She'd pictured a basement-level flat in a white brick terraced house. Not a home like this!

"There's a private garden entrance?" she sputtered.

"It shouldn't come as that much of a shock. You live in a palazzo with a private courtyard," Lucas joked.

Matthew took pity on Nora. "The building has been converted into three dwellings. Two apartments and one wing. The flat Lucas claimed for himself when he purchased the property is number two, which consists of the raised and lower ground-floor levels."

This was what he had meant by a smart investment.

Her muscles twitched. "Can we go in?"

Lucas and Matthew laughed. "Yes, we can," Lucas said.

"Good luck, mate." Matthew bade them goodbye, then climbed into the car and drove off.

"Welcome home." Lucas opened the black wrought-iron gate.

Passing under the shade of four trees, they followed the pathway around a fountain, which contained water lilies. A short but neat carpet of grass filled the remaining space. Nora shifted her backpack to one shoulder and followed Lucas down two steps to a black door with a gold number two on it.

"I had Matthew install a number pad. It's much more practical to memorize and type in the code than to carry a key." The black door clicked open. Lucas entered and turned the lights on. An electric hum filled the flat. "I didn't realize it was *this* bad," he said under his breath.

Nora's eyes widened. An endless wall of boxes of varying shapes and sizes filled the length of the entry hallway clear to the back door of the kitchen. So tight was the space that only one person could pass through the hall at a time. Lucas turned his body sideways and shuffled into the first room on the left.

"Oh my," Nora said as she placed her backpack on the ground and her hands on her hips.

This must be the flat's main sitting room. On two sides of the room, boxes were stacked about two meters in height and ran the expanse of the wall's length. From what she could make out, the flat had been converted to modern standards, yet it still maintained some of its period features. There was a beautiful white marble fireplace and mantel, two glass chandeliers, crown molding, and highly-polished wooden floors. A red velvet chaise and black side table were the only pieces of furniture in the room.

Lucas walked over to the window and pulled open a set of sheer white curtains to let in some much-needed natural light. There were three lovely sash windows. Nora could picture herself curled up with a good book on the chaise near the fireplace, with Lucas working on his computer and Rex napping at their feet.

"I'm so sorry, Nora; I never would've brought you here if I'd known the true state of it." Lucas's face flushed a deep shade of black-cherry red.

She opened and closed her mouth. "What is in all of these boxes?"

"I don't know." His ears burned crimson as well. "This is a culmination of things from uni, rare and limited-edition dinosaur toys, bits of furniture, kitchenware, and other odds and ends. I never formally moved in and unpacked the place."

"So when you told me that you'd sorted out your flat before you left for Australia and that you didn't need help packing, what did you actually do?" Her eyebrow twitched.

"I made the piles neater." He pulled at his cravat.

"And your idea of a romantic weekend was to bring me here?" She couldn't contain herself. Her body shook with laughter, ringing out through the flat. "And how many rooms are there in total?"

"Down here, not counting the loo, there is the kitchen, the reception and dining rooms, and upstairs there are two bedrooms and a library—so six rooms in total?"

"And they are just as full of boxes?"

"All but the kitchen," he admitted.

She wiped a tear from the corner of her eye. "Is this where we're to spend the night?"

"No, I made other arrangements." He glanced at his watch. "Gah, we're a little off schedule because of the train mishap. I have reservations for us somewhere special at two. I need to jump in the shower and change if we're going to make it on time." His eyes met hers. "Unless you'd like to get ready first."

"Is what I'm wearing appropriate?" Nora gestured to her outfit. She wore one of her favorite little black dresses with a white belt, over a pair of black tights and ankle boots. She'd paired the ensemble with a pink, gray, and white-checked Burberry scarf, and white overcoat.

"How you are dressed now is perfect."

"Then no, I won't need to change." She pointed to the boxes. "Do you mind if I open some of these? My curiosity has gotten the better of me."

"Be my guest." He clicked his heels together, bowed, and left Nora to her own devices.

"It's like Christmas." She rubbed her hands together. "Where to begin?"

She was tempted to explore, but if Matthew considered this room tidy, she was afraid to see what state the other rooms were in. She might not even be able to fit inside the rooms if they were packed floor to ceiling with boxes as tightly as the hallway.

Lucas returned about twenty minutes later, showered, shaved, and hair still damp. He had exchanged the period clothing for a pair of gray slacks, a baby-blue button-up shirt, and a black jumper. "Have you found anything interesting?"

Nora sat on her knees. "A set of copper kitchen pans, a

food processor, a nineteen ninety- five *Jurassic Park* limited edition T-Rex and velociraptor figurine set, a ceramic border collie wall clock that resembles Rex, and my personal favorite…" She tossed a plastic package in his direction. "A pack of Stegosaurus men's boxer briefs."

Lucas covered his face with his hands.

"You will purchase anything with a dinosaur on it, won't you?" She stood and laughed as she crossed the room to hug him. He smelled of fresh lemon-scented soap.

"I have no sales resistance whenever I see something that is both practical and has a print of my reptilian friends." He sighed.

"At least my knowing that you'll buy things like that"—she pointed to the boxers—"makes it easier for me to pick out your birthday and Christmas gifts. Are we ready to go out, then?"

Lucas nodded. "I just need my coat."

CHAPTER 26

What a Wonderful World

They took a short stroll to Pittville Park. Lucas was keen to show Nora the boathouse and the lake. A trio of adult swans glided across the water. Families sat on picnic blankets and folding chairs. The white tip of a red fox's tail disappeared into a clump of bushes.

"Do you remember how you were explaining the premise of the new BBC adaptation of *Sanditon* to me? Well, Pittville is very much like a real-life version of *Sanditon*," Lucas said.

He told her how a well-to-do man named William Pitt had once aspired to turn his estate into a lucrative private spa retreat. Naming the town after himself, he had dreamed of constructing five hundred villas, ornamental lakes, parks, and other green spaces. Yet his plans were never to come to fruition. After a slew of devastating financial losses, Pitt lost his fortune. The Court of Chancery seized his assets and sold them off to pay his debts. He died not long after.

"It's such a sad story. I feel for Mr. Pitt, just as I did for Mr. Parker in *Sanditon*." Nora laughed. "All I can say on the matter is that they had better produce a second series. I will be most seriously displeased if they choose to leave Miss Charlotte Heywood's romantic storyline unresolved. All Austen ladies deserve a happily ever after."

Lucas slipped his hand into Nora's. It was warm and fit just right. "Does that include the likes of Lady Susan, Miss Lucy Steele, Miss Lydia Bennet…"

"Point taken. I amend what I said earlier. All Austen heroines deserve to have romantic closure." She squeezed his hand.

Through the clearing of the trees, the path led them to the rust-colored building with Greek columns. Nora's eyes traveled up to the roof, taking in the dome and statues of Aesculapius and Hygieia, the Greek god and goddess of health and medicine, and Hippocrates, the founder of medicine. All symbols of health.

They ascended a set of steps. Ever the gentleman, Lucas held open the glass doors. "After you, my Lady Nora."

A woman in a white regency gown and a turban held a clipboard. She curtsied. "I was beginning to wonder where you might be. Are you Lord Merrick?"

Lucas took a moment to realize she was addressing him. He cleared his throat. "My apologies. I was distracted by the serene beauty of my stunning girlfriend. I am Lucas Malcolm, Lord Merrick." He extended his hand to her.

Nora much preferred Lord Malcolm. Lord Merrick sounded too formal.

"I'm Lisa." The woman fanned herself with her clipboard. "Everything is as you requested. If you two would please follow me." She motioned with a gloved arm. "We have you set up in the ballroom."

Nora tilted her head to the side. What did Lucas have planned? She didn't have long to ruminate. He offered her his arm, and they followed Lisa from the foyer to a set of tall wooden doors. A pair of footmen in powdered wigs and servants' livery inclined their heads and opened the doors to the ballroom.

"I hope you two have a magical afternoon tea," Lisa said.

Nora gasped. Three cantilevered glass chandeliers shimmered from the white-and-gold vaulted ceiling. Elegant white Grecian colonnades lined the room between tall sash windows. A red carpet extended from the doorway to the center of the room, where a round table was set for two. The sound system played soft classical music from the soundtrack of the 2009 television adaptation of *Emma*.

Lucas planned this for me? She rested her head on his shoulder.

He puffed out his chest. "You're speechless. I take that as a sign you approve?"

Nora nodded.

When they reached the table, Lucas pulled out her chair. "Grazie," she said. "I can't believe you arranged for all this."

"Only the best for you, my lady." After he took his seat, the two footmen brought out a tea service and cake stand full of delightful culinary confections. "Thank you, that will be all." Lucas dismissed the men.

Nora unfolded her napkin and helped herself to two scones, strawberry jam, and a cucumber sandwich.

"I love that you aren't afraid to tuck in," Lucas joked, opting to pour himself tea first.

"I'm half Italian and half Isola Nostrani. Two cultures that are renowned for their love of food."

"Tea?"

"Yes, please."

He poured the steaming liquid into her cup.

"I wish I had known where we were going to spend the day. I would've taken care to dress *properly* in a fancy ball gown," she said.

Lucas placed the teapot down and reached for two finger sandwiches. "I didn't think of it until we were leaving the flat. I didn't wish to spoil the surprise."

She placed her hand on top of his. "I forgive you, Lord Malcolm. Next time, however, I won't let you off so easily."

He chuckled. "I'll remember that for the Jane Austen Festival's Masquerade Ball."

Nora's pulse raced. "You're coming to the ball?"

He arched an eyebrow. "I thought my attendance was mandatory."

"It is," she replied quickly.

"Good, because I cleared my schedule and am giving up some highly *valuable* presentation prep time for it. It's the last bit of fun I'll have until I submit my thesis."

She placed her knife and jam down. "I wish you could remain with me until the ball. It's only three weeks away."

His facial expression softened. "You know I would stay if I could."

"I know."

"I thought my presence would be helpful to Lorenzo. He's been incredibly antsy about Sabrina's surprise."

"So you're not planning to attend solely for me?" she teased.

"*You* are my priority," he sputtered. "Not even a stampede of sauropods could sway my mind. Mind you, they could easily with their sheer size, which I—" Lucas caught himself and smiled coyly.

"I'm only teasing." Her lips curved up.

Sabrina had texted her this morning that Rome agreed

with her and Lorenzo. The ball should settle any lingering doubts between the pair of star-crossed lovers.

Lucas gestured to the food. "Everything will be cold if we dally any longer."

When the candles had burned low and the tea had long been cleared away, Lucas stood and offered her his hand. "My Lady Nora, would you care to dance with me in this grand ballroom before our next adventure?"

"I would, except we don't have any music." She gestured to the wide-open room.

Lucas's eye twitched. "Music, you say?" He clapped his hands together. "Maestro. My lady requires music!"

As she opened her mouth to make a snarky retort, she heard the telltale sound of a string quartet striking up the opening notes of her special song, "Leonora's Waltz." In the corner of the room, a footman pulled upon a gold tassel cord. A red velvet curtain was peeled away to reveal the musicians watching the pair from the corners of their eyes.

"There. Now we have music. Is there anything else, or will you finally consent to dance with me?"

The legs of Nora's chair squeaked against the wooden floor as she rose. "As my Lord Malcolm commands."

Lucas all but swept her off her feet as he guided her around the table. They stood across from one another. Her eyes locked on to his twinkling agate-blue orbs, reminding her of the color of the sea surrounding Isola Nostrum.

He bowed.

So this was to be a Regency dance. And not just any dance, but Emma and Knightley's. She recognized the steps from the film. *Well played, Lord M. Well played, indeed.*

She curtsied. They glided forward, and their hands touched. Without the fabric of gloves, she could feel every movement and touch his fingers made. Every breath he took. Nora swore her heart was beating so wildly that Lucas would be able to hear the pounding through her chest.

Her mind transported them back in time. She saw Lucas in a perfectly-tailored navy tailcoat, crisp white shirt, cravat, and black breeches. Herself in a light-cream silk gown. Candles burned low around them. The only sound would be the rustle of the fabric. She licked her lips.

Dancing was always intimate, but Regency dancing, especially, was on another level.

Just like Mr. Knightly, Lucas was an excellent dancer, carrying himself with a surprising amount of poise and grace. She saw a faint patch of pink on his cheeks. The folds of his eyes crinkled with pleasure and the fringe of his sandy locks bobbled up and down as they let their bodies go through the dancing motions, weaving in and out of one another's embrace.

He was, without a doubt, Mr. Knightly. Lucas was a rational man, but he could also make impulsive and spontaneous decisions. She thought he was indifferent to her for the first few years of their fake engagement, but the moment he told her he loved her, everything changed. At first, her love for him was young love, but over time, it had grown and matured, much as their relationship had. *You are my one and only, Lord Malcolm.*

The last note of the music played. They continued to stare at one another, each breathing heavily. They moved toward each other, and Lucas placed a soft, chaste kiss on her lips. Nora's eyes fluttered closed. She sighed in deep contentment.

When she opened her eyes, Lucas had knelt down on one knee. The string quartet played the much more contemporary Bruno Mars song, "I Think I Wanna Marry You." From behind his back, he brought forth a strawberry-red box and opened the lid. It held a dainty yellow-gold pendant with sapphires and diamonds. Examining the item closer, she noticed that the sapphire formed the body of a long-necked Brontosaurus and the cluster of diamonds a flower.

The one type of sauropod she recognized by name and shape.

"Principessa Leonora. You have already captured my heart, my mind, my body, and my soul. You are the only woman I can picture myself having a future with. Will you put this obstinate, headstrong man out of his misery, and at long last transform our fake engagement into a *real* one?"

Nora giggled. "Don't you have another question for me too?"

A moment of confusion passed behind his eyes.

"Something about becoming your wife?"

"Of all the things to forget." He facepalmed. "Leonora. Nora. Will you marry me?"

"Si." She nodded. "I want nothing more than to become your Lady Malcolm."

He breathed a deep sigh of relief. They kissed again, deeply and passionately, to the tune of "What a Wonderful World."

CHAPTER 27

A Magic Carpet

Lucas's afternoon plans to rent a small gig carriage and take them up into the hills above Pittville for a romantic picnic had disintegrated after a heavy downpour of rain. On a whim, they'd discovered the Cheltenham Racecourse and rented a suite.

The sound of thundering hooves pounded against the racetrack as the pack of brown thoroughbreds turned the final corner for home. The small crowd cheered, jumping to its feet and urging their favored horses and jockeys on. Mud splattered in every which direction.

Nora placed her binoculars down. "The winner of the sixth race was Rags to Riches. A fitting name, don't you agree?"

"Yes, except that I picked Daddy Longlegs to win." Lucas tossed his losing betting slip onto the table and sat across from Nora. "It's a good thing I only wagered two quid. You and I are terrible at picking winners. Between the two of us, through the fifth and sixth races, we've only managed to pick one horse that has placed in the top three."

"That's what happens when you pick the horse you're

betting on based on its name or its appearance," she laughed.

Nora angled her body so it faced her fiancé. The next race wouldn't begin for another twenty minutes. Her fingers played with the delicate gold chain she was wearing. She was thrilled to bits Lucas had given her a necklace. He'd declared it would've raised too many questions if he had opted to give her another engagement ring.

"Shall we address the elephant in the room? What are we going to do about our wedding now that our engagement is officially official?" Nora asked.

Lucas leaned back in his chair. "What did your mum and wedding planner say the last time you spoke to them?"

Nora grimaced. "Mama was frustrated that your mum wishes for us to hold a pre-wedding reception at your family's chateau in France in addition to the two wedding ceremonies and two receptions they've already agreed upon. The working timetable is set for eighteen months from now."

Which was longer than she'd like to wait, but beggars couldn't be choosers.

Lucas winced in sympathy. "My mother can be a handful. I can't imagine what you've had to put up with."

"It hasn't been so bad until recently because it wasn't real. I was more concerned about how we were going to inform the matriarchs that our engagement and the wedding were a farce."

"Would you like me to call a meeting with our mothers and the wedding planner?" Lucas ran a hand over his jawline. "I don't like that they are calling *all* the shots."

"We can't deny our mamas. Let them have their fun." Nora folded her hands and placed them on the table. "You are an only child. Susan has spoken several times about how exciting it is for her to be involved in the planning process. And my mama… she started planning the moment you spoke to Papa. She's been dreaming about the dress I'd wear, location, and all the minute details about it since I was a little girl."

"It isn't fair to you. It's your day." Lucas leaned forward in his seat.

"If it were my prerogative, I'd like something simple. Just a few of our closest friends and family members." Nora's eyes danced. "So long as I am with the man I love, that's all that matters."

Lucas rubbed his hands together. "We could elope? Fly to Las Vegas and be done with it all in a day. I'd be in the proverbial doghouse forever, but it would be worth it to avoid the stress of it all."

Nora cocked her head to the side. "What do you have to stress about? The mamas are doing all the work."

His cheeks colored. "You know what I mean."

The public address speaker announced the horses for the seventh race would proceed to the gate. Nora stood, opened the window, and leaned over the railing. She smelled the scent of wet grass and mud. Heard the buzz of conversation of those sitting below in the grandstand. Lucas joined her a moment later, rubbing her elbows. The calluses of his fingers were rough against her smooth skin.

"If you truly meant what you said earlier about meeting with the matriarchs, in my heart, I would prefer they toned down the extravagance of the affair to one pre-wedding dinner, one ceremony, and one reception," she admitted.

"That sounds fair. We can broach the subject with them the weekend of the Jane Austen Festival. Mother will throw a fit, but I'll see to her."

"Thank you." Nora rested her head on his chest.

Sitting on the chaise at the Cheltenham flat, Nora found the inspiration she sought to at long last write an ending to *Entering the Marriage Mart.*

Miss Kennington dropped the bucket of chicken feed and rubbed her eyes. Lord Malcolm was jumping off a powerful brown thoroughbred horse, clad only in his shirtsleeves, trousers, and boots. Her pulse quickened.

"Miss Kennington, I have ridden through the night to reach you. I could not bear to be parted from you for a single moment longer. I have come here today to beg for your forgiveness and to try and make amends."

Jogging to close the distance between them, Lord Malcolm dropped to his knees. "I have never been more ashamed of myself. I should never have taken the word of my staff against your own. You have come to mean so much to me. To my sister Alice. I love you, and I know that you shall never endeavor to return my affections, but if you could find it in your heart to forgive me . . ."

"Lord Malcolm." Miss Kennington knelt down beside him. She gently placed her hand under his chin and lifted it. "I am still very cross with you, indeed, but from the moment you rescued me from that odious rake, Mr. Fletcher, you had my heart. The longer I spent in your presence, the deeper my affection grew for you and your dear sister. The moment I fled your home, I knew that I would never be able to love another. You have bewitched me in mind and spirit."

Lord Malcolm's hand clasped hers. "Miss Kennington. Against all odds . . . that is . . . if I were to ask for your hand in holy matrimony, would you . . . would you . . . consider . . . I . . ."

"Yes, Lord Malcolm. I would consider it."

Lord Malcolm swallowed hard and tried hard to focus his mind to find the words evading him. He cleared his throat. "Miss Kennington, would you do me the great honor of consenting to become my wife?"

"I will."

Lord Malcolm smiled as wide as the River Avon and cupped her cheeks. "You have made me the happiest man in all of England. I shall spend the rest of our lives trying to earn your forgiveness."

"You have made me the happiest woman alive. I love you, Lord M. Just as you are."

They kissed, and all was right in the world again.

Lucas glanced over her shoulder. "You've named the hero of your first non-Austen story Lord Malcolm?" he asked in a bemused tone.

Nora quickly locked her computer screen. "You weren't supposed to see it until I'd finished editing the draft."

Lucas crossed his arms. "Out of all the names in the universe, you couldn't think of *any* other than Lord Malcolm?"

Her face burned. "I needed *some* way to fulfill my Austen fantasy, and using you as a source of inspiration filled the void," she sputtered.

"And what have you named your heroine? Miss Nora?"

Nora wished the ground would swallow her up. "Miss Amelia Kennington."

He stroked his jaw. "I suppose if you used the name

Leonora or Nora, it would be too much of a dead giveaway that you modeled her after yourself."

She swallowed hard. "My pen name is Nora Bennet."

He sat on the chaise and reached for her laptop. "When you were mad at me, did you take your anger out on the poor fictional Lord Malcolm bloke?"

Nora muttered under her breath in Italian and hugged the computer closer to her body.

"What's that? I couldn't *quite* hear or understand you."

"I said I wrote two entire chapters where Lord Malcolm's sensible sister Alice, the person he loves most, cuts off all ties with him. Before you appeared on my doorstep, I was going to alter the plot to also have him lose his fortune."

His fingers drummed against the arm of the chaise. "And when shall *I* be granted leave by your alter ego to read said story?"

"I'll send the file to you before you board your plane to fly home. How does that sound?"

This story was very personal. She wanted him to be able to spend the time reading it properly in private. It was a love letter to their relationship as much as it was a debut story. *Entering the Marriage Mart* represented the day Lucas decided that entering an engagement of convenience with her was a brilliant idea.

His shoulders deflated. "Very well."

Certain Lucas wouldn't steal her computer from her possession, she placed it to the side. "What do you have planned for us this evening? It'll be hard to top the proposal at the pump rooms."

Lucas's eyes sparkled with mirth. "What would you say to me taking a dip in a pond and climbing out in a wet shirt?"

Nora covered her mouth with her hand. "I'd say it's raining, and that the lake in Pittville Park was infested with mosquitos."

"After living in Brisbane for the last four years, mosquitoes are nothing." He wrapped an arm around her. She rested her head on his shoulder. "My dear Lady Nora, you and I will be spending the evening at a Jane Austen improv show. There is a comedy troupe in town who's received rave reviews for their reenactments of the lost Jane Austen stories."

Nora's eyes widened. "Lost stories?"

"As Matthew explained it, the audience suggests a title and the troupe will improv a story in the style of Jane Austen based on that suggestion."

"Ugh…" Nora was at a loss for words. "I don't know… Austen improv?"

"Matthew promised it was both witty and hilarious. No two plays are ever the same. And tomorrow morning, you and I are going to take a romantic sojourn through the Cotswolds from up above."

Nora furrowed her brow. "We're taking a helicopter ride?"

"No. Nothing of the sort." Lucas chuckled. "It's a hot air balloon ride. A mate of mine offers them to the public as one of the ways he supports his estate."

She sat up taller. "That sounds incredible."

"Nothing but the best for my principessa. It's the closest we might ever come to taking a magic carpet ride together."

∼

". . .the principle is a very easy concept based on the ideal gas law. There is a mathematical principle between the volume, temperature, and pressure of a gas. Thus, because a cubic foot of air is roughly twenty-eight grams when the air is—"

"I get the gist of it, Lord M." Nora squeezed Lucas's hand. "In layman's terms, hot air rises. When the balloon has been filled with enough hot air, we'll become airborne."

She glanced over her shoulder to the man in charge of piloting the balloon. He chuckled at hearing their exchange.

"Sorry to bother you, but is there any coffee on board? We were running a little late this morning, and my mad-scientist fiancé missed his daily dose of caffeine. Unlike most people, coffee seems to calm him down."

The pilot kept his eyes trained on the gauges connected to the propane tank. "There should be a picnic basket in the corner with some snacks and a thermos of coffee straight from Lord Renbrook's kitchen."

"Grazie." Nora wiggled her hand free from Lucas's.

Maintaining a firm grip on the inside rail, she shuffled over to the far corner, easily finding the snacks. The basket was much wider than she'd imagined. It could easily accommodate fifteen people. The wicker rims came up to about the level of her shoulders.

"Do you need some help, Lady Nora?" Lucas turned and leaned his back against the rail.

"No. I've got it." Carefully, she knelt down, twisted the top of the metal container, and poured the still-hot liquid into a plastic mug. "Mmm. . . it's a dark roast."

"Oy. I can smell it from here. Renbrook knows what he's about." Lucas sniffed the air.

Nora passed the cup to him. Then she asked the pilot, "Can I get anything for you, sir?"

"It's Phil, and thank you, but no, ma'am. I had a cuppa before we took off."

Nora blinked twice. "We're already airborne?"

"Indeed," the pilot said.

She sprang to her feet and wiped her hands against the rough fabric of her jeans. The world below had grown smaller. As if straight out of a fairy tale, they floated over an expansive field of lavender cloaked by a thin layer of fog. The tips of the plants swayed gently in the breeze. Golden rays of light from the rising sun peeked out from behind a curtain of clouds, illuminating the flowers. There were shades of lilac, lavender, and a royal purple so dark that some might argue it was a shade of blue.

"It's beautiful."

Lucas joined her, draping an arm around her shoulders. "It is, but I'm standing next to the most handsome woman in the room." He kissed her cheek.

"It's not really a room," Nora giggled.

"A mere technicality." Lucas sipped from the mug.

Phil stopped filling the balloon with propane, and for the first time, all Nora could hear was the sound of birds. They drifted over a thick grove of trees. She saw a trio of deer jumping and disappearing into a thicket.

"We're up so high. Almost tall enough to touch the clouds."

"Are you still afraid?" Lucas asked in a low tone.

She shook her head and rested it against his shoulder. "I thought I'd be frightened, but now that we're up here, I'm exhilarated. The balloon is so smooth, and it's like . . ."

The intonation of his voice rose. "A magic carpet ride?"

"Si . . . but now that I think about it, it's more like we're sailing on Peter Pan's ship."

A smile tugged at the corner of Lucas's lips. "Do you mean Captain Hook's ship?"

"Was it Captain Hook's ship at the end of *Peter Pan*? My memory is a little fuzzy. We might just have to watch the Disney film together to refresh it. *Aladdin* too."

He rubbed his arm up and down hers. "Whatever my Lady Nora wishes."

As they ascended higher and higher into the clouds, Nora's gaze traveled up to his pair of mischievous blue eyes. They sparkled like brilliantly cut diamonds. This was the man she was going to spend the rest of her life with. The man who had become her best friend. The man who would always take care of her. Her heart was full.

She swallowed hard. "I love you, Lord Malcolm."

"And I you, my Lady Nora." He brought her hand to his lips and softly hummed the tune to the song "A Whole New World." "When I'm way up here, it's crystal clear, that now I'm in a whole new world," he sang.

"And it's one we'll explore together. You and me."

The balloon continued to drift over the rolling fields of the Cotswolds, carrying the two lovers off to a future full of hopes, dreams, and possibilities.

Part Five

CHAPTER 28

Epilogue—A Royal Wedding

Five months later, Lucas was done with his program. After spending some time volunteering with the fire service, he moved back to the UK. As luck would have it, just after the last set of boxes in his Cheltenham flat had been sorted, Lucas received an invitation to take part in the excavation of a newly discovered set of sauropod remains in Dorset. Inspired by Nora, in the long term, he hoped to find a job at the National History Museum in London.

For Nora, *Entering the Marriage Mart* had done far better than she'd ever expected. After the launch of the book in paperback form, by the end of the first week, it had topped the best-seller list in the Regency romance category. The second book in the series was due to launch in a matter of weeks. If the pre-sales were any indication, it would also be a best-seller. She was proud that the proceeds they raised from the books would be donated to charity. Although she was no longer employed at the museum, she still maintained a full schedule and divided her time between being a working royal, writing, and spending time with Lucas.

~

Thirteen months after that, their wedding day arrived.

An electric buzz hummed through the air in the town of Ananostrum. Purple-and-gold flags with the Toscani family crest were displayed in every shop window and from the bow of every boat in the harbor. The streets were overflowing with crowds of well-wishers. Papa had declared the day to be a national holiday.

In her dressing room at the palace, Nora's father kissed her on the forehead. "Leonora, you have never looked more beautiful. Lucas won't be able to take his eyes off you once he sees you."

"Grazie, Papa."

From the vanity table, Mama removed the top of a battered box. Tissue paper crinkled as a handcrafted lace veil was removed. With a light touch, Nora's mother inserted the veil's combs into her daughter's hair. "Your dress is new. Your necklace is blue. Your grandmother's veil is both old and borrowed." Mama dried her eye with a tissue. "I am crying already."

Nora turned and stared at her reflection in the full-length mirror, scarcely recognizing herself. Staring back at her was a woman with loose, wavy caramel-brown locks, wearing an ivory Regency-inspired empire-waist gown. The sleeves were sheer and puffy, the skirt adorned with crystal-and-pearl beading and scalloped lace.

"Leonora, we have one more gift for you," Papa said, presenting Nora with a large black leather box.

Her hands shook. She pressed the silver clasp to unlock it. With a click, it opened to reveal a ruby, pearl, and diamond platinum tiara. Her eyes widened. "Papa. Mama.

This is too much." Her fingers traced the intricate points, swirls, and flower forms.

"Your papa and I had this tiara commissioned ages ago. We had hoped to have it in hand before you performed your first official public duties as the Principessa dei Fiore, but c'est la vie."

"Your Highness?" Nora turned her head toward her hair-and-makeup artist. "May I?"

"Si. Si." Nora sat down.

Mama removed the tiara from the box and settled it on top of her head. The hair artist immediately set to work securing the tiara and veil.

"I'll meet you two ladies in the sitting room." Papa dismissed himself.

Lucia entered the room. As one of the two bridesmaids, she and Sabrina both wore the same wine-colored one-shoulder ball gown. Lucia had been particularly happy to find that her dress contained pockets.

Lucia walked around her sister and stood next to the mirror.

"How are Lorenzo, Lucas, and Matthew doing?" Nora inquired. She winced as a bobby pin was jammed into the tender skin by the nape of her neck.

"The men were discussing some fancy luxury car that one of Lucas's friends, the Earl of Renbrook, just bought. It was either a Porsche or a Ferrari. I forget. Boys and their toys." Lucia shrugged.

"They didn't appear nervous?"

"Not in the least." Lucia grinned. "Sabrina told me about the gathering you and Lucas are throwing next weekend at your new home in Cheltenham. I assume I'm invited."

"Of course you're invited," she whispered. "I was going

to tell you more about it when we were alone." Nora's eyes darted to her mother across the room. "It's an *intimate* party, just for a few close friends and family. *Don't* say a word to Mama or Papa."

An hour later, Nora was handed up by her father into a white open-topped carriage. "I'll see you at the church," he said, placing a soft kiss on her forehead and flipping the veil over her face. The carriage door was slammed shut.

"Salute!" a voice commanded. The guard of honor, a team of eight members of Isola Nostrum's cavalry, snapped their heads to the right and saluted the king.

Papa returned the salute.

"Forward," the squadron leader cried.

In unison, both the soldiers and carriage began advancing toward the palace gates. Nora waved to her father and the members of palace staff flanking the drive.

"Congratulazioni, Principessa!" they shouted.

She flashed a wide smile and nodded to them until the carriage turned the corner and initiated its descent down the mountain toward the town of Ananostrum.

Nora sat tall with her hands on her lap. For the first time in two weeks, she was utterly alone. She heard the steady clip-clop of the horses' hooves and the jingle of their bridle chains.

This was the last time she'd leave the palace as Nora Toscani. The next time she was here, in private, she'd be Mrs. Lord Dr. Lucas Malcolm, the Countess of Merrick. How well that sounded.

She wondered what Lucas was thinking about. Would he admire her dress?

She twisted the tiger's eye ring on her hand. Off to her left, the agate blue of the sea, dotted with a smattering of white vessels, reminded her of the color of Lucas's eyes.

It was the same shade of blue that locked onto her eyes the day they became a fake engaged couple at the Natural History Museum. It seemed like ages ago that they were discussing how he could pull it off so he could complete his studies in Australia.

Lucas was worried it would be a terrible idea. He was concerned she would be putting her love life on hold, but in reality, they were writing the prologue of their lives together. She had always known he was a very special man, and she was right. He was her best friend. Her anchor. Her soulmate.

In the distance, like a clap of thunder, she heard the resounding cheers of the assembled crowds. The first carriage with Lucas, Lorenzo, and Matthew must have reached town.

Her palms grew sweaty. Her carriage slowed as the foliage flanking the road thinned, and the noise level shot up ten decibels. Then she saw them. Standing shoulder to shoulder, holding camera phones and waving purple-and-gold flags, was the largest assembled crowd she had ever seen.

It was an endless sea of people. Nora couldn't believe all of them turned up to see her and Lucas. There were more people here than lived on Isola Nostrum. Where had they all come from? Her family wasn't like their British counterparts. They didn't normally ever attract this much attention.

She bit her lip and hesitantly gave a small flick of the wrist. A royal wave. The crowd screamed in delight.

The poor horses. How could they stand all the noise? It was taking all her self-control not to cover her own ears. It was deafening.

The carriage took the scenic route, conveying Nora up

and down nearly every street in the town. Finally, she spied the cool-gray stone exterior of the church. The carriage slowed and came to a stop.

The taller of the two drivers climbed down and lowered a set of steps.

"Good luck, Principessa," she heard him say in a hushed tone.

Through her veil, she observed the dancing brown eyes of her longtime security guard. "Angelo… always hiding in plain sight."

He winked and handed her down.

"Nora!" Sabrina squealed. "You look so regal. Every inch the crown princess of Isola Nostrum." Her maid of honor passed her a bouquet of white, pink, and orange orchids. "Take two steps forward so you're fully on the purple carpet. Lucia and I need to straighten the train."

"Si. It must be perfect," her younger sister added.

The two women made quick work of adjusting her skirt.

Lorenzo and Matthew appeared in her field of vision, wearing dove-gray tuxedos.

"Are you ladies ready?" Lorenzo asked.

Sabrina looped her arm through his. "As ready as we'll ever be."

"Lorenzo, you and Sabrina will enter first, then Matthew and I will enter right behind you. Do you remember where you're supposed to stand?" Lucia asked.

"Si, Lu. I remember." Lorenzo rolled his eyes dramatically. "Mama made us practice for over an hour last night."

Lucia huffed.

Matthew chuckled. "Lucia only wants what's best for her sister." He offered his arm to her.

"Lorenzo, Lucia. Behave." The voice of their father cut sharply through the air.

"Si, Papa," the siblings responded in a resigned tone.

Nora once again took in the sight of her father in full military dress uniform. He wore a navy-blue tunic trimmed in gold braiding and a white sash. Although he may have retired from active duty, the ribbons on his chest, tunic buttons, and shoes were shined to the highest standard. Papa was so handsome. Would Lorenzo take after him when he was older?

"You four, go on ahead. The wedding planner will direct you to enter when it's time." Her father slipped on a pair of white gloves. "Leonora and I will follow directly."

The bridal party ascended the steps.

"Leonora. How are you managing?"

She breathed deeply. "If I am being honest, Papa, I can't feel my limbs. I feel like I am having an out-of-body experience. Does that make sense?"

"It was the same for me when I married your mother twenty-eight years ago." He smiled, showing off his dimples. "We married in the morning, and none of it felt real until I set eyes upon Mama walking toward me in a bridal gown with the puffiest sleeves and longest train I'd ever seen."

She settled a hand on her stomach. It was fluttering with the wings of a thousand butterflies.

"Your Lucas, or Lord Malcolm, as I've heard you call him, is a good man. I know he will take excellent care of you, my little principessa." Her cheeks warmed at hearing her father call her by her nickname. "Every time I see the two of you together, I can sense the deep love and affection that you share with one another."

"I love him so much," Nora confessed.

"Then we should get you inside. You two have a few vows to exchange."

She leaned on the arm of her father and was guided up the steps on trembling legs. Entering the foyer, Nora smelled the scent of fresh roses, freesia, and lavender and heard the harpist playing "Ave Maria." She and her father stood off to the side. The wedding planner gave the signal.

Nora watched in fascination as one hundred guests turned their bodies toward the aisle, watching the page boys and girls, then Sabrina, Lorenzo, Lucia, and Matthew walked toward the altar. Her mother sat in the front row in a gown of seafoam turquoise with a matching fascinator, opposite the Duke and Duchess of Trent. Lucas stood with his back turned to Nora.

The music changed. Two violinists and a cellist joined the harpist. The guests all stood. She and Papa nodded to one another. Nora took a deep breath and entered the church. The guests whispered to one another. Her eyes soaked in the dancing flames of the candles, the decorative floral arches, and the soft light of the stained-glass windows.

Suddenly, Lucas turned. Their gazes locked. He beamed at her and mouthed, *"You look beautiful."*

He looked handsome himself. Lucas wore dove-gray trousers, a black morning coat, a royal-blue waistcoat, and a baby-blue tie, making his agate eyes pop. Each step she took brought her closer, until they were finally beside him. Papa carefully lifted her veil and placed her hand in Lucas's, then made his way over to the front pew.

"Am I living a real-life fairy tale?" she whispered.

"My dear Lady Nora, I can indeed confirm we are standing here, and it isn't a dream. It's been a long time coming."

Nora smiled.

The congregation was seated, and the officiant began the ceremony. Nora, however, couldn't focus on what was being said. All she could do was stand there and marvel at her husband-to-be.

"Do you, Lord Lucas Anthony Malcolm, take Her Serene Highness Principessa Leonora Amelia Beatrice Toscani to be your lawfully wedded wife, to have and to hold from this day forth, as long as you both shall live?"

Lucas nodded, the corners of his lips curving up. He let out a resounding, "I do."

Chills traveled through her body. Lucas reached down and retrieved her ring from a purple velvet pillow held by Rex. Nora hadn't noticed the canine, appearing dapper in a black bowtie, until now. His tail wagged wildly.

"Thank you, Rexie," she said.

Lucas slipped a thin yellow-gold band over her ring finger.

"And do you, Your Serene Highness Principessa Leonora Amelia Beatrice Toscani, take Lord Lucas Anthony Malcolm, to be your lawfully wedded husband, to have and to hold from this day forth, as long as you both shall live?"

"I do."

Nora's hands shook. She took Lucas's ring from a matching pillow held by Lucia and placed it on his ring finger.

"I now pronounce you husband and wife. Lord Lucas, you may kiss your bride."

He wrapped his arms around her, and they kissed. To Nora, time seemed to slow. She felt as if she were standing on a cloud, lighter than air. In Lucas's embrace, everything was perfect.

Time resumed its normal speed. The guests cheered.

The harpist, violinists, and cellist began to play. Arm in arm, Nora and Lucas floated up the aisle, radiating joy and happiness.

As Jane once said, a lady's imagination was very rapid. It jumped from admiration to love. From love to matrimony in a moment. Jane knew how to give her characters a happy ending. *Here is to hoping that my own story is only just beginning. A tale written for the love of dinosaurs.*

Dear Reader

Thank you for taking the time to read "For the Love of Dinosaurs."

If you enjoyed this book, please take a moment to leave a review on Amazon, Goodreads, Bookbub, or whatever platform you may have discovered this book on. It helps Tomi connect with readers like you!

Love her books? Become a part of her treasured community here.

Stay connected with Tomi by scanning QR code, or by visiting her official website.

Https://TomiTabb.com

Acknowledgments

Writing the story of Nora and Lucas has been an absolute joy. Thank you, my readers, once again for taking the time to read through another one of my books. Your support means so much to me. Without you, none of this would have been possible.

To Kaylee Baldwin, Ranee Clark, Joanne Lui, and Charity Chimni, thank you to each and every one of you for all of your words of wisdom and keen eyes. You ladies are the absolute best.

To my beta readers. Thank you so much for your valuable input and in helping this story continue to grow and evolve.

To my rainy day partner in crime and fellow author, Brooke Gilbert...thank you for your positive words of encouragement in keeping me going on the tough days.

To all of the amazingly kind, talented, and smart geology and paleontology professors and graduate students I reached out in the UK and in Australia, thank you so much for taking the time to answer my seemingly endless list of questions. I have so much respect for what you do.

Lastly, to my friends and family. Thank you for putting up

with the long hours I put in sitting at my desk writing away.
This is for you.

About the Author

Tomi's publishing journey began in 2020 with the release of her debut novel, *Dancing With a Royal*. Although she's always loved writing fictional stories, Tomi's background is in academic writing. She holds an MA degree in History and is currently pursuing her doctorate degree in the same subject.

In her rare free time, Tomi enjoys figure skating and hunting for new pumpkin flavored foods to try. It's one of the many reasons fall is her favorite season.

Tomi is a California native where she resides with her family and one very spoiled cat.

Website: TomiTabb.com

Also by Tomi Tabb

The Unexpected Royals

-Dancing With a Royal

-Jiving With a Royal

-Designing for a Royal

-More Than a Passing Shot

Friends of the Unexpected Royals

-Designs on Love

-Engineering Love

Novellas Related to the Unexpected Royals Series

-Pointe Shoes and Sugar Plums

-A Game of Small Victories

The Skaters of Sequoia Valley

-The Rules of the Rink

-The Sloth Zone

The Royals of Isola Nostrum

-The Great Austen Adventure

-For the Love of Dinosaurs

Historical Romance

-The Mysterious Mr. Marcellus